S0-DQX-335

Phil entered the Patricia Hotel and sat at an empty table. The clientele consisted of an intoxicated, somnolent crowd of misfits. Phil ordered two half-pints for four dollars and pretended it was nineteen forty-two.

He shut his eyes, leaned back and reminisced. Hearing movement near him, Phil opened his eyes. Three grungy-looking biker types had quietly seated themselves at his table. They stared at him and he stared back.

If an old fart gets rubbed out in a sleazy bar on East Hastings, Phil wondered, does anyone hear his screams?

"A great read! [Sisson's] plot was as twisted as a box full of Slinkys, dialogue sharper than a scalpel, and [his] many 'life observations' made me laugh out loud."

— Laurence Gough

Also by Hal Sisson

A Fowler View of Life
Coots, Codgers and Curmudgeons
(with Dwayne Rowe)
The Big Bamboozle
Caverns of the Cross (Arsenal Pulp Press)

A
Fat Lot
of
Good

Hal Sisson

Salal Press
Victoria, BC

Copyright © 2002 Hal Sisson

This book is a work of fiction. Names, characters,
places and incidents are either the product of the
author's imagination or are used fictitiously, and
any resemblance to actual events or locales, or
actual persons, living or dead, is entirely coincidental.

National Library of Canada Cataloguing in Publication

Sisson, Hal C., 1921 -
   A fat lot of good / Hal Sisson.

ISBN 1-894012-06-2

   I. Title.

PS8587.I79F37 2002   C813'.54   C2002-902347-5
PR9199.3.S5363F37 2002

Cover photo: Bjorn Stavrum
Cover design: Faultline Communications + Design
www.faultline.ca

Printed and bound in Canada
Transcontinental Printing Ltd.
Louiseville, Quebec
First printing: June 2002

Salal Press
Box 36060
Victoria, BC V9A 7J5

To all my old friends, legal or otherwise, who have a great sense of humour, particularly Bill Fowler and Mike Delano, who inspired the character and moniker of one of the sleuths in this novel. And to my family, Doreen, Ted and Lindy.

Special thanks to Clare Thorbes, Linda Field, Pearl Baldwin, Jim Moffat, Glen Acorn, Don McAllister, and any other friends I've missed, for their constant encouragement of my writing efforts. Well, none of them ever told me to quit. Thanks also to Dwayne Rowe, my former law partner and collaborator on two books, *Coots, Codgers and Curmudgeons* and its forthcoming sequel, *Garage Sale of the Mind*. And to Al Pease, bon vivant and contender for the title of best wind instrument musician in Canada, for graciously agreeing to pose for the cover photo.

Yet, ah! why should they know their fate?
Since sorrow never comes too late,
And happiness too swiftly flies.
No more; where ignorance is bliss,
'Tis folly to be wise.

Thomas Gray (1716 - 1771)

Prologue

Dr. Richard Poindexter, Jr. didn't have the heart to live in his Marine Drive mansion anymore. That organ had been removed from his body by crude and bloody surgery, while the good doctor lay strapped down and screaming on his massage table.

When Dick Poindexter was born, he'd cried on entering this great stage of fools. As he grew, he came to realize that life can become a variety of jokes perpetrated by friends and enemies, governments, corporations and religions.

In response, perhaps in retaliation, Dr. Dick, or Dex, as some called him, had often played some of life's more rotten tricks on others, never expecting his own life to end with such a dirty joke being played on himself. His existence bled to infinity in a haze of pain, punctuated by his shrieks of agony and outrage that he had been so thoroughly duped.

Fate, for its own diversion, was about to play a host of jokes on other parties closely connected with the life and death of Doctor Dick—parties who sought to obscure their connection with the crime. A fat lot of good it was going to do them!

One

Poindexter's home, complete with ocean view, was one of several exclusive domiciles in the area, all well screened from the surrounding community by tall stone fences and taller vegetation so neighbours could not easily observe each other's comings and goings. The grounds were spacious enough to render the sounds of nighttime revelry faint, if not inaudible.

Murder, however, was another matter. Someone should have heard the screams of the dying doctor, but if they did, they continued to mind their own business, a reaction that was *de rigueur* in the very English provincial capital of Victoria on Vancouver Island.

The body lay undisturbed throughout the weekend and into the following week.

When Dr. Dick didn't turn up at his office that late November morning, his staff tried to raise him by phone. They weren't alarmed when he failed to answer. Poindexter often arrived at work only after sleeping off the last traces of a pounding head and sour-breath hangover from the all-night parties he sometimes hosted on weekends. His receptionist calmly implemented Plan B, cancelling the cardiologist's appointments.

Nancy Cavanaugh embarked on her first task that same morning, cleaning the Poindexter mansion. Nancy and a few friends ran Good and Cleaner Services, a well-regarded firm among the fussy well-to-do of the district. Nancy liked to think that their meticulous attention to each client's special requests was one reason their business was in such high demand.

Dr. Dick had a fetish about keeping his exercise room smelling of anything but sweat, so that was Nancy's next stop after she finished the dining room and kitchen. As she approached along the short hallway, the vague sweet-and-sour smell she'd noticed as soon as she stepped into the house became a powerful stench. Accustomed to removing vomit and other fluids and solids of bodily or other origin, Nancy simply held her breath and pushed open the door.

One quick look confirmed that no dusting was required here. Her employer was in no condition to criticize, as he was all over the massage table like a dog's breakfast, his blood and guts strewn above, beside and around him.

Nancy's breath expelled in a loud groan. Her shoulders shook violently, her eyes snapped wide open in fright and she backed quickly from the room. Her haste to escape the carnage turned into a mad dash for the nearest telephone. Instead of calling 911, her first thought was to call her brother Wade in hopes of catching him before he left for work. Wade Cavanaugh was a Victoria police constable desperate to make detective, and Nancy was sure he'd know what to do.

Wade responded with alacrity to his sister's panicked call. In less than twenty minutes, his old Mustang beater squealed to a stop outside the Poindexter residence.

"I'm not going back in there," Nancy declared, so Wade explored on his own. He seemed to take forever, and Nancy was beginning to worry, when Wade rejoined her in the living room.

"What took you so long?" asked the distraught Nancy.

"I was trying out his exercise bike," Wade deadpanned. He clicked his shoulder microphone and radioed for backup and a crime scene unit. He told Nancy to stay where she was and began to check the rest of the house.

Three police cruisers and a crime scene van sped to the Poindexter home, closely followed by a *Times-Colonist* reporter who made a practice of eavesdropping on police radio traffic. He cell-phoned a friend at *C-FAX*, the local all-news radio station.

No sirens; the cops glided silently up the street and approached the house on foot. Fanning out slowly and keeping their voices low, the backup team drew their guns and began searching the premises. They didn't find anyone outside, but what they discovered inside was downright bone-chilling.

The victim lay in a pool of congealed blood on a narrow padded table in the centre of a white-tiled exercise room, the gaping hole in his chest exposing lacerated lungs. Sloppy cuts from whatever lethal instrument had created this aperture continued down into the victim's belly. Intestines draped like a slimy curtain toward the floor, where a large puddle of blood gathered around the table.

The killer had used some of the blood to scrawl an upside-down cross on the wall behind the body. Rigor mortis had set in, and the coroner estimated that Poindexter had been dead for about sixty hours.

The police search failed to turn up the weapon, the doctor's heart or any other clues. In fact, they found sweet essence of bugger all, with one exception: Poindexter's appointment book on the desk of his study revealed that someone named Annie Chance had been scheduled to massage the medic at five the previous Friday afternoon. That made her the last person to see him alive, or a prime suspect in his murder.

Two

Christmas was fast approaching, and Philip Figgwiggin, Q.C. (retired), wanted to bake a Red Velvet Cake in the worst way. That's the way I'll likely do it, too, he mused. The cake was a family tradition and Figgwiggin's effort would be a tribute to his beloved wife Daisy, who had died four years earlier.

Phil risked sliding into the same depression he'd faced the previous yuletide season, unless he made a concrete effort (but not a concrete cake, he hoped) to create an upbeat atmosphere. He had decided that baking just might take a bite out of his fear of loneliness, old age and death.

Phil held the cake recipe the requisite distance from his eyes and wondered whether he'd bitten off more than he could chew. After all, the only baking instruction he understood was *Lick bowl.*

The main ingredients he either had already or could easily obtain: sugar, eggs, flour, oil, vanilla flavouring, vinegar and bicarbonate of soda. *Better check my supply of bicarb,* Phil thought. *I might need extra, and not necessarily for the cake.*

But where to find the key item—the one that made Red Velvet Cake so special, the one that gave it the rich, deep, dark lustrous red colour that Phil loved, a sensual, even erotic red? Daisy was a purist, so she had always used the authentic colouring extracted from dried insects. But she'd stopped making the cake when she read somewhere that the natural dried bug extract could provoke life-threatening allergic reactions in some people.

Phil read the footnote to the recipe. *Carmine: a natural red dye derived from the crushed bodies of cochineal insects, Cactylopius coccus, found on the prickly pear cacti.* Phil had never had a reaction to the cake, but no doubt thanks to the same article his wife had seen, most cooks now substituted artificial red food colouring in Red Velvet cake.

Phil's recipe included instructions for making the dye: *Grind the bugs to a fine powder; a little bit goes a long way.* Well it always does, doesn't it? thought Phil. *Place one tablespoon of the powder into a cup of water and bring to a rolling boil for fifteen minutes. Strain through a fine sieve. Boil and strain twice more to concentrate the liquid. Refrigerate to prevent mould formation, or allow all moisture to evaporate and store the powder in a sealed container. It should keep indefinitely.*

Phil daydreamed about taking a trip to Mexico to get the bugs, gathering and crushing them himself (stomping them in a bucket, maybe) and making his own powder. He'd heard the little buggers were in short supply in Mexico, though, so perhaps he'd have to travel to Peru. He could work in a visit to Machu Picchu and take his friend Mike Fowler along. Mike was game for anything, but age was a factor for both of them, so maybe the trip wasn't such a hot idea.

Phil Figgwiggin was a reformed lawyer who had retired from the rat race of a practice in Victoria and Vancouver because the rats were winning. He did miss, however, the cut and thrust, the hand-to-hand combat that was courtroom action, the pitting of his intellect against complex legal issues. Aging, if not unexpected, had come at a bad time in his life. Daisy's death had made him feel even more keenly the lack of purpose in his daily routine. He'd done a stint in the R.C.A.F. during the war and a short fling in show business in later years, albeit of the amateur burlesque and music hall variety. Neither of those occupations was viable at his age.

Phil dropped the recipe on the kitchen table, went to the bathroom and looked in the mirror. As always, his split-second reaction was, who the hell is that?

He saw a tall, portly, stoop-shouldered man with a full head of curly grey hair, deep blue eyes behind rimless spectacles, a neatly trimmed moustache and goatee and a pallid complexion accented with a few liver spots. His features conveyed a serious mien, but that was belied by the laugh lines around his baggy eyes.

He was in reasonably good shape physically, his long-standing heart condition alleviated by a quadruple bypass five years earlier. But he had to admit his youth had disappeared, the figure in the glass proof that he was an old man. He longed for some kind of action to relieve the tedium of old age.

Phil turned on *C-FAX* radio. Bad news

travels fast, he thought. The media can't wait to fill you in on every political fiasco, genocide, disaster, famine, and every bit of corruption in Christendom. Phil's favourite bad-news purveyor specialized in local crap, with car crashes, rapes, robberies and murders always leading off the news. Today was no exception.

In major news today, Dr. Richard Poindexter, Jr., a well known Victoria heart surgeon, was found dead at his home this morning.

"The hell you say!" Phil shouted at the radio. He sank into a chair, stunned. Poindexter was his heart surgeon.

Police are treating the death as a homicide. They have few leads, says spokesperson Jane Trimball. "We don't know how many assailants were involved, but we're asking the public's help in locating the person or persons responsible. Anyone with information should contact the police department at 555-1432."

That was Constable Jane Trimball of the Victoria Police Department. Dr. Poindexter, a College of Physicians and Surgeons official, was a well-known and respected member of the medical profession in Victoria. He assumed his father's general practice when Poindexter Sr. died in 1980, but later specialized in diseases of the heart.

Phil tuned out as the newscaster went on to

other stories. Murdered? He couldn't believe it. But by whom and why? Self-interest took over briefly as Phil wondered where he was going to find another doctor, and what would happen if he had another heart attack. He had now lost the only two doctors he'd ever had, his old buddy Dick Sr., and now his son.

He sat for another few minutes, his cake forgotten. "Son of a bitch!" he exclaimed. Jumping up from his chair, Phil grabbed his coat, scarf and hat from the hall closet and hurried to his car.

By the time Figgwiggin arrived at 2635 Marine Drive, the police had already strung the yellow crime scene tape and a cop was keeping curious onlookers and the media at bay. Phil approached the officer.

"You can't go inside, sir, this is a crime scene," said the cop.

"It's okay, I'm the victim's godfather," Phil replied

"Doesn't   qualify. You'd have to be his father, maybe an uncle."

Phil knew that silence is the only real substitute for brains, but he kept trying anyway. "I'm one of his heart patients."

"The doc's dead!"

"I'm his lawyer."

"That clinches it," the cop said in disgust.

"Can't you make an exception? I just want to make up my own mind about how this might have happened."

"Cuts no ice with me. Now, sir, I'd like you, as it says in the Good Book, go forth and multiply..."

"Are you telling me to fuck off?" Phil couldn't believe his ears.

"You said it, not me, but you got that right, buster." The constable turned his back and walked toward the house.

As a lawyer, Phil understood that advisability is distinct from necessity and in this situation he had no alternative but to obey the cop's instructions. The cop had the hammer, as they say in curling, but Phil figured to get in the last word. "What can you expect from pigs but grunts," was the lame remark he directed *sotto voce* at the policeman's receding back.

He shook his head as he walked back to the car, muttering the famous Newfie saying, "Whale oil beef hooked!"

Never easily discouraged, Phil sat in his car and watched the parked vehicle bearing the *Times-Colonist* logo. Before long, he was rewarded by the appearance of a reporter. Phil hustled over to intercept him

"Wait up, young man. I'd like a word, if you don't mind."

The young man stopped next to his vehicle and gave Phil the once over. Phil stuck out his hand and introduced himself. The reporter responded with the name Vaughn Bostrum, which Phil recognized from articles he'd seen in the newspaper.

"I'm Poindexter's godfather, actually," said Phil, "and his patient. They won't let me in there. Can you tell me what's going on?"

Vaughn proved quite loquacious. "The cleaning lady identified the body," he told Phil. "I talked to her earlier. The cops aren't saying much, as usual, but from what I can gather, this one's pretty gory. The doc was tied down to a massage table while someone performed a multi-by-pass on him."

Bostrum's eyes gleamed. "How about that for a switch? This is front-page stuff, lots of room for follow-ups, too. You can read all about it in the *T-C*."

"Thanks, I'll watch for your byline," Phil said, astounded by the man's callousness.

Three

Buck naked, Annie Chance stared at herself in the bathroom mirror, then raised her arms above her head. Could her boobs still pass the pencil test? she wondered. Moot point!

Annie bent over to run hot water into the tub. She was looking forward to a long soak after a tough day at No Lipshtick Traces, Inc. Her back ached. So did her hands, arms and legs. She enjoyed her work, but the physical demands of giving massages and providing corollary services like S & M games took its toll each day. Most of the services she offered were strictly legit, like massage therapy. Some others weren't offered at the YM-YWCA and were considered by some—wrong-thinkers, in her opinion—to border on the illegal.

Annie's apartment was a new addition to the old main house on Seaquay Crescent that housed her business endeavours, a very handy arrangement.

The sudden ringing of the doorbell was an unwanted intrusion. Struggling quickly into a bathrobe and binding it tightly about her, Chance answered the door. Two men were firmly planted on her doorstep, a little one and a big one. Mutt and Jeff, she mentally dubbed them.

Annie stared at the official-looking badge that the tall plainclothes detective shoved into her face, then at the search warrant his companion held out toward her.

"What is this?" she asked "I wasn't expecting company."

"Annie Chance?" the bigger one asked.

"Who wants to know?"

"Victoria Police, ma'am," the detective replied as he brushed past her into the hallway. "We'd like to ask you a few questions."

"Why?"

"You read the warrant, we'll search the house. We have reason to believe you have illegal drugs on the premises."

"That's ridiculous," Annie spluttered. "I don't have to put up with this."

"We can talk here or down at the station,"

the big cop said, staring at her breasts. "Tony, take a look around, see if Ms. Chance is entertaining anyone."

The other cop was smaller, narrower, with small, deep-set dark eyes framing a thin, hooked nose. Not waiting for an invitation from Annie, the little cop set off toward the back of the apartment.

"Are you guys charging me with a crime? I've got a right to know."

"Did you give a massage to a Doctor Poindexter last Friday afternoon?"

Annie's sphincter muscles tightened. "As a matter of fact, yes I did," she said. "What's that got to do with the price of tea in China?"

"Maybe a lot," said the cop, "maybe a lot. What was his condition when you left him?"

"He was relaxed, maybe even asleep. I give good massage. So what?"

"So he was alive when you left him?"

"Of course he was!" Annie exclaimed, her breath now coming in gasps. "Wha...what are you trying to tell me?" She could feel sweat starting to trickle down her bare back. "Is he dead now? What happened?"

"That's what we're here to find out. We want to know everything that happened at his house on Friday."

Annie held back any further protest until

she'd read the warrant, then stammered, "What's this got to do with drugs?" With sudden resolve, she declared, "I'm sorry. I have no comment. I refuse to answer any more of your questions."

Then, her voice rising in anger, she continued, "I demand to see my lawyer before you do anything else. Now tell your buddy to stop rooting around in my underwear drawer for non-existent drugs. And you can both get the hell out of my house, you flat-footed, lame-brained bastards."

"Just relax, lady, and no one will get hurt," was the big cop's loud response as he took a menacing step toward her.

The search was getting out of hand. Hearing the loud discussion taking place near the door, the thin cop returned to help out his partner.

Tony LeBlanc had always been a groper, as any of his female classmates in high school could attest. Joining the police force hadn't changed his basic instincts when certain situations presented themselves, such as the present one, a big blonde in a tight dressing gown with her backside toward him. Acting on some inexplicable, lecherous compulsion, he goosed Annie.

Bad move. Her knee-jerk reaction was to

pivot and slam her knee into Tony's groin. With an agonized grunt he doubled over, clutching his gonads. Annie followed with a right uppercut into his descending head, rearranging Tony's already broken nose, which started to spew blood as he collapsed to the floor. One hand now clutched his face, the other cupped his balls.

The big guy jumped on Annie's back and they both fell on top of Tony in a messy tangle on the tiled entranceway.

That's when the fun and legal games really started and the wheels of justice began to slip off.

Four

Sergeant Harry Muldoon glowered at Wade Cavanaugh from under heavy black eyebrows. Harry's squad hadn't found enough evidence to please the detective sergeant, who was just back from a Mexican holiday and getting a firsthand look at the crime scene.

"What's your opinion, Wade? You're the hotshot who wants to be a detective."

"We didn't find the doc's heart," Wade replied, "so maybe this is a case of organ theft. Someone literally stole his heart away."

"When Irish eyes were smiling, I suppose." Harry's voice dripped sarcasm.

Constable Cavanaugh winced. He'd heard Muldoon was a bear, and realized he'd have to work with him every day if he were assigned to homicide. Cavanaugh eased his ample frame onto the edge of the jacuzzi and surveyed Poindexter's workout room.

White tile covered the sides of the jacuzzi and the floor around it and extended into the adjoining shower and toilet. Mats covered the rest of the floor and Nautilus equipment sat against one wall. French doors framed by blue draw-curtains opened onto a patio. The walls and ceiling were covered with mirrors tinted a smoky blue.

Cavanaugh's mouth fell open as he contemplated the ceiling and the kinds of exercise-room games the mirrors might have witnessed. He looked over at the massage table, from which Poindexter's body had already been removed, then back to Muldoon, who was pacing the floor in frustration.

"Holy goddamned graffiti! As if we needed that little extra touch!" Muldoon growled at the inverted cross smeared on the mirror. "Robbery's not the motive, there's all kinds of expensive stuff in this house but nothing's missing, at least not that the cleaning lady can tell. No murder weapon, no dope. Whoever did this knew the doctor pretty well, and Annie Chance sure fits that bill. But you idiots jumped the gun, didn't you?"

Cavanaugh assumed a noncommittal

expression as he absorbed the misdirected verbal abuse.

"Picked up the prime suspect in a murder charge before there was enough evidence to make a parking ticket stick," Muldoon continued. "Alleging possession of drugs to get a search warrant." Harry rolled his eyes at his reflection in the mirrored ceiling. "Then the dummies goose her, cuff her too tight, and snicker, 'Oh, sorry, ma'am.'"

"So she claims."

"I wouldn't put it past those knuckleheads."

"I see what you mean, Sarge, but I wasn't there."

"They held her for three hours before they let her make a phone call. Shit! I can't stop to scratch my balls on a tropical beach without coming back to find everything screwed up."

"I didn't have the authority to stop them, Sarge, but they did get a legal search warrant."

"Yeah, a warrant obtained from their friendly justice of the peace, who's about as much use as a condom in the Vatican. This whole thing is a disaster. If it didn't make police work that much harder, I'd say we should have to get all our warrants from a Supreme Court judge, like we have to do for a phone tap. It would stop all this warrant shopping. Now we're going to have the media on our backs accusing us of sexual abuse, foul-mouthed ignorance, excessive force and God knows what else, and I'm supposed to fix it."

Cavanaugh feared the sergeant might blow a head gasket, so he tried to divert his attention from the bungled search. "If Annie Chance didn't do it, who did?"

"I didn't say she didn't do it, I'm just pissed at the way this thing's been handled. Had to cut my holiday short. I'm pretty damn convinced Chance is guilty. She runs an S & M operation out of her house. Those people are all sick, if you ask me."

Harry continued to pace. "Talk about your die nasty! The doc's killer must have been involved in some deep-seated pathological assholery, and everything about this business points to Annie Chance. I'll bet she was smiling when she did it."

"What makes you say that?" asked Wade.

"'One may smile, and smile, and be a villain, and cut your heart out with a bloody axe.' I heard that in an old movie recently, although it wasn't likely an axe that cancelled Poindexter's ticket."

"How about a chainsaw? Or one of those small skill saws, that would do it."

Harry stopped pacing. Slowly he turned.

"Maybe there's hope for you, Cavanaugh," he said in a low voice. "Something nasty and damnably sharp, at any rate. Okay, let's stop wasting time. This case is getting colder by the minute and I need extra bodies. So for now, you get to play detective. Although I wouldn't have hassled Chance just yet, I do think the dame's the most likely one to use that type of a weapon—the one you haven't found yet. So start checking all the hardware and medical supply places, find out if Chance bought a skill saw in the last couple of weeks. I wish to hell the killer had used a weapon we could trace."

Watching Muldoon in a foul mood made Wade as nervous as a long-tailed cat near a rocking chair. Trying to attain detective status wasn't going to be easy with Muldoon as both his alleged tutor and his superior. Muldoon's reputation was that of a domineering bully when an investigation wasn't going well, and this one sure as hell wasn't.

No snitches had come forward in the first two days; no witnesses to suspicious activity had turned up, either. Victoria police were under heavy pressure to solve the murder—particularly Harry, who was now in charge of the case, and who desperately wanted to convict someone for the crime. Anyone. Soon.

Muldoon badly wanted a promotion before he lost more hairline and gained more waistline; wanted to be a chief and not just one of the Indians. In a city, not in the boondocks.

Wade had gone down to the station when he heard they'd brought Chance in. She hadn't struck him as the type to commit such a savage crime. Tough around the edges, sure, but not a cold-blooded killer. In fact, he had been quite taken with Annie and the fight she had put up against the narc squad. That little Tony LeBlanc got what had been coming to him for a long time, but there could be repercussions from the botched episode.

Wade tried to lighten the mood, even at the risk of taking some flak himself. "Your mind's like concrete, Sarge, all mixed up and firmly set," said the constable. "Sure she's suspect and could have knocked the Doc off, but someone else could just as easily have been the killer."

"That's your take on it, eh? Good-looking dame with the big boobs didn't do it. Typical. Place scoured for evidence, no forced entry. We've canvassed the neighbourhood; nobody heard a fight or a dispute. No line on anyone but Annie."

Muldoon walked over to the French doors and stared out at the garden and the curve of the driveway beside it. "The way I figure it," he mused, "Annie gave the doc more than just a massage. She gets him on the table, she straps him down and they proceed to some sort of sado-machismo thing. Probably just part of the regular routine. But what if Doctor Daddy Warbucks and Little Orphan Annie were lovers, but Annie finds out she isn't the only one he's getting a leg over? Maybe this time she really attacks him and rips his heart out with something she stashed in the house for the purpose."

"I agree that if someone other than Annie did it, they sure didn't leave many clues."

"Whereas Annie left plenty."

"But can you call them clues?"

"We could get a hernia jumping to conclusions, but it sure looks like the big blonde with the phony name did Poindexter in. Last to see him alive, her prints all over the place."

"But where does that get us?" Wade ventured. "She's a masseuse and she gave him a massage. As per usual, she says. We didn't find any of his blood on her clothes or in her car or apartment. If she did the job, then she must've been naked, and the fact that she was in the buff didn't spook the doc."

"Then the doc should have kicked her ass when he got her panties down, instead of boinking her." Harry hitched his pants up over his pot belly. "Her clothes were well away from the crime scene and that's why they don't show any blood contamination."

"Other people, friends of his, over time, worked out or showered here," said Wade, gazing around. "So anything the lab finds might be inconclusive. They didn't even leave any towels we could check for hair."

"Theory: Chance and Poindexter showered together before the murder," said Muldoon, "but only she used it afterward. He wasn't known as Doctor Dick for nothing. Poindexter was likely doing missionary work among the virgin population of the hospital. Annie finds out about it and sets him up. They have a knee trembler in the shower using the saucer and bucket method of birth control."

"What's that, Sarge?" Wade interrupted. "Never heard of that one."

"Works best if the woman's taller than the man," Muldoon answered with a laugh. "He stands on a bucket, and when his eyes get as big as saucers, she kicks the bucket out from under him. Personally, I've always found knee tremblers a big strain on the whole anatomy. I'm speaking contraceptively, of course. You can't keep it up for long."

Wade laughed along with Muldoon, but

couldn't resist saying, "With your weight, Sarge, yeah, you could hurt yourself."

"Your belt doesn't go through all the loops either, Wade. I told you, I'm going to lose twenty pounds. You should do the same. A room gets fatter every time you enter."

Wade didn't reply. He got down from his perch on the edge of the jacuzzi, went over to the exercise bike, got on and started to pedal.

Muldoon frowned. "Sure like that bike, don't you? Maybe Santa will bring you one for Christmas."

Wade ignored the needling and offered up another theory as he pedalled. "The cross on the wall bothers me. Upside down, drawn in blood. You can scoff, but some crazy cult could do a thing like that."

"Don't make me laugh," Muldoon replied, annoyance creeping into his voice. "I don't want to hear that devil shit. Doesn't wash anymore. Ritual murder was popular in the eighties, all media hype but no resemblance to reality. Cops even bought into that theory, saw cults everywhere, but it's no longer a growth industry in our business. So forget that line of crap."

"Okay, okay. I'm not about to attack religious groups, they're protected by law."

"A bizarre crazy did this? More likely a

smart, cool-blooded loner who had a bone to pick with Dick Poindexter. Picture this: Annie's already naked..."

"I'm picturing it, Sarge."

"She puts on a shower cap, rubber gloves, plastic cape, kills him as he's strapped to the table. Knows there'll be lots of blood, so she spreads it around, makes the crazy cross to make it look like some religious nut did it. Maybe she's a closet psycho herself. Then she takes a long shower. None of the blood stays on her, techs checked the shower trap, but came up empty. Annie ran the water so long the trace evidence is all down the drain and out in Juan de Fuca Strait on its way to Seattle with the rest of Victoria's sewage."

Muldoon continued to stare out into the dull overcast November day. The first drops of rain started to splatter on the stones of the patio. Harry wished he were still in Mexico—one tequila, two tequila, three tequila, floor!

Wade waited for him to continue.

"They did find some spots of blood on the patio, so somebody carried something out this way. I figure Annie gets dressed at some other location in the house, likely the bedroom, then leaves, hauling everything away with her in bags—the murder weapon, clothing, towels—deep-sixes the lot, Lord knows where. Tells us she left the doc sleeping peacefully on the massage table."

"Record shows she's been giving him a massage on the same afternoon every week for months," Wade declared. "She was a nurse and has an R.M.T. certificate."

"What's that stand for? Registered Meat Tenderizer?"

Wade grunted. "Annie said in her statement that it was strictly a business arrangement. Massage only, to help him relax."

"She may deny the sex bit," Muldoon said, "but as a regular visitor to this house she can leave any number of prints, hair and other stuff all over the place."

Harry held up his hand before Wade could object. "And I agree, that doesn't make a case." Muldoon rocked back and forth on his platform shoes, his big jaw thrust forward as he processed his thoughts.

"It's the best theory we got at this point. No one lives here but the doc, so she had lots of time, a whole weekend, and she dumped anything connected with the murder somewhere. Where? Yeah, Annie Chance is a suspect, all right, but how do we prove she did it?"

"This is still a whodunit, if you ask me."

"I'll keep that in mind. In the meantime, let's

try to find out if this tough broad and Doctor Dick were lovers. Maybe she felt she was getting screwed, booed and tattooed in more ways than one and did something about it."

"A crime of passion, but planned ahead and with deliberate intent. We'll stick to that theory till something better comes up. So, Wade, go find me something proving Annie Chance rubbed him out."

Wade jumped off the bike, his landing surprisingly light, given his six-foot height and extra girth. "Or something that would change your mind," he mumbled.

Wade knew his height bothered Muldoon, who secretly suffered from a short man complex. Cavanaugh also knew he'd have to tread carefully around his new boss's easily bruised ego and hair-trigger temper. He was determined, however, to find the real culprit, and hoped it would destroy Muldoon's pet theory.

Sergeant Muldoon pretended not to hear the remark. Shrugging his shoulders higher into his expensive black leather jacket, he barked at his subordinate, "Find something!"

Five

Phil threw the newspaper down in disgust. Vaughn Bostrum's article described Poindexter's murder in gory detail, almost to the point of performing the coroner's autopsy. Just like a coroner, though, the story got the who, what, where and when right but didn't even take a stab at the why. Phil favoured the old adage: Believe half of what you see, and none of what you read in the newspapers.

Victoria's staid reputation as a minimum security facility for old people was largely an illusion. An entire region of three hundred and thirty thousand people came into town to drink, sample the astonishing variety of escort services or do deals in the thriving drug market. Add in the no-goodniks from

Vancouver who crossed the water to do business in the capital's drier and more laid-back climate, and the result was a crime rate well out of proportion for a city of Victoria's size. Even Phil, who'd specialized in conveyancing, estate work, civil litigation and company law, had defended a healthy share of blue- and white-collar criminals in his day.

Citizens could anticipate a few strange deaths in which the terminally ill or desperately sick relieved themselves of a pain-wracked life. Poindexter's death was different, however, certainly not part of the random violence that plagued the city. It was a focused attack; the murderer probably knew the victim, and had some deranged reason for committing the crime. Phil was too short on facts and background history to speculate further. It was death from unnatural causes by an unknown assailant.

Some of his former adversaries in the crown prosecutor's office were still around and still friendly, since Phil had only retired four years earlier. That would be the best place to begin his inquiries.

Usually Phil looked forward to a daily visit with his buddy Mike Fowler, but not today. Mike, who had a condo in the same block, was leaving for a visit with his daughter and her family in Edmonton. He'd be gone for an indeterminate period, and barely had time for a coffee with Phil before he left for the airport.

As he awaited Mike's arrival an old rhyme ran through Phil's mind, one which more or less described their relationship:

Damon and Pythias together went round,
Wherever was Damon, Pythias was found,
One day Pythias called Damon a skunk,
And Damon went out and got Pythias drunk.

Mike was a tough, bandy-legged old hombre, a survivor who took long walks to keep in shape, although as Mike himself said, he was now qualified to give lessons in doddering. He'd shrunk to five-ten and a hundred and sixty pounds, still with most of his hair, but none of his own teeth. On days when he was running low on gas, Mike hid his pallor behind his trademark ear-splitting grin and ready humour.

At eighty-five, Mike described himself as a retired lover, explorer, gourmet and amateur gynecologist. During World War Two he'd served in the merchant navy, where he learned to jerry-rig all kinds of devices. After the war he'd made a good living splicing and rigging steel cable in the oil patch and on ski slopes in the Pacific Northwest.

Deep-water diving and demolition were

among his other talents. The prototype jack-of-all-trades, explosives became Mike's specialty. He could implode buildings, blow out basements or take out underwater pilings. In his heyday, he used to pass out business cards that read: *Small wars fought, bridges destroyed, uprisings quelled, revolutions started, tigers tamed, saloons emptied, orgies organized, virgins converted and elephants bred.*

A latter-day soldier of fortune, Mike was testy, raunchy, iconoclastic and the closest friend Phil had ever had.

Phil left the lock off the condo door and Mike walked in, saying, "Packed and ready to go. The limo's picking me up at ten-thirty."

"Sit down and take a load off. I'll pour the coffee. Do you want a shot of Bailey's Cream in it?"

"You're thinking clearly for this early in the morning. Sure, why not? I'm down a quart and we gotta get the motor started." Mike plunked himself down on the sofa.

"How's your fear of flying?" asked Phil, handing Mike a hot mug of mocha.

"It's a short flight, so I'll be okay. But the longer ones, now they scare the pants off me."

"Why would that be?"

"More danger of the plane blowing up."

"You mean because of terrorists?"

"No. More often it's methane gas inside the plane."

"I don't understand," said Phil.

"Well, you take your typical 747 with four hundred-odd passengers all ingesting that rotten airline food they serve on those long flights. That generates a whole lotta flatulence and the forward motion of the plane drives the gas toward the back. It gets so dense in the last few rows, they oughta issue gas masks to the passengers."

"I see." Phil was beginning to feel a strong pull on his leg.

"You get so nervous back there, you feel like a Christian Scientist with acute appendicitis."

"For God's sake, Mike..."

"Some idiot tries to light a cigarette in one of those rear cans and *kaboom!* The whole tail end of the plane gets blown off."

Phil's mouth twitched as he tried to restrain a grin. "So terrorists aren't to blame in most cases?"

"Hell no. The airlines blame them, but they know different. They just won't admit it's the slop they serve that's responsible."

"Glad we cleared that up, Mike." Phil was chuckling openly at this point. "I won't worry about you, then."

"Please don't," Mike replied. "So what's eating you?"

"This Poindexter murder, for one thing, and I could use your help if you get back anytime soon."

"Yeah, I saw this morning's rag. You're going to look into it, then?"

"Figure I should. Have to, really."

"A pig's ass is pork. I knew you would, him being your doctor and all that. Well, who knows? I was planning to be gone for a month, maybe six weeks, you know, stay until they get so sick of me I don't have to go again for a couple of years. But the trip's turned into a real gathering of the clan, so there'll be lots of rug rats and ankle biters underfoot. If they start to get to me, I may come home early. Either way, you can count me in for whatever you've got in mind. Till then, good luck!"

They clinked their mugs, then Mike got to his feet and headed for the door, sketching a farewell salute as he left.

At one-thirty the following morning, Phil was resigning himself to another sleep-deprived night. He was nestled into his recliner, staring out the window with a medical magazine dangling from his fingers. In the daytime his condo looked out over Dallas Road at the distant Olympic Mountains of

Washington State. All he could see now were the lights of a freighter that was gliding through the Strait of Juan de Fuca into the greater black vastness of the wide Pacific Ocean. He was recalling a twelve-year-old conversation with Richard Poindexter, Sr. in a restaurant near the doctor's Oak Bay office.

"Lust drives men to an early grave," his old friend had said. "Like other mammalian species, human males exhaust themselves chasing females. That, plus maintaining social status, requires considerable energy. So if you want a long life, stay home and abstain from booze, butts and broads. But if you wait till your sixties to do so, it won't help."

"So once I qualify for the old-age pension, giving up my vices won't help me live any longer, is that it?"

"I didn't say giving up those habits doesn't count," the physician countered, his eyes following the legs of a passing waitress. "What I am saying is that an unhealthy lifestyle takes its toll during youth and middle age, not after people reach the golden age."

Philip was certainly interested in longevity, but not at the expense of quality of life, so he'd told his doctor and friend that he'd certainly consider his advice, but intended to carry on as usual.

Now he was finding that his bad habits were waning without any deliberate action on his part. His tolerance for late nights and alcohol wasn't what it used to be, and his libido had settled into semi-retirement. The last years of his marriage to Daisy had been virtually platonic.

Phil glanced again at the medical magazine he had been reading. It cheered him considerably, for the article was on something called the Testoderm Potency Patch, designed to top up testosterone levels in older men. The patch secreted five milligrams of the hormone into the bloodstream over the course of twenty-four hours—about the same amount a healthy young man would produce in a day. Voilà, hard-on city! By nature a skeptic, Phil was nonetheless tempted to give the patch a try. His flesh might be weak, but his spirit was still urging him not to give up the hunt.

Phil had obtained the magazine from a usually reliable source, the locker room of the YMCA. An alleged satisfied user had told Phil that a few days into the treatment, he had found himself fixing things around the house. A week later, spontaneous erections had become somewhat of a nuisance, and after two weeks his sex life had returned to normal, surprising himself, to say nothing of his wife.

Phil wondered if the wife wasn't about to pack her bags and leave home. His informant said that his voice was deeper and more authoritative and he could touch his toes again. He even thought the hormone infusions had reduced the size of his pot belly.

"That's for me!" had been Phil's reaction, even though on further inquiry he could see three problems which might prevent similar success. The first was minor: the patch was not available in Canada, so he'd have to go to Seattle to obtain a supply. Secondly, his informant had been in his late fifties, so would the stuff work on someone twenty years older, with a serious heart condition to boot?

The third problem was the greatest of all. The patch had to be attached to a hairless scrotum. Who could Phil trust to shave his testicles? He'd always had more balls than a eunuch and didn't want to alter that condition. It wasn't as if he could do it properly himself, and he couldn't go into a barbershop and ask for that kind of a haircut. When he took down his pants and asked for a shave, they'd throw him out into the street.

There was his absent friend Mike, but could he trust him to do it? Mike was a man

of many talents, but no scrotum shaver he.
He'd probably want some of the patches, too.
Maybe they could shave each other. The idea
of hands prone to involuntary tremors
approaching his family jewels almost made
Phil nauseous. Maybe an operating room
nurse would be more to the point?

Phil rose, his hand rubbing a small lesion
and scaly spot on his forehead, the result of
overexposure to the sun early in life. He stood
over the bathroom sink applying ointment. As
he did, his thoughts returned to the murder.

He tried to convince himself that he wasn't
crazy for wanting to involve himself in finding the killer. Why should he concern himself? Because if he ceased caring about another's demise, he might as well be dead himself. Also, Poindexter, Jr.'s death affected Phil
personally. Poindexter was his godson, after
all. Phil had admired the cardiologist and
enjoyed Dex's sense of humour, even though
it often came with a nasty edge.

So many doctors were little better than pill
pushers for the pharmaceuticals. Not so the
Poindexters. After all, Dick had stuck two
fingers up Phil's ass when he'd asked for a
second opinion as to the condition of his
prostate. Now Phil not only had the hassle of
finding another physician, he ran the risk

that a new doctor would fuck up his medication, making him a guinea pig for the drug companies' latest wares.

Newscasts of the past two days had covered the murder, and Phil was reminded of his own quadruple bypass operation. Like Poindexter, he'd been opened up from arsehole to appetite, but at least he hadn't felt a thing, and he'd woken up after the procedure.

Two of the hardest things to do these days, he thought, are going to sleep at night and getting up in the morning. You need less sleep the older you get, so they say. Who are *they*, those sons of bitches? *They* say a lot of things—mostly fiddlesticks, is what you finally figure out.

Phil repaired to his small, centrally located kitchen, cursing his inability to sleep. A graveyard stew was what he needed. He heated some skim milk in the microwave and toasted a slice of multi-grain bread. He buttered the toast, then placed it across the top of a small bowl, sprinkling a bit of brown sugar and cinnamon across the surface. Then he slowly poured the milk through the toast. Sometimes he could do it without having the bread fall into the bowl. That was as satisfying as breaking wind just as you got off a crowded elevator. You don't have to care as much about what you do at seventy-six, he mused. A lot of people say *Excuse me* after they fart. Why don't they just say *Look Out!* before they do? Be more to the point. Most young people think you're an old fart anyway—so why try to make liars of them? Senior citizen be damned, he thought, what I am is just plain old. The toast collapsed into the bowl of warm milk just as he set it down on the dining room table.

Phil's condo complex was handy for walking to his favourite downtown haunts, like the Y, movie theatres, the library, coffee bars and Herman's Dixieland Inn, the best jazz bistro in town. The jazz joint had been torched by some arsonistic arsehole, but had since been rebuilt.

Phil was close to Cook Street Village, a two-block-long "town centre" boasting the city's best video store, Pic-a-Flic, a Starbucks and its rival Moka House across the street, two grocery stores similarly facing each other and a few other small businesses.

He set off for his daily stroll. A hundred years earlier, the Cook Street area was a skunk-cabbage bog, then later, a rich bottomland of Chinese market gardens. Now the street was graced by a botanical archway of giant chestnut trees. In March, the trees sprouted their umbrella of leaves, followed by masses of white flowers standing upright on their limbs like fat scented candles. The falling petals dusted the street like wind-blown snow.

But this was late autumn, and Phil walked among the horse chestnuts, their pulpy burrs breaking on impact. Glistening brown nuts lay thickly along the boulevard.

Phil circled back through Beacon Hill Park to the waterfront. He sat on a bench to watch the breakers rolling up the strand and the hang-gliders catching updrafts from the cliffs along Dallas Road.

Exercise or die, according to the cardiologists, and Phil tried to get as much as possible. He thought it best to avoid the other golden agers in the parks. They only wanted to talk about health problems, preferably their own, the actions of their pacemakers, or indulge in the coulda-shoulda-woulda game. Boring. Phil didn't need anyone else nudging him further along the path of depression. Nor was he interested in the "things were so tough" gang, who'd tell you that when they went to school they had to walk uphill both ways, that their neighbourhood was so tough that loners had to walk in pairs, or that their town had been so small that the local prostitute was a virgin. Worst of all, some of the older women were determined to succeed in Victoria's second-time-around romance jungle. Phil always made sure to wear his widow-repellent aftershave.

And for God's sake, stay away from the World War Two veterans, Phil thought, and the nightmare of Canadian Legion beer halls full of army, airforce and navy types of old. Those bastards will terrify you with their tales of derring-do—or didn't, as the case may be. Some of them talk of nothing else but the times they went A.W.O.L—After Women or Liquor. Tell you they were in the toughest fighting force in the world, the naval airforce! Don't scoff, they say, and maybe they're right—if you've ever tried to force air through a navel you'll know what they mean.

A man sat down on the bench beside him. Recently retired, by the look of him. He wore a heavy cardigan and a scarf. His Alberta farmer's cap was pulled tightly down on his head, forcing his grey hair more sharply out from his ears, lending him an Einstein-ish air.

"You look like a fellow grandfather, sir. Am I correct?" Not a good opening conversational gambit with Phil.

"As a matter of fact I am," said Phil, "but I

hope we're not about to start bazooing about the glorious achievements of our respective little turd-droppers."

Taken aback by Phil's attitude, the gent replied, "An apt description for kids at a certain age. How old are yours?"

"Well past that stage, thank God. Not that they've stopped getting into a lot of crap I'd rather not hear about."

"Mine are very young. The four-year-old's a smart little tyke; took him to Playland the other day..." Phil had already tuned out and was plotting a polite escape. "...and he said, 'You're not going to die yet, Grampa, but soon...'"

"Well, let's hope the kid isn't as smart as you think he is. Better ask him his definition of soon. Well, I've got to get going. And a good day to you, sir. Try to make a liar out of the kid." Phil rose, nodded and hurried off.

Phil proceeded to the Professional Building on Quadra Street to check out a youngish old gal—well, she was considerably younger than Phil—who had served as Poindexter's office manager for several years, then suddenly switched to working for a blood clinic in the same building. Mary Podalchuk ought to know where Dex had kept his old medical files. If he could have a look-see at the files, he might find something. Or she might just remember someone who'd had a run-in with young Poindexter.

Phil took the elevator to Fitch & Curie Research Incorporated on the third floor. There wasn't a disease or a condition that a person could contract or inherit that didn't require a blood test of some sort. These bloodsuckers did a booming business, and Phil bet that physicians and surgeons owned the privatized clinic. He was well into an internal rant about government cutbacks to universal health care and the insidious creep of the expensive privatized alternatives when he arrived at the waiting room of Podalchuck's office.

"I'd like to speak with Ms. Podalchuk, please," he politely informed the receptionist.

"She's very busy right now, sir," the guardian of the inner sanctum replied.

"Then would you tell her that I'm sorry I accidentally flushed her winning lottery ticket down the toilet," Phil deadpanned.

A sharp inhalation from the receptionist as she jumped from her chair. "I'll see if I can find her."

Phil took a vacant pew in the reception area next to a glass-and-chrome coffee table. Fluorescent lights overhead gave the room a hard white glare. He scrutinized the magazine selection on the coffee table. He passed over editions of *CARP News* and *Canadian Geographic*, reaching for *Macleans* magazine. He might as well lighten up and read an old Allan Fotheringham article while he was waiting. Foth's columns demonstrated an acidulous wit, from which you could learn things in a back assward way. As the elephant said as he danced among the chickens, "It's every man for hisself." Was that an apt analogy for globalization?

He wondered whether Mary had changed from the last time he'd seen her. He used to call her Mary-Mary Quite Contrary, or the Polish Princess, because of her contrarian views and oft-expressed disdain for human foibles and frailties. She had no compassion for those she felt had wronged her world.

He was just reaching for another issue of the magazine when a solidly built woman approached, bearing a serious mien. Mary had put on some weight. Taller than average and in her late forties, she had salt-and-pepper hair pulled back too tightly from her face, exceedingly white teeth and deep brown eyes under heavy eyebrows. Her steel-rimmed glasses glittered as she fixed him in her sights. This was likely the appearance she chose to adopt in a business office. When she let her formerly red hair down, Phil knew she could be attractive, though he'd never considered her beautiful.

"Hello, Mr. Figgwiggin. Still the same old joker," said Mary. "I might have known it was you."

"We've got to stop meeting like this, people will get the wrong impression," said Phil, smiling as he got to his feet.

As they shook hands, Mary replied, not returning his smile, "Will they now, and what impression might that be?"

As always when he encountered Podalchuk, Phil found himself rising to the challenge of coaxing a bit of humour out of her. *"I'm shy, Mary Ann, I'm shy,"* he crooned, *"so put your arms around my waist, I promise I won't scream or cry."*

"Behave yourself. Those old songs never worked on me, you know that. So?"

"So you never take a coffee break, and maybe you didn't eat much for breakfast, so maybe you'd like to break some bread with me, or a piece of cake."

"And where and when might an event like that take place?"

"Maybe down at the Contessa Bakery, anytime you say."

Mary looked at her wristwatch. "Why do I get the feeling this is more than just a social call?" Phil shrugged amiably.

"Okay, I'll join you there in ten minutes."

"Right on," Phil replied.

He walked to the nearby bakery, a bit of old Tudor architecture on Fort Street's Antique Row. There were gobs of great pastry at the Contessa—to look at only, as far as he was concerned. He got a coffee and took a seat at an outside table so he could watch the passing browsers and inhale the sparkling fall air.

Mary soon joined him, and he went back inside to order another coffee and two microwaved sugar-free muffins. If he ordered anything else Mary was sure to berate him for not sticking to the heart-healthy diet she would assume he was on.

"You're looking good, Mary," he told her as he sat back down.

"Mr. Figgwiggin," she stated acerbically, "there are four ages of man: childhood, youth, middle age, and *You're looking good!* When you hear that phrase you know you are in deep trouble. So forget the flattery, what did you really come to see me about?"

"It was always tough to fool you, Mary," said Phil, sighing. "Okay, I'll cut to the chase. It's about Dick Poindexter, who could have killed him and why. I thought you might have some ideas along those lines. You knew most of his patients. Maybe one of them had reason to want him dead."

Mary stared intensely at him for several moments over the rim of her coffee cup. She took a sip and slowly set the cup down before she spoke. "It was a terrible thing to have happened. Since I used to be his receptionist, the police naturally had questions for me, but I couldn't help them. And I don't think I can help you, either."

"Maybe you've had some time to think since you talked to the police. Maybe you remember disagreements with patients, nutbar cases, something out of the general run of doctor-patient relationships?"

Mary continued to sip her Irish-raspberry coffee, the frown lines between her eyes deepening. "Richard was on the Discipline Committee of the College of Physicians and Surgeons. There were some doctors..."

Mary paused, "and others who had reason to dislike him, maybe even enough to kill him."

"Bears looking into. Anything else?" Phil pressed. "Doctors can't cure everybody. Didn't he have the usual number of patients who shuffled off this mortal coil while they were under his care?"

"That happens all the time," Mary admitted.

"Yes, but they can't talk and they can't come back from the grave and cut your heart out."

"Oh, Dick could cut your heart out all right," exclaimed Mary, then quickly added, "after all, he was a surgeon, but I'm speaking figuratively as well."

"Are you implying that perhaps it was tit for tat?"

"I'll tell you this, Philip. Life is a natural, never-ending cycle of birth, death and reincarnation. Our body is only the home that our spirit, our soul if you like, has formed for us. The dead may return to lead a better life the next time around." Phil couldn't remember ever hearing such philosophy from Mary before. "But in the meantime," she continued "the dead have relatives who aren't too happy about the manner of their passing."

"Good point. So maybe we find a patient who's now in the sweet bye-and-bye, who has a near and dear one who is mightily pissed off."

"We do a lot of urinalysis at the clinic, so that kind of language doesn't bother me at all."

"Well, I hope you washed your hands before you broke our muffins in half. So, can you think of anybody who might have had reason—"

Mary finished his sentence, "To want him dead?"

"Yes."

"I can think of several, but they would only be my suspicions about any possible animosity."

"Mary, if I could get a look into the files, something might turn up, some lead that I could follow. It might only be a possibility, but I feel I have to do anything I can to get to the bottom of his murder."

"Why should you get mixed up in this? What you're proposing is...well...an invasion of privacy or something. As a retired lawyer, you should know that better than anyone. And I'd be equally guilty in helping you."

Phil thought for a moment. "Can't we just put it down to trying to solve a murder?"

Mary suddenly laughed out loud. "Death comes to us all, Mr. Figgwiggin. Saints and sinners alike, and some people deserve it. We're living in a burning house and there is no fire department coming to our rescue."

"As Woody Allen once said, 'I don't mind dying per se, I just don't want to be there when it happens.' Especially if it comes in such a horrific form, as it did for the doc. Who, incidentally, is going to find out that I looked at some of his files?"

Mary sat silently for several moments, her eyes following the pedestrians walking up and down Fort Street. Finally she answered, "You can't tell anyone where you got the information, assuming you do find something."

"If I find nothing, no harm done," Phil hastened to reassure her. "My lips are sealed regarding the details of someone's gall bladder operation. I'm only looking for a lead I could follow to some conclusion. I'd still have to prove it some other way, or find some way to get the law to find what I already knew was in the files." One thing about Contrary Mary, thought Philip, she'll either go for this or she won't, but she won't dither.

"Let me check my schedule." Mary consulted the small day planner she extracted from her purse. "End of November, beginning of December. Hmm. A time of great change. Two very powerful planets are locked in opposition. Mars with its aggression, Pluto showing powerful obsession. People feeling the need to transform something."

Phil's eyebrows rose as Mary's recitation continued. "Very aptly put," he commented, "but what's with the horoscope routine, Mary?"

"Tonight would be a very auspicious time to search for evildoers. The veil between the spirit world and the living is very thin on this date and the two worlds become transparent to each other."

"Does that translate into 'I'll do it?' "

"These are not ordinary times—change is about to erupt. Yes, I'll do it," Mary agreed, "as long as I don't get dragged into anything. I'll make up a short list of the files you should check, and I can get you into the file room after the janitor goes off duty. I always meant to turn in that extra set of Dick's keys that I have kicking around in a drawer someplace at home."

"Good."

"Meet me in the parking lot about twelve tonight."

Once Mary let him into Poindexter's office and showed him the filing system, she left Philip to read the files she had selected. "If I'm going to have to hang around for a while," said Podalchuk, sounding resigned, "I might as well get some work done."

All was quiet on the midnight front as Phil made himself comfortable behind the dead man's desk and picked up the first of the files.

He found little of interest at first. Most of the entries were cryptic, apart from descriptions of the medical problems involved.

Phil paused to read more carefully when

he reached the Shivagitz file. Early in his career, Poindexter had been assisting Dr. William McCarthy in an emergency appendectomy upon a fellow physician of Lebanese extraction, Dr. Don Shivagitz. McCarthy suffered a nervous breakdown during the performance of the operation, slashing the patient's stomach muscles in two directions.

Poindexter came to the rescue. He pushed McCarthy aside and stuffed Shivagitz's guts back in as best he could, then stitched him up and hoped for the best. McCarthy was taken away in a straitjacket. Everyone involved, hospital included, became prime targets for lawsuits, as Don Shivagitz hadn't been a happy camper. The doctors were insured, and typically, the medical profession closed ranks. The matter was settled out of court with barely a ripple of publicity.

Several files later, Phil came to Martene Jennings, age fifty-four, who died of heart failure on the operating table during a bypass operation. Phil shuddered involuntarily at the thought that while he had survived his own bypass, such operations still entailed a fair degree of risk.

Jennings was a widow with a couple of grown kids. No indication of anything strange. As it happened in a percentage of

cases, fate seemed the likely cause of death.
Something had to get you in the end.
Nothing here, thought Philip, as he came to
the last pages on file.

Then he found a copy of a letter of condo-
lence from Poindexter to a Riley Eldridge.
Why not to a Jennings? Poindexter was asking Eldridge not to take Martene Jennings's
death so hard, that the heart team had done
all they could on the bypass operation, but to
no avail. Poindexter's letter affirmed that the
advice he had given Eldridge about other
treatments for Jennings's condition was med-
ically sound.

Obviously someone had a grievance,
thought Phil, scratching his goatee, because
the general tone of the letter smacked too
much of an attempt to placate, rather than
console, an angry recipient regarding some
previous advice or circumstance. Nothing
much to go on from that, but Philip wrote
Riley Eldridge's name below that of Don
Shivagitz in his notebook.

The rest of the files yielded even less. Mary
had primarily listed cases that involved
death due to a heart condition, since
Poindexter's killer seemed obsessed with
that organ. Replacing the files, Philip
switched off the desk lamp and let himself

out through the main office and into the hallway. He stopped by to collect Mary and they
left the building together.

In her car, Phil turned to Podalchuk. "This
Jennings woman. Tell me about her."

"She was a treat, no doubt about it, in more
ways than one," Mary replied.

"Meaning?"

"A very pleasant lady, old-fashioned, pretty,
and I took to her immediately, something I
couldn't say about her male friend."

"A guy called Eldridge, Riley Eldridge?"

"That was the name, yes. A sullen type, in
my view. She was too good for him. He pro-
fessed much love and concern for her well-
being, if you could believe him."

"How did he take her death?"

"Hard."

"Did he blame Poindexter?"

"He did. He was very unhappy, very angry.
I just remembered—before the operation, he
used to come to the office with her and discuss her heart problem with Richard."

"Did you ever hear what was said?"

"Not much. They talked about a treatment
called chelation. I can't remember anything
specific that the doctor may have said about
Eldridge afterward, except that they had quarrelled. This is normal, by the way. Doctors

usually don't reveal much about their patients, except to other doctors."

"How about Don Shivagitz, what happened to him?"

"Well, he eventually healed after that fouled-up operation, got feeling better and tried to carry on his medical practice. But he was never the same."

"I wouldn't think so. Shivagitz would have trouble for a long time with all his stomach muscles cut like that."

"That's right. There are some sports and activities he wouldn't be able to do," Mary agreed. "He was not happy with Richard, I can tell you that, and maybe with good reason."

"What happened to the head surgeon, McCarthy?"

"He was in a rubber room for a while. I don't know what eventually happened to him. There's a lot of pressure on doctors, some of which is their own fault because of their lifestyle. The devil only knows why he snapped, and at such a bad time, too. Richard stepped in before McCarthy could do more damage, but Shivagitz didn't seem to appreciate that. With McCarthy out of the way, maybe Poindexter was the only target he had for the grudge he was harbouring."

"It's a theory," Phil said with a sigh. "Not

much to go on, but I'll follow up on these leads. Thanks for your help, Mary."

"That's all right," said Mary, a decided edge to her voice, "but really, why do you want to play private eye? Are you sure you're up to it? You are meddling, and the way of the transgressor is hard. Remember, you're looking for a vicious killer and things could get dangerous."

"Granted, it's not my line," Phil replied, "but I have this strange compulsion to get involved, to try to find out the who and why. Don't ask me to explain it."

Mary looked at her watch and yawned. Phil took the hint. "Sorry for the late night. If you think of anything else, let me know. Drive safely, and good night, nurse!" Phil got out of Mary's car and headed for his own vehicle.

Six

Richard Poindexter's demise left a vacancy on the Discipline Committee of the College of Physicians and Surgeons of British Columbia. The committee members gathered at the Vancouver office for an ad hoc discussion.

"We'll have a hard time replacing him on the Board," said Raymond Giles.

Avery Sutherland, fidgeting in a corner, nodded in agreement as he stared into his coffee cup. "Dick supported the College's position on a lot of controversial subjects. Gave us strong leadership, did some good works. We're going to miss him."

George Penner grimly shook his bald head. He looked like a character out of *The Pickwick Papers* as he peered over the horn-rimmed glasses perched on the end of his nose.

"Normally, I'm a very caring person," he said, his gruff delivery contradicting his words, "but in Dick's case, for some reason I don't give a damn. At the risk of speaking ill of the dead, for my money he was too opinionated and prone to embroidering the truth; many of our rank-and-file practitioners would certainly agree with me. Constipation of the brain and diarrhea of the mouth is my diagnosis."

"Let's not lose our perspective," the registrar, Barry Logan, broke in. "Poindexter may have been a nuisance in some ways, but he was very effective on the committee. Maintaining the high standards of the medical profession isn't a piece of cake, as you well know. Sure, there are some members who won't lose any sleep over Dick's untimely death, and some may even be happy he's no longer sitting in judgment over them."

"But surely not to the extent they would..." Bill Portman paused, "No, I can't imagine. Still, someone did him in. Whoever it was knew a bit about bypass surgery."

"Damn little, from what I hear," Penner quipped. "Sounds like one of your jobs, Portman."

"Get stuffed, Penner," the other shot back.

"Is that one of your medical opinions?"

"Enough, gentlemen, enough," said Logan,

running a hand through his blitzkrieg of grey hair. "Our Dick has to be replaced and I've drawn up a list of potential candidates for you to study. I'll initiate the election process right away."

"You'll have no trouble finding a replacement, Barry," muttered Portman. "No shortage of doctors eager to look down the throats and up the rectums of their colleagues."

"How's that business about chelation therapy coming along?" asked Jock McNeill from his easy chair by the window. "Chelation was one of Dick's concerns, wasn't it?"

"Didn't you hear?" Logan sounded surprised.

"No. I've been on holiday—South America, Santiago and a side trip to Easter Island."

"It was a bit odd," said Portman. "Dick went off the boil on that subject about six months ago. He literally stopped talking about it. So what happened in that lawsuit against Robert Madigan? Wasn't Poindexter the one pushing for legal action?"

The registrar bristled. "Yes, he was. And we established our legal position at the examination for discovery and subsequent court hearing. Madigan was ordered to comply with the terms of the Medical Practitioner's Act, and we're in the process of obtaining the medical records of the patients involved. Then we can conduct our summary investigation. Too bad Madigan refused to provide access in the first place. Would have saved himself a lot of trouble."

"To say nothing of the legal expense," Portman remarked. "Madigan shouldn't have gotten mixed up in that quackery anyway. We had plenty of complaints from other doctors, as I recall."

There was a momentary silence as the assembled healers contemplated the last remark. "We haven't stopped Bob Madigan," said Penner. "He's still chelating people, and not for lead poisoning, either."

"If I thought chelation would take the lead out of my ass and put it in my pencil," McNeill quipped, "I'd try it myself."

"They tell me he's taking this lawsuit extremely badly," said Penner. "The stress is getting to him. He may quit, but he's not someone you want to fool around with. What are we going to do next?"

"That's what the disciplinary committee is for," Logan chimed in. "We'll decide whether Madigan's use of EDTA chelation therapy is an appropriate treatment for atherosclerosis."

Penner spoke up again. "Bob Madigan's one doctor who's not sorry to see Poindexter check out. You can bet your medical practice on that."

Seven

If Phil was going to try the private eye bit, there was only one way to start—by asking questions. He decided to see an old acquaintance, a former adversary really, Crown Prosecutor Justin Thorndyke. Maybe Thorndyke could clue him in on whatever murder theories were extant in the Poindexter killing.

It was a perfect morning, the air crisp and clear, the sunshine flickering through the remaining leaves of the oaks lining the avenue and ricocheting off the wet pavement. Victoria was swept by westerly winds that brought waves of showers, then blew away the clouds to again reveal bright blue skies. The city was usually spared the socked-in drizzle that plagued Vancouver through the winter season.

Phil walked north from Beacon Hill Park. He reached the seawall of the Inner Harbour via Thunderbird Park, a collection of totem poles of various native nations, then strolled past the Parliament buildings, the Royal British Columbia Museum and the Empress Hotel.

Seeing the Empress reminded him of a Canadian wartime joke that depended on the locale for part of its humour. The Douglas Street site directly behind the Empress Hotel—the famous Crystal Gardens—used to boast the world's largest heated salt-water swimming pool.

An RCAF pilot from the airbase at Patricia Bay, just married, checked into the Empress with his new bride. They were shy about making love in the daylight, so to pass the time till evening, the groom suggested a dip in the Crystal Pool. He was an expert swimmer and eager to demonstrate his prowess to his bride, who'd never seen him swim. She elected to watch from the stands. Her husband rented a one-piece cotton swimming garment. When wet, the swimsuits left little to the imagination. In fact, they revealed a great deal of everything. After showering, the groom emerged from the locker room showing off his manly form at the deep end of the pool. Waving to his nearby bride, he dove in and churned the pool for several lengths, using the Australian crawl and several other strokes, likely saving the breast stroke for later in the evening.

When he looked up again, to his consternation, his bride was gone. Disgruntled, he exited the pool, dressed and rushed to their honeymoon suite, where he found his bride stretched out naked on the bed, completely zonked out, unconscious. Good Lord, what was the matter? Then, in her handwriting, he saw a note on the dressing table: *The vaseline's on the bureau, the shoehorn's on the shelf; I saw your tool at the Crystal Pool and chloroformed myself.*

The Law Courts Building on Burdett Avenue at Blanshard Street was Phil's destination. An overcrowded, poorly designed rabbit warren, the place suffered from serious security problems. To accommodate the overflow until a new facility could be built, the Crown was renting space in the nineteenth-century courthouse in Bastion Square that had long since been converted into a maritime museum.

If Thorndyke wasn't busy, Phil planned to invite the man for a pint of draft in one of the local pubs. The nearby Old Bailey Pub, perhaps, or the Cherry Bank Hotel just across the street from the courthouse, the ambience

in either being more conducive to the sh
of any views Justin might have on ...e
Poindexter murder.

Crown counsels were housed in a cramped
corner on the first floor. Employees shared
old desks, as they had for years, and the
equipment appeared as rundown as Phil
remembered.

He was ushered into Thorndyke's private
office by a prim female secretary, her neat
appearance in sharp contrast to the clutter of
her boss's office.

A bookcase against one wall was jammed
with legal texts, photos, a bowling trophy.
Files and papers were stacked on every available space, including the two chairs in front
of a large dingy green metal desk and the
tops of the several filing cabinets.

On a corner of the desk underneath an old-
fashioned reading lamp, one framed photo
showed a smiling fisherman proudly displa-
ying the prize salmon he'd caught, and another showed a woman with two children mug-
ging for the camera. Justin apparently
worked from the small clear circle on the desk
in the centre of the desk and pushed papers
outward onto the stacked files at the edges.

The secretary noticed Phil's scrutiny and
remarked with some asperity: "He doesn't

allow me to touch any of this stuff, says he knows where everything is. And if you believe that, you'll believe he'll be along any minute. Make yourself comfortable. I've told him you're here."

Phil removed a law book from a straight-backed chair, easily resisting any latent desire to peruse its contents, and sat. Thorndyke burst through the door, halted suddenly and stared at Phil in disbelief. "Figg, I haven't seen you for what—four, five years?—you obviously haven't died, and here you are. How the hell are you?" Justin forcefully pumped Phil's hand, then plumped his large frame into his padded swivel chair.

"Ignorant, no change," replied Phil, "but I lie a lot. Never discuss your physical condition with anyone. It's a pain in the ass."

"Same old Figgwiggin, I see. Then you'll want to get right to the point. You must have a reason for coming to call on me. We were never bosom buddies, but you know, I always respected you as an adversary."

"Opposite sides of the fence. You were offence and I was defence."

"I knew enough not to skate between you and the boards. What can I do for you, Figg?" asked Thorndyke.

"You know Richard Poindexter, Jr. was murdered?"

"Of course. The police haven't laid any charges yet, so we're not involved in any prosecution in the matter. Sergeant Harry Muldoon's handling the investigation, and under the charge approval process, our office has to assess the evidence involved in any case the cops bring us, then okay the charges."

"Numb Nuts Harry! I remember him," said Phil, stroking his goatee, "but not with a lot of affection. Wrong-headed and arrogant."

"I'm not a big fan myself, but that's off the record."

"You talk to all kinds of people down at the cop shop, so I wondered whether you might have heard some theories as to who did that job on Poindexter."

"What's your interest? You can't be chasing ambulances. You were struck off the law list as inactive a few years ago, if I recall. At least, I hope you were. And that's a compliment," added Thorndyke.

"Poindexter's father was a close pal of mine. After he died, Dick, who was my godson, became my doctor. I don't like what happened to him and I'm determined to do what I can to help find his killer. I tried to talk myself out of getting involved, but I couldn't."

"Not your line of work, remember?" Thorndyke declared. "You used to *defend* murderers."

"I did, true, but I've got brains I haven't even used yet. I need to put them to work."

Thorndyke picked some lint from the Irish tweed jacket that accentuated his boyish good looks. He ran his fingers through hair just beginning to turn grey, then leaned his leather-patched elbows on the desk. "It's good to see you hanging in there, Phil," he said warmly.

Phil detected dejection behind Thorndyke's usual energetic manner and there was a tired look in the prosecutor's eye. His moustache could have used a trim, and his glasses sat slightly askew on his face. "How are things going in the justice department?" Phil felt constrained to ask.

"Ask me some questions," said Thorndyke, "and I won't tell you some lies. Morale's low in the office and I'm worried about the health of my staff if current conditions persist. We're sinking under an enormous workload, and poor management. There's no support from the Attorney-General's office. The stress is terrific and I'm afraid our best people are going to burn out if the caseload issue isn't addressed soon."

"Sounds bad," Phil sympathized, as much as an ex-defence counsel could manage when commiserating with the prosecution.

"I'll tell you confidentially. Headquarters down in that Gotham City bureaucracy in the Sussex Building houses a bunch of interfering, autocratic bastards, in bed with the politicos. They rarely come down here. They don't get into the nitty-gritty of court work; they just issue directives on how things should be done. I've got to tell you, the stress is getting to me, too."

"I sensed that," Phil said. "It's a shame."

"Everyone here's afraid of fallout, so we keep our heads down." He pursed his lips and sat back in his chair. "Sorry to belabour you with my problems when you're here on other business. I don't often get a chance to speak frankly with outsiders. I don't know much about the Poindexter case now, but I may hear something later that I could pass on to you, so long as it doesn't jeopardize the investigation."

"I hope your relationship with the police doesn't blind you to some serious reliability problems with the force."

"Harry Muldoon?" When Figgwiggin nodded, Thorndyke added, "It won't. You're in the book, I take it? I'll get back to you."

"How often have we said that to clients, Justin? That's nearly as bad as saying, 'I'm here to help you' or 'Everything's under control.' Have you got time for a libation over at the Cherry Bank Hotel?"

"I'd love to take you up on that, Figg, but I've got some urgent business. I'll have to take a rain check."

"Okay, I have a bit of my own business to attend to in a couple of days. I have to take a driver's test."

"I'm sure you'll pass," Thorndyke said reassuringly. "Didn't you used to be chauffeur for the Hell Drivers?" He paused for a moment, then said, "You know, you might be interested in this case—at least it'll be good for a laugh. Got time to come on a short trip with me?"

"Why not? What's up?" Phil asked as they headed out of the office.

"There's a line-up at the police station. You're not going to believe this."

"What's the crime?"

"You remember those protests in front of Len Amberson's office?"

"The federal minister. Sure, something to do with forestry or fish, wasn't it? What else in B.C.? The Raging Grannies and other shit disturbers were likely present and accounted for."

"Too true. Several of the protesters mooned

Amberson when he came out to speak to the crowd. The cops arrested half a dozen of them, charged them with public mischief and indecent exposure. All but one were found guilty. Fined five hundred dollars each."

"What about the other one?" Phil smelled a possible client, then felt a pang as he remembered he was no longer in the game.

"He's maintaining his innocence. His lawyer and the cops asked for and got a court order requiring the minister to come down and take a look at his bare bottom to certify whether or not he was among the mooners."

"Oh, I surely don't want to miss this," Phil said, chuckling. Too bad Mike Fowler couldn't be in on the fun.

As they got on the elevator bound for the basement, Phil said, "I wonder whether Amberson will recognize a real asshole when he sees one?"

"Well," replied Justin Thorndyke, "he should. He's had lots of practice in the House of Commons."

It was Thursday morning. Phil had no work-out scheduled at the Y, so he decided to check out Don Shivagitz, the accidental disembowelling victim he'd read about in Poindexter's files. When he called the number, the answering machine informed him Shivagitz was in the Middle East on an extended vacation. *If you require immediate assistance, please contact Dr. Pindar Dundat at 555-0686.*

So much for that for the nonce, Phil thought. File it under abeyance. He checked the weather from his bedroom window—a lowering sky, slight drizzle, wet streets, dripping trees and hedgerows; the kind of day the local tourism bureau never mentioned in their glossy brochures. Phil didn't feel like wetting his pant legs in the thin mush of trampled autumn leaves on the street below. His driver's test was still a day away, so should he risk driving to the police station anyway?

He'd just discovered that his driver's licence had expired nearly a year previously. He couldn't remember getting an expiry notice in the mail. Now that he knew, he'd have to be more careful. He hadn't been asked for his licence in a driving situation for a long time, but he was over seventy-five and had to take a driving test before he could obtain a new licence. Those Motor Vehicle bureaucrats were going to give him a bad time. In Phil's own mind, he drove just as well as he'd ever done. How well was that, certain wrong thinkers might ask, but Phil was convinced the test was a lead pipe cinch.

First item of business—breakfast at Tim Horton's. He drove onto their lot and parked directly in front of the cafe windows, a tad close to the adjacent car; close enough so that when he opened the door to get out, the leading edge gently touched the side of the car next to him.

A short wait to get his doughnut and cup of java. He also bought two apple cinnamon bagels and a jelly bismarck to throw in his fridge for future snacking. Finding a newspaper, he proceeded to eat his completely non-nutritional breakfast.

On returning to the lot, he placed the bag of bagels on the roof of the car. He got out his keys and opened the door. Again the door touched the side of the car parked next to his. At this point a young stud with long black hair streaked with yellow, wearing a Vancouver Grizzlies jacket, a two-day stubble and a bad attitude, came marching out of Horton's toward him.

"Hey," the stud said loudly, "do you realize that your car is hitting my car every time you open your door? Don't you have any respect for other people's property?"

"You mean to tell me that my car touched your car?" Phil replied, glancing down. "I don't see any damage, not even any marks. You've got a metal protection strip along the side."

"That's not the point. Your car's banging into mine. Not touching, banging. You gotta cut that out."

"Me? I didn't touch your car," Phil protested, even more loudly. "You said my car touched your car."

"No, it's you that's doing it."

"Wrong. It was my car that did it, like you said," Phil replied gruffly. "You said that!"

Suddenly rage and anger shook Phil's frame. Slamming his door shut, he started kicking the side of his own car with all his might, although his rubber-soled shoes weren't doing any damage, all the while shouting, "Bad, bad, bad car! I'll teach you to touch this man's vehicle, you son of a bitch. He loves his car. He regards his jalopy as a projection of his penis. And you're doing this kind of crud all the time, aren't you! Trying to get me in trouble again, aren't you, you piece of shit. I've never liked you, you rotten lemon. I'll show you, you inconsiderate bastard, you can't get away with this kind of crap. Getting me into these situations. Just take this shit-kicking and learn something from it."

"Your car's not doing it, you nut, it's you," the young man yelled.

"Are you crazy?" Phil loudly continued,

launching into another wild tirade. "I didn't touch your goddamn car. My car did. You said it did. Now I'm going to teach this car a lesson it won't forget in a fucking hurry!" Phil administered more kicks to his own vehicle. "You exhaust-retentive piece of sna-fued dog defecation," he yelled, the veins in his neck protruding.

His accuser started to back away. Phil opened his car door and was about to get behind the wheel.

"You've left a package on the roof, sir," said the macho in a conciliatory tone.

"Thank you," said Phil, quietly and politely, as he reached for the bagel bag. "Our cars are now even with each other. A good day to you, sir." He backed out and drove away.

"Well, that was satisfying, if I do say so myself," Phil said aloud as he headed for the police station. He again wished his sidekick Mike had been with him. Mike would defi-nitely say Phil's method acting was improv-ing, but that playing these kinds of head games could be dangerous. Phil only wished he had more chances to perform.

The new police headquarters on Caledonia at Quadra put the old Fisgard Street police sta-tion to shame. A modern three-storey building, a combination of reinforced concrete and steel with aluminum composite brown panel cladding, the sixty-five thousand square feet of space provided ample room for the officers, including a private office for Harry Muldoon.

With fingertip pressure on his temples, Harry tried to ease the fitful throbbing of a tenacious hangover. He reached under his hair and—*pop! pop! pop! pop!*—in a few seconds he held most of his thick russet locks in the palm of his hand. All that remained on his scalp were four gold snaps embedded deep in the bone of his skull.

A victim of inherited baldness, Harry had no wish to be called a slaphead by the younger women he liked to date. They wanted guys with a full head of hair and Muldoon had found the ideal way to provide it.

For four thousand dollars, a plastic mould was made for Muldoon's head. Human hair was sewn into it and cut to suit his style and to blend in with his remaining fringe of hair.

The titanium sockets had fused with his skull in three months. Gold snaps screwed into the sockets held his wig in place. The hairpiece was supposed to last four years and stand up to regular shampooing. Muldoon figured a thousand a year wasn't too much to pay to solve what had become a traumatic emotional problem.

What he needed now was more sleep and less nightlife, he thought, yawning and flinching at the pounding behind his eyes. Yet Muldoon was savvy enough to admit, at least to himself, that he wasn't about to change his lifestyle.

His abrasive attitude infuriated his fellow officers, but Muldoon had put away his fair share of run-down hustlers and bag snatchers, home-invaders, muggers, rapists, bank and condo robbers, fraud and forgery artists and arsonists.

First-degree murder happened less often, but despite the Poindexter case being little more than a week old, his superiors were getting antsy for results.

The public relations office was working overtime to allay public fears that some madman was running loose in the city, and urging tipsters to call Crimestoppers. Despite the two-thousand-dollar reward, no useful information had been called in to the hotline.

A half dozen police officers were working on the file, including Harry's new gofer, Wade Cavanaugh, but they still had no promising leads and Harry was feeling desperate.

He snapped his rug back into place and

levered his broad-bellied, five-foot-eight fire-hydrant frame out from behind his desk in search of a fourth cup of coffee. He had big teeth, a craggy nose and errant eyebrows, but he dressed well, both on and off the job. His expensive wardrobe, along with his title, worked magic on a succession of women.

Unfortunately, the effects were temporary, as witnessed by the two marriages he'd bombed out on during his rise through the ranks and the fact that none of his subsequent relationships had lasted more than a couple of months.

Just as Muldoon reached the drip coffeemaker on a corner table by his office door, his receptionist buzzed him to announce Philip Figgwiggin's unexpected arrival. Muldoon remembered the lawyer from a few years back, but the memories were no more fond than those concerning his ex-wives. Muldoon retreated to his desk and asked her to show Figgwiggin in.

"Do you want a cup of coffee while you explain why you're here?" was Harry's brusque greeting.

"Just had one at Horton's," Phil replied and sat down uninvited. "But a second one wouldn't hurt. Thanks."

"I remember you cross-examining me in a

few courtrooms in years past," Muldoon remarked. He poured two mugs of coffee and handed Phil's over, then sat down heavily. He rubbed his temples again, then took a long sip from his mug. "Cops don't like defence lawyers, you know, probably never will."

"Not feeling too well, Sergeant?" Phil ignored the barb.

Harry muttered his assent. "Actually, I've got sexual concussion."

"What might that be?" asked Phil, smiling.

"A fucking headache!" Harry drained the rest of the cup and sighed. The brew did make him feel better. "What can I do for you?"

"The Richard Poindexter case. None of my business of course, but—"

"You got that right," Muldoon interrupted.

"—as a friend of the Poindexter family I'd like to see the perpetrator caught, and I think I can help. I've got time on my hands, and—"

Harry didn't let him finish. "Do you happen to have a private investigator's licence?"

"As a matter of fact, no."

"Any experience in this line of work?" asked Muldoon. "Because I have about as much use for private investigators as I have for a second belly button."

"About as much time as I've had in bed with virgins," Phil shot back. "But if you consider that I've had plenty of experience as a criminal defence lawyer, then I think I qualify."

"The regs are that you have to get a licence from the Security Programs Division of the attorney general's ministry."

"What are they going to ask me? Whether I have a grade twelve education and the ability to say 'Have a nice day?'" Phil replied.

"You need two years experience in investigative work in a private firm or as a police officer. Has someone hired you to look into the murder?"

"Not yet, but it's a possibility. I just wanted to talk to you. Volunteer to do some legwork, something to help." This was the point, Phil later remembered, where Muldoon had thoroughly pissed him off, and cemented his decision to investigate on his own.

"My advice to you, Mr. Figgwiggin, is to stay completely out of the matter. We're dealing with some kind of psychopath and you could get hurt."

"I agree, but it's likely a psycho with some connection to Poindexter. I thought maybe I—"

"Don't think, okay?" Harry bristled.

Damn this Muldoon, thought Phil, he never lets me finish a sentence.

"That's our job," the cop continued, "and

we don't need any help. We have some leads and we're working hard on the case. Don't take this the wrong way. I appreciate your offer to help, but the best thing I can do for you is to wish you lots of sex and travel."

"Meaning?"

"Fuck off, Figgnewton!" Muldoon added, grinning wolfishly.. "And I say that advisedly and without malice aforethought, for your own good."

Telling Phil what to do and where to go was becoming a habit with the cops. From now on, he'd treat them like he would an elephant with diarrhea—give them lots of room.

"Okay, Harry. Keep working on that friendly attitude." Figgwiggin picked up his coffee mug, returned Muldoon's grin, and reached across the desk to clink mugs with the cop. "A toast, then," he said, "without malice aforethought and for your own good: 'A man may kiss his wife goodbye, the rose may kiss a butterfly, the wine may kiss the frosted glass, and you, my friend, may kiss my ass.'"

That brought Muldoon out of his chair, but Figgwiggin was already at the door and slamming it shut on his way out.

Eight

Daylight in the swamp, or at any rate, in this godforsaken hellhole I call home, were Phil's first thoughts as he got out of bed. Should he breakfast or shower first? Never too hungry on first arising, he decided on the shower.

Towelling himself afterward, Phil proceeded to put on his shorts, pants, shirt and slippers. As he did so, he noticed the *Important Information* notice on his dresser, placed there as a precaution against forgetting the next day's road test. Not checking the expiry date of his old driver's licence before he was seventy-five had been a bad career move; now the bastards had him by the short and curlies.

Bring a vehicle that is roadworthy and complies with the requirements of the Motor Vehicle Act, he read from the sheet, *two forms of identification and your current driver's licence.*

He was sure he'd pass the test. How hard could it be?

In any case, he'd be able to accomplish two missions simultaneously, since Riley Eldridge was going to be his examiner. An old friend who was head honcho in the Motor Vehicle Branch had waived the rules and granted Phil's request to have Eldridge assigned to him.

The buzzing of the condo intercom startled him from his musings. He wasn't expecting anyone. Was he supposed to be doing something this morning? He lifted the handset off the wall and said, "Yes, what is it?"

An unfamiliar woman's voice came through the speaker. "Could I have a few words with you, Mr. Figgwiggin? On a business matter, a legal problem."

"No longer in the business, ma'am. I'm technically retired. Sorry."

"I was told you could offer some good advice."

Phil paused, then against his better judgment and out of politeness, he replied, "I'll come down." He buzzed her in, checked his fly, locked his door and grabbed the elevator.

A handsome woman was waiting for him

in the lobby. Her age was hard to guess, but about forty, give or take. She was beautiful in a Rubenesque way. Phil got the impression she could throw you some really big curves and that her fast ball still had plenty of heat. Maybe he should bunt and try to get to first base. Then he remembered the hardball rules: If the count is two strikes and you bunt foul, you're out; and if you're too old to play, you can still be a coach.

Her plumpness was carried on a large-boned frame and Phil got the impression of underlying strength. She wore her glossy blonde hair long, her lipstick a bit bright on a pretty pair of lips.

Her pale clear skin was stretched tightly over high cheekbones. A red coat featuring black leather banding was thrown open to reveal a long black skirt and a tight green lace blouse over a white camisole. He knew he shouldn't stare, but those mammary glands were brobdignagian.

"Could we talk, Mr. Figgwiggin?" The woman's direct, blue-eyed gaze noted his scrutiny and challenged him to raise his own eyes to her face. "May I come in?"

"Ah, there's a problem there," Phil said with a wide smile. "You're in the right place, you're just forty years too late. I'd rather you didn't come up. One of my idiosyncrasies happens to be that I don't allow women in my bachelor rooms." In truth, the opportunity hadn't arisen lately, but his place was a mess.

"It won't take long." She flashed him a quick warm smile of her own.

"Just tell me what you want right here."

"They said you could be cantankerous. Okay, then, where could we go to talk? My name is Annie Chance, and—"

Phil interrupted, a loud bell ringing in his brain pan. "Now that's a different ball game. I think I know what you want to talk about."

"I need help," Annie said, staring at him intensely. "I've got to talk to someone other than the cops, and a retired lawyer seemed to be a good choice."

"But why me?"

"I heard you were asking questions about Dex's murder."

Phil thought that one over. "Who told you that?"

"I have my sources. Look, my car's parked right outside. Maybe we could go for a drive."

"Best offer I've had all day," Phil said affably. "Wait in the car, I'll get properly dressed and be right out. I haven't had breakfast yet, we could go somewhere and eat."

They drove a few blocks down Dallas Drive and parked along the seawall near the Ogden Point Cafe. They lined up inside "The Dive," the name by which the eatery was generally known.

Phil opted for scrambled eggs, toast and coffee. Annie, stating she had already eaten breakfast, settled for a hot chocolate. Since it was too chilly for the outside balcony, they chose a table adjacent to a front window, overlooking the shipping docks.

Chance eased into a chair with a slow, graceful arrogance, ignoring the stares of the male customers. She sipped from her drink then leaned toward Phil, her alto voice cutting easily through the hubbub around them. "The police have given me a real good grilling. They think I did it, you know."

Phil knew better than to ask whether she had. Easily slipping back into old habits, he kept his face blank and let silence coax the story out of Chance. Never force people to lie, but try to find out if they're telling the truth.

Chance related her shock and outrage at finding herself a suspect and at having her place searched and her person fondled by the cops.

"If they had enough evidence, the cops would have charged you by now," he reassured her.

"Sergeant Muldoon figures I had a motive."

"What's his theory?" Phil asked. As the fitful sun spilled through the window, it revealed the dark circles under Chance's eyes, which she'd tried to conceal with makeup.

"A few days after the raid, the police wanted to talk to me again, and foolishly, I agreed. Figured if I co-operated, they'd leave me alone. Muldoon thinks I'm a tart. He suggested I'd seen more ceiling than Michelangelo, and that I use the massage business as a front for prostitution."

"He said that?"

"Yeah, and to my face. I'm no angel, that's for sure, and a woman has to make a living. But Muldoon's got no class. He also said my bedroom was known as the O.K. Corral. They've gone over my car and apartment. They still have the car, so I've had to rent the one I'm driving. Can I confide in you, Mr. Figgwiggin, off the record?"

"I'm not in the father-confessor business, but you can rely on me not to breach a confidence. What's on your mind?"

Chance waited until the waitress deposited Phil's breakfast on the table.

"Okay, then. I was sleeping with him. I'd known Dex—Dick, I mean, I called him both nicknames—for a long time. We shared some interests and had a thing for each other. Then he started cheating on me, not living up to his promises."

Annie was becoming agitated. "I was plenty mad, but that's all. He was no bargain, anyway. I knew I couldn't count on him, he'd done the same to other women. He could be fun and he could be generous, but some of the things that man did..."

"That's interesting, Ms. Chance. He was my godson and my doctor, and his father was a good friend of mine, but you obviously knew Dick better than I did. I'd like to know more about him, if you don't mind."

"I don't know that it means anything, but Dex upset a lot of people, maybe enough to make them want to kill him."

Phil poured some ketchup beside his scrambled eggs and tackled his breakfast as he thought over what Chance had said. "What did Poindexter do?"

"He'd play practical jokes on people he didn't like or saw as enemies. Some of his pranks were pretty vicious. Not exactly good behaviour for a doctor, so he was careful to keep that side of himself hidden most of the time."

"Can you give me an example?"

"Well, for instance, a Jehovah's Witness

team came to the door once. I was there, we'd been drinking. Dex saw them coming down the street so he went to the door naked, with blood smeared all over his face and body. It looked as if he'd been eating a fresh sacrifice. Then he said he'd like to contribute to their church. He'd bought a beef heart at the meat market, and he was hiding it behind his back. He stuck out his hand and offered it to them. They took off in one big hurry."

"It's a bit gruesome, but I doubt the Jehovah's Witnesses would come back and cut his heart out," Phil said as he opened a little tub of orange marmalade and spread it on his toast.

"No, but it's typical of the gags Dex would pull. So if Dex did something really bad to someone, something they figured had ruined them, whether they deserved it or not, then how is that person going to react if they were to find out who did it to them?"

"Likely not too well. Did something like that happen?"

"Maybe. And I'd like to get the police off my back and onto a productive track. If they don't catch this murderer...

"They haven't had much luck so far and maybe they won't. Some cases are impossible to solve."

"My own reputation and my safety are at stake. My massage business is going down the tubes already."

"So what else can you tell me?"

"So, while we were having our massage sessions and I was giving Dex a vanilla oil rub or showing him the Viennese oyster position, we used to get pretty snapped up on white lightning—"

"On what?"

"Champagne and vodka on ice, no mix. Powerful. He told me some things that he did to people he didn't like."

"Did Dick say who they were?"

"No, he never told me that. But he had to brag to someone, and sometimes he'd get so drunk he wouldn't remember some of the things he'd talked about. But I remember once he said a guy had done him dirt and he wanted to get even real bad. I'm not sure that it involved drugs, but there was big money in it, and I vaguely recall that this guy had done something which cost Dex a lot of money, a lot of concern."

Annie paused to sip her hot chocolate. "Dex knew how to get anything in the drug line." she continued. "I never did figure it out, but there was some connection between the same guy and some bigshot down in San

Francisco, a mafia boss maybe, who was serving time in jail."

"Those types seem to have a lot of pull even while they're in jail," Phil interjected.

"Yeah, well anyway, Dex knew what was going on between the two men, so he wrote a nasty letter to this mob boss, who's a real nutcase, apparently. Dex insulted the guy's mother and his whole family, threw in the Catholic Church and the guy's parish priest for good measure and he signed the other guy's name. He wore gloves and typed it on someone else's computer. He was careful not to leave fingerprints on the letter, and he sealed and stamped it using a wet sponge."

"Good thinking. Nowadays they can get your DNA from any bodily fluid. Was this guy a friend of Dick's?

"No, more like a business associate he had some kind of a deal with."

"Did the letter get results?"

"Dex said it did. The victim was visited by some very large gentlemen with no necks who beat the living shit out of him. Put him in the hospital for a good long time. Maybe they thought they'd killed him, but they failed. Dex said it saved him from doing it himself."

"Did Dex, as you call him, say where this happened?"

"Yes, in Vancouver."

"Well, that would certainly be a motive for retaliation, if that guy ever found out how Dick set him up. If the victim wasn't paranoid before, he could be afterward. Funny thing, a truly dedicated paranoid can switch from victim to aggressor very quickly, especially if they strike in retaliation. Or they may strike first, in order to prevent some perceived persecution or hostile action. Maybe Dick was a little paranoid himself. I didn't see him often, but I didn't detect any signs of that, Ms. Chance."

"Call me Annie, please. Dex had a great bedside manner and he was a good actor. He was also an expert in the use of additives."

"Meaning?" His breakfast finished, Phil reached for his coffee cup.

"Ever hear of Rohypnol?"

"That's the date-rape drug, isn't it?"

"Yes. Related to valium and halcion, a derivative of benzodiazepine. Tasteless, odourless, dissolves in anything and works like a powerful sleeping pill. A guy slips it into a girl's drink, she blacks out. Since another effect of these 'roofies' is memory loss, she's not even sure if she's been sexually assaulted."

"Do you mean to tell me Poindexter used that on people?"

"Yes, at least once that I know of. He also spiked one guy's drink with medroxyprogesterone acetate. I used to be a nurse but I had to look that one up. It's a powerful prescription drug that deadens the sex drive bigtime. If a stud gets even a bit of that, it's limp dick time."

Phil winced as this phrase registered. Maybe someone was slipping him some of the stuff. Couldn't be old age, could it? No, old age is when getting lucky means you've managed to find your car in the parking lot. "Who was the guy?"

"A local Lothario who was doing the horizontal mambo with some lady Dex took a shine to, or so he told me. Someone Dex knew socially. Did it to him over a long period of time, so the guy got more and more depressed as he lost his libido."

Annie smirked. "Then to top top it off, Dex started slipping him some methylene blue, pulverized pure niacin vitamin tablets, and some phenolphthalein."

"What do those things do?" Phil asked.

"Methylene blue passes through the body without changing colour, so your urine comes out blue. About a half an hour after taking the niacin, you get hot flashes and your skin turns bright red. Phenolphthalein is a white crystalline substance used as the active ingredient in chocolate-based candy laxatives. You put all those together in the right proportions and the victim starts to get hot flashes as he races for the men's room before he craps himself, his skin turns red, he pisses blue, and he can't get a hard-on." Annie grinned broadly at him.

Phil, about to finish off his coffee, suddenly lost his taste for it. "My God, think of the trauma that would have caused!"

"Yes, wouldn't it! And what do you think you'd do if you ever found out who'd done that to you?"

Annie had turned serious again. "I thought if you're looking into his death anyway, maybe you could find out who some of his dirty tricks victims were. Maybe there's some hospital or police record. Either way, like I said, I want the cops to stop hassling me."

"You couldn't predict the results of doing those things, it would depend who you did it to. I don't know whether I can help you, Annie, but I appreciate everything you've told me."

"Thanks for hearing me out," said Annie. "Just so you see that Dex Poindexter wasn't always Mr. Nice Guy, as most people thought. He could be a real prick, but you had to get to know him well before you found that out. And I should know."

"You're sure you don't have any names to go with these stories?"

"Sorry, I don't. But someone like that could have gone around the bend and done him in after I left him sleeping that day. If you could find out who it was that Dex beat up, then that could be the person who murdered Dex."

"You have a point there."

"Do you suppose we could meet again?"

"Yes, if you like. *Don't know where, don't know when, but I hope it is some sunny day,*" Phil half crooned the words, though not as well as Vera Lynn, then added, "unlike this one." He nodded toward the overcast sky, which had begun to leak. Returning his companion's smile, Phil's thoughts turned wistfully to baseball once again, wondering what it would be like to beat out a bunt to first base.

Nine

Riley Eldridge didn't feel like doing a damn thing, but he had to go to work in ten minutes. Placing the back legs of the wooden office chair just the correct distance from the wall of his private cubicle, he tipped back until his muscular shoulders were in a comfortable leaning position, and stretched his long legs across the top of the metal desk. From the breast pocket of his yellow shirt he pulled a pack of Spearmint gum. He unwrapped a stick, popped it into his mouth, closed his eyes and began to chew slowly as he rested his head against the wall.

Autumn was long gone. Frost had struck and the season's unusually bright red, orange and yellow leaves had disappeared in a succession of wind and rain storms driven in off the Pacific coast. Victoria's weather never failed to surprise, and although Christmas was everywhere in the stores, the city was now basking under blue skies and balmy breezes. Eldridge heard the cawing of crows in the bare branches outside his office window in the Ministry of Transportation and Highways building.

Riley didn't think of himself as lazy, he preferred to think he worked so fast that he was always finished. The monotony of his job was getting to him and he tended to take out his frustration on the people who came to him seeking a driver's licence. Putting the boots to the clowns always made him feel better. It got rid of his inner rage and he did his job at the same time.

Nobody in this fucking town knew how to drive, anyway. Especially the pisse-pauvre stubble jumpers and those combine pilots from the prairies, who migrated in droves to the West Coast. All their licences should be revoked, they should be forced to learn to drive all over again. If they couldn't learn properly, then walking was good enough for the bastards.

Only a few more years to go on the job and

then, as he often said, "the government can kiss my Royal Canadian ass goodbye."

His Motor Vehicle Branch colleagues didn't call him the Terminator for nothing, and his exacting standards now dovetailed with the get-tough policy of the Insurance Corporation of B.C., the government-owned insurer of vehicles and drivers in the province.

At eight-thirty Riley straightened up and reached for the daily schedule on his desk. Who's on first, Riley said to himself, what's on second—and I don't know who on third. Ah, yes—a Philip Figgwiggin's first up.

Eldridge was surprised at the notation that Figgwiggin had specifically asked for him to conduct the test. Why me, Riley wondered, I don't know him. He consulted his computer. Over seventy-five, expired licence, retired lawyer. They always think they're shit-hot drivers. We'll soon find out.

Riley sang a bit of doggerel, sotto voce, as he left his cubicle for the public waiting room: *Here they come, the daily scum, their bloodshot eyes aflame...*

Phil Figgwiggin waited in the main office portion of the building. Riley called his name over the intercom and Phil stepped up to the counter. They exchanged brief introductions but did not shake hands. Figgwiggin's right to drive was in Eldridge's back pocket and they both knew it.

Riley relished a wimpish attitude in an applicant. He wanted to see the ingratiating smile, the whipped-dog attitude before a bureaucrat who has total power. No such body language was evident in Figgwiggin, and this really riled Riley.

For his part, Phil regarded the whole exercise as part of the general process calculated to make older Canadian citizens lose any lingering self-respect. He therefore adopted an attitude he had developed going through customs, where you truly were dealing with the bottom of the bureaucratic barrel: Don't cringe or supplicate. Stand tall, look the agent straight in the eye and don't smile. Your demeanour should not be that of a child waiting to be scolded, but of an objective scientist studying a familiar but unappealing insect. Don't volunteer anything, don't make small talk. Never lose your cool. Don't look for trouble.

Phil figured he's been driving perfectly well for fifty years, the carping of some detractors notwithstanding, so he was simply going to maintain your space and his integrity. That should be quite enough to come out on top of the situation.

They went for a fifteen-minute drive in Phil's car, through the usual routine of a driver's test, gradually relaxing in each other's presence. Eldridge asked Figgwiggin to perform certain driving operations and Phil complied. Returning to the Motor Vehicle Branch office, Phil placed the vehicle in park but didn't apply his emergency brake.

Riley drummed on his clipboard with his marker pen while scratching his thigh with the other hand.

There was one aspect of his job that Riley loved: the look in their eyes when they got the results.

"Mr. Figgwiggin," he said with a crooked smile, pausing for greater effect. "I'm going to have to fail you."

Phil stared at him for a moment in astonishment, but managed to suppress outright chagrin. "Is that your opinion, sir? I would have thought otherwise."

"You have one hundred demerit points against you for infractions against safe driving. Forty-five is the maximum allowable. I'd like to go over your mistakes." Eldridge did just that, and Phil grudgingly recognized some of the errors he'd made.

"I'll give you a learner's licence," Riley said with a smirk. "You can take the test again, but until you pass, you have to have a fully qualified licence holder with you whenever you drive. Do you understand, sir?"

"Certainly, Mr. Eldridge," Phil said through clenched teeth like Kirk Douglas. Bureaucrats all have two things in common, he thought. They have opinions and they have rectums and they should try to shove one thing up the other. But he had to keep his mouth shut if he wanted to beat this jack job and eventually get his licence renewed.

"Could I have your expired licence, please?"

"You could, except for the fact that I lost it. Don't know how it happened," Phil fabricated. "Damned inconvenient, I must say. Likely what caused me to miss the expiry date. I was such a good driver, no one ever asked for it. So you see, I didn't know it was gone for the longest time."

"Well, now you have a learner's licence you can use."

"Thank you for those few kind words. Now, if we're finished with this driving business, Mr. Eldridge, I wonder if I could take a few more minutes of your valuable time?"

"Of course," said Riley, disappointed at the non-reaction he was getting from this arrogant customer. Why hadn't he started the usual brown-nosing? "What did you want to talk about?"

"You've probably heard by now about Dr. Richard Poindexter's murder. I'm aware that you had some contact with the doctor in relation to a friend of yours, Martene Jennings."

Eldridge's smile faded and was replaced by a frown. After a slight hesitation, he answered, "Maybe so. Why are you asking?"

"Poindexter Senior was a good friend of mine, and his son was my godson and my doctor. I'm looking into his death and I thought you might be able to clear something up."

"What's that?" asked Eldridge.

"I understand that you wanted Ms. Jennings's medical problems—her heart condition—dealt with through some other kind of treatment. I have to assume that you and Poindexter disagreed about what the treatment should be. What can you tell me about that?"

Struggling to control his rage, Eldridge finally spoke. "You could say we had a difference of opinion. No, not even that. I suggested an alternative therapy, chelation, and Poindexter said it wouldn't be effective."

"And?"

Riley took a small cigarette case from his

breast pocket, extracted a roll-your-own and lit up. Taking a deep drag, he gazed across the parking lot. "And he downplayed the success stories I'd heard about chelation, said it was nothing but quackery and that Martene should have nothing to do with it. I wish now that we'd at least tried it before the operation."

"That being the unsuccessful open-heart bypass that was the immediate cause of your friend's death?"

"Yes."

"Did you hold Poindexter responsible for Ms. Jennings's death?"

"Look," replied Eldridge with some agitation, "if you're asking if I killed him, then the answer's no."

"I'm just trying to eliminate you as a suspect," Phil hastened to say.

Riley took another drag. "Okay, I'll tell you the rest, not that it'll do any good. I booked an appointment with Poindexter. I wanted him to check out some growths on my face and neck, probably just too much sun, but I wanted to rule out cancer. And I wanted a copy of Martene's medical records, because she was considering chelation. We'd both read articles that said chelation cleaned out plaque or helped prevent formation of free radical particles that clogged veins and arteries. I would've tried anything to keep her from going under the knife."

Phil felt a pang of sympathy, remembering his own surgery.

"Poindexter gave it to me with both barrels. There's a lot of garbage being printed these days, he said. Studies show the treatment's useless, EDTA chelation has no measurable effect on arteriosclerotic plaque or other arterial disease, blah, blah, blah. He said doctors were making a ton of money peddling something that didn't work, and that they should watch their ass, because the College of Physicians and Surgeons was going to come down hard on them."

Riley's lip curled. "He also talked about dangerous side effects, possible kidney damage, and that doctors' medical insurance wouldn't cover them if they got sued. Anyway, I wanted him to let her try some other alternative remedies, because bypass surgery doesn't always work, either, or not for long."

"What did he say to that?" Phil asked.

"He said throwing chelation at the whole body was like firing a shotgun at the side of a barn—you might hit something and you might not. The fact that you might hit the barn seemed to escape him. He told me to talk to the College and I did, but I didn't get anywhere with them, either. I guess they've got so much money tied up in drugs and mainstream procedures that they feel threatened by alternatives."

"So what happened then?"

"So Martene had the surgery. And died right after. Then I find out Poindexter's changed his tune. He took his sister to the States for chelation when she got some sort of heart disease and a terminal diagnosis, just like Martene. Now she's playing golf, and I've seen her at the Y. She must've swum thirty lengths!" Riley fell silent.

"What did you do when you found out about his sister?"

Eldridge's anger bubbled up as he answered. "I went apeshit, got roaring drunk. I don't remember anything I did for a week after I found out about that sister. But that was a long time ago. I was pissed at Poindexter, still am, but not enough to kill him. The fact that someone else hated him enough to murder him neither surprises nor bothers me."

"Got any ideas whose anger might have carried that far?"

"No, and I don't appreciate your using this

driver's test to badger me about it," Eldridge snapped. "Come into the office and I'll book you for another test. By the way, you didn't put on the emergency brake when you parked here. That's another ten points against you," he remarked triumphantly.

"The car is in park on level ground," Phil protested.

"You're supposed to put it on when you park, no matter where you are."

"Yeah, and burn out the brake when you forget to release it next time you drive off." Phil did his best to hide his irritation, given the hell Poindexter had put Eldridge through. Then he remembered the ninety-one-year-old woman on oxygen support in his building. She still had her licence and was still using it.

Eldridge gave him a date three weeks hence. Phil protested the delay.

"Sorry, that's the best I can do," said Riley, not looking sorry at all. We're booked solid with everyone trying to get their licence before Christmas. Here's your copy of the test results and a booklet on safe driving, which I suggest you read before your next test. I'm going to do you a favour and let you drive home from here."

Phil's control deserted him at that point.

Wound up like an alarm clock, he snatched the papers from Eldridge's hand, turned on his heel and stalked toward the door.

"You didn't say thank you," Eldridge called after him.

Phil didn't look back. He called over his shoulder, "That saves you having to say you're welcome," and kept on walking. I don't thank muggers either, he thought.

Riley Eldridge stared at the door long after Figgwiggin was gone and said in a low voice, "And fuck you too, mister, fuck everybody that looks like you, and fuck the car you drove in with." Martene was the only person who'd ever brightened up his miserable life, but she was dead, damn it, and nothing was going to bring her back. "So just butt out. It's none of your damn business.

"Hold the next driver," he said to the receptionist. "I need a short break."

Back in his office, Eldridge sank dejectedly into his chair and lowered his arms and head onto the desk top, even though he knew he should get back to work. "He deserved what he got," Riley muttered under his breath.

Ten

Victoria's trees were now entirely bare, city crews having swept the foliage into piles and removed it in a desultory manner to some giant compost heap somewhere in Sooke or elsewhere in the hinterland. The fall days had passed in pleasant disarray, only sporadic rain showers marring the self-satisfaction of the denizens of Lotusland, who each year so bravely eschewed the rigours of Canadian winter as experienced by the suckers who remained in Winnipeg, Medicine Hat and Moose Jaw.

Christmas was at hand and people were still buying cut flowers and poinsettias from the corner grocery stores and taking their eastern friends to Butchart Gardens. They always gave lip service to Bing Crosby and a White Christmas, while fervently praying they never got one. Many Victorians never even thought about snow, Phil Figgwiggin among them.

But this time around, Victorians didn't have to dream of a white Christmas; they got one. Before it started, Phil was visiting a favourite haunt, the Stonehouse Pub in Sidney near the Swartz Bay ferry terminal linking the peninsula to the mainland. Originally a Tudor-style private residence in a wooded region on Canoe Cove Road, the all-stone alehouse featured a sunny patio, large flower gardens and a lawn where cro-quet addicts could take on the charming but recalcitrant Irish host, Simon Deane.

Jazz was featured that Saturday afternoon, and a goodly crowd was on hand. Jim Moffat was on piano, while Hughie Ketcheson, Glen Acorn and the more famous Roy Reynolds from Vancouver alternated on saxophone, vying with each other in what was billed as the Battle of the Saxes.

When the snow began to fall, Simon, in a burst of generosity, ordered rum eggnog all around to celebrate the rare sight. By then, Phil had already had his quota of two pints of the best house brew. The snow just kept coming and the temperature continued to drop.

Deep down Phil knew better, but he insisted he wasn't too high to drive. Like so many of his former clients, he got behind the wheel full of Dutch courage and headed for home.

The road conditions were a piece of cake for an expert driver like himself. But he hadn't figured on the rapid approach of a monstrous snowstorm, unheard of among the pampered denizens of Victoria and environs. It would enter the record books as the worst blizzard and the most snow since 1915. People would have to struggle to reach food and medicine, risking frostbite to get to the coffee shops for a latte fix.

The storm was still in its early stages, though, and Phil managed to drive to within a few miles of the Victoria city limits when he spotted the police. A Drinking Driving CounterAttack! Damn! One too many for the road and now the cops for a chaser. Then he cursed again, remembering the licence he no longer possessed.

Phil swung off the highway onto a side road and into a small farm yard. The dirt was wet and his tires spun deep into the muck. Stuck! He had no choice but to abandon the mired vehicle.

Phil tramped back toward the highway through the bone-chilling wind and increasingly dense snowfall. He felt like Good King Wenceslaus, tramping through the snow that lay all about, deep and crisp and even. The moon didn't shine brightly on this night, but the frost was pretty damn cruel.

But joy of joys, a cab approached, heading into town. Hurrah! Frantically waving the taxi down, Phil talked to the driver.

"Yeah, I'll take you into town, buddy, for fifty bucks."

"What? That's a rip-off!" Phil spluttered in protest.

"Take it or leave it," the cabbie whined. "You're drunk, you could throw up in my cab, you're all wet, I got other fares coming out my ying-yang. Cash in advance or get lost."

And then Phil remembered that after quaffing at the Stonehouse, he didn't have that much cash left on him. "I'll take it, but unless you'll accept my credit card, I'll have to pay you most of it when I get back into town. Okay?"

"No, it's not okay. I said cash on the barrel head or no go."

Never should have told him that, Phil realized. "Look. I'm in a jam, you can trust me, you have to help me out here."

"No, I don't, man. Goodbye." Tires spun in the snow and the cab shot away in a white cloud of swirling snow. Phil's jaw hung open in disbelief.

Phil cursed the son of a bitch, and he kept up a barrage of cursing as he walked desperately through the storm blowing in off the Pacific Ocean and slamming into the lower tip of Vancouver Island. His anger and a few shots of nitroglycerine spray under the tongue kept him going. Eventually he got a lift, but only after he was wet through, cold to the bone, and covered in slush. The more he thought about the cab driver, whose face he'd never forget, the madder Phil got. God, he hated that bastard.

On the heels of his harrowing experience, Phil was plagued with fatigue, back pain and shortness of breath. Those were the symptoms he dreaded. Was his heart condition launching a warning shot across his bow? Flu, a touch of pneumonia? He convinced himself that he was simply over-fatigued. His only consolation was the driver's test coming up the following week, between the holidays.

It was the season of peace and goodwill, but anger takes many forms, from teeth-grinding rage to silent smouldering. Phil knew he had to stop thinking that way, didn't need to like the situation but had to accept it or let the thing stress him out even further.

A couple of days after the storm, much of the snow was gone, cars were back on the street in droves and the paralyzed city was gradually returning to normal. Phil was walking uphill towards the YMCA when an angina attack hit him.

His face flushed, he worked hard to breathe through flared nostrils. He felt like someone was squeezing the blood from his heavy heart like a sponge. Damnation! Phil reached for the nitroglycerine spray container he usually carried in his jacket pocket. Wrong jacket. Damn again.

The low stone wall near Rose Manor beckoned and he sat down.

How long since his last bad case of angina? Except for that walk in the snowstorm, four, maybe five years, wasn't it, since his quadruple bypass at the university hospital. He was lucky he'd had the operation before he had a heart attack. Nothing lasts forever, he mused. Except death, which I'm trying to evade, and taxes, which I'm trying to avoid.

The angina recurred with increasing frequency over the next several days. Phil reflected that he'd lived through the depression, got caught in the war, missed out on free love and now the old-age pension plan was going broke. A run of hard luck. Now he was going to have to do something more about his dickie ticker.

Shit happens, Phil thought as he lay dead still on his back in the hospital bed, Nurse Ladi Dodd's hand pressing hard into his crotch. What a way to spend Christmas. But then, maybe Dodd's ministrations were his Christmas present.

The nurse was using a ten-pound canvas bag of lead shot, trying to staunch the flow of blood from the angioplasty entry wound in the artery in his groin. Ladi's dark wavy hair fell across his right arm, which lay at his side between them. She bent over him as she sat by the bed; his hand was tantalizingly close to the pendulous breasts outlined by her uniform.

Another angiogram had indicated to his new cardiologist that blockage in one of the veins used in the bypass was causing the trouble. Phil was informed they could fix that with an angioplasty operation. They would insert a balloon at the location of the blockage and blow it up, widening the diameter of the vein and increasing the flow of blood.

In the middle of the night before the operation, the surgeon had come to him and told Phil that he wanted to insert a stent rather than rely on the balloon business. Was that okay? When the medic explained that a stent was a small wire mesh gizmo to be inserted at the site of the blockage that would hold the vein open, Phil could only say, "Okay, you're the doctor."

The job was performed the next morning, where he got a close-up look at the chaotic state of the country's healthcare system: stretchers lined up in the hallways, overworked staff scurrying back and forth and accident victims being turned away for lack of space.

The aftermath required that Phil lie perfectly still on his back for three days, in order to lessen the chance of blood clots and give the stent site a chance to heal smoothly. All of which had created the circumstances in which he now found himself, alone with Nurse Ladi Dodd at three-thirty in the morning.

Nurse Dodd had been doing her rounds on the graveyard shift when she found Phil lying in a pool of blood. She was out of the room like a shot, returning seconds later and slamming the bag of buckshot onto the incision, pressing home the weight into his inner thigh just to the right of his family jewels to stop the bleeding.

Phil felt a brief stirring at this unexpected pampering of his privates, and almost of its own volition, although there was little room to put it elsewhere, his hand rubbed lightly against Dodi's breast. She shifted position slightly but otherwise made no comment.

I'd better say something if this situation is to go on much longer, thought Phil. Make light of the situation. "I think I'm getting excited, Ladi, so would you mind if I used the palm of my right hand as a platform for your left breast?"

Nurse Dodd broke into a laugh. "Well, if it would make you feel any better, go ahead."

"We've got to stop meeting this way," said Phil, smiling.

His hand was just inches away, so he gave her left boob a quick friendly touch. These days it was difficult to know the exact legal meaning of either sexual harassment or consent, unless you got it in writing, so it was best not to press his luck.

It was fortunate that she had checked him out, because Phil hadn't known he was bleeding. His blood was extremely thin from the warfarin rat poison the cardiologist in this

Jack the Ripper trade school had prescribed to keep his blood from clotting.

The drug prevented new blockages where the angioplasty had been performed and the stent inserted. Less chance of a stroke. That was the general idea, but Phil felt like a car whose engine had run over two hundred thousand klicks and was down a quart of oil. For a day and a half now, he'd been lying here on his back, shagging the dog and selling the pups, with still another day and a half to go.

"Ladi, can I ask you something?"

"I'm already married, Mr. Figgwiggin, so I hope that's not it."

"Ah, too bad, you've dashed my hopes. No, I was wondering how you got a name like Ladi. Never heard it before."

"It is unusual, I'll admit. My great-grandmother, also Ladi Dodd, was a famous tennis player. True story. She was the British ladies tennis champion for one year back somewhere in the 1890s or early 1900s. But I never met anyone who knew that."

"I'll be jiggered. I keep meeting nurses with strange names. Did you happen to know a nurse named Annie Chance?"

"Yes, she's the one they talked about in the Poindexter murder. I didn't know her personally. She nursed up and down the Island before she went into business for herself as a masseuse, and from what I hear, she offers other services on the Q.T. as well. But good for her, I say. A lot of us would like to get out of this racket and into something more lucrative. What about her?"

"Is she what you'd call reliable? What do you know about her?"

"She had a reputation as a good nurse. She worked operating rooms for awhile, and you've gotta be on the ball to handle that."

"So she would've assisted with a lot of heart operations of all kinds."

"Sure. As a matter of fact, I think she worked on an operating team with Poindexter. Heart operations were one of their specialties. That's likely how they got involved with each other. Annie was younger then and very pretty. Judging from the *Times-Colonist* photo, Annie's still got a lot going for her."

"What about Poindexter's, what was his reputation?"

"Dick? Just like his name," Dodd said dryly. "He fancied himself a swordsman, but he never came on to me."

"Picked on the easy ones?"

"Why, thank you. Yeah, we once had a nurse here they called Tonsils—you know, because so many young doctors took her out..." Phil chuckled in appreciation as Ladi continued. "Sorry, a little hospital humour. Anyway, Poindexter and his wife apparently separated a long time ago, but he never wanted to commit to anything permanent. I think he and Chance had something going between them. That's my theory, if you're asking for my opinion."

"I am. Was there anything, well, strange about Poindexter?"

"How do you mean?"

"Was he ever depressed? Did he act hyper or manic? Any eccentricities at all?"

"I never heard anything like that, just that he was a sexist jerk. I was glad I never had to work with him. Understand, I hardly knew him."

"Did you ever hear any scuttlebutt around the hospital circuit as to his playing nasty practical jokes or dirty tricks?"

"No, none that I ever heard." Dodd removed the bag and inspected the wound. "The bleeding's stopped, but just keep that bag in place for another half hour, just in case. Try not to move for a while, okay?"

She patted Phil's hand as she rose from his bedside. "I've gotta go now, Mr. Figgwiggin. We're short-staffed and I've got a lot of other patients to see. Buzz the nurse's station if you have any problems. It's been fun talking to you." She left Phil flat on his back and alone with his thoughts.

Could Annie Chance have been lying to him about Poindexter's pranks, perhaps to cover her involvement in the murder? He was inclined to believe she was telling the truth, though. She'd been part of Poindexter's operating room team, and she'd been dumped by her erstwhile lover. That and her business gave her both opportunity and motive, but also a legitimate reason for her presence in his home.

Muldoon's fixation on Annie as the prime suspect was understandable, but there were many other possibilities lurking out there in the boondocks somewhere. Phil's mind was like a parachute—he had to keep it open if it was going to function properly. A number of people had reason to hate Dick Poindexter. But Phil, as he said to himself, first had to vamoose, 23 skidoo, get the hello out of this hospital and back into the land of the living. He hoped Mike was back from Edmonton, for then he'd have an intelligent sounding board for his theories, a great good friend with whom to discuss the case.

Phil won his release from the hospital five days later, the staff's stern admonition about taking it easy following him off the ward. That wasn't his style, although he wisely cancelled his driving test. He did realize the need to convalesce after the insertion of the stent, but felt his recuperation this time would be faster than after his horrendous bypass operation of several years ago.

"Take it easy" might be good advice, and some old farts subscribed to the theory that retirement itself was a form of taking life easy all the time. Phil didn't think so, always feeling the urge to do something, anything, in an attempt to keep his future in front instead of behind him. Having had little in the way of exercise for a period of time, his muscles were weak and sore, but day by day he began to feel better.

Apart from his exercise regimen, maybe this was the time when he could straighten out the mess in the den he called his office. Go through the files and the bookshelves and the computer. Throw some things out perhaps, get rid of the crap, restore some order to the rest. Then maybe he'd be able to find stuff when he wanted it, not a few days or weeks later. Or never. At least he wouldn't have to spend half his time searching for something he knew he had around the place somewhere but couldn't locate.

Good idea, but then the phone rang and he picked up the receiver. His chum Mike was back. Great! Come down for a visit, Mike invited. Of a surety. Pronto. Good thing Mike lived in the same condo block. A visit to his apartment would make Phil's appear to be in apple-pie order by comparison, which might kill this strange house-cleaning urge.

The welcome between the two friends was warm. "Hope you're feeling okay. You're looking thinner," Mike said with some concern as they shook hands and clapped each other on the back.

"Thinner but better," Phil replied, as they sat on the worn sofa on Mike's enclosed balcony. "I did a short hospital stint while you were gone, but I'll fill you in on that later."

"I lost fifteen pounds myself," Mike declared. "Bet you can't even tell."

"That's a lot, how come?"

"I got circumcised."

Phil guffawed. Mike reached for a bottle of whiskey from a sideboard, which he opened then tipped into the mugs he'd set out on the table. He went into the kitchen and came back with a coffee pot, topping the mugs up with the brew. "Don't laugh. I asked the doctor what they do with the foreskins. Know what he told me?'

"No."

"Said they sent them over to Ireland where they planted them in the old sod. And when they got to be six feet tall they sent them back to Canada as Mounties. If they didn't grow very big, they sold them for dinky toys."

"You don't change," said Phil with a grin, hoisting his spiked coffee. "So what else is new and startling?"

"I've been working on a theory of mine. You know how we old guys have a hard time getting it up?"

"Problem all right, I'll admit. Old is when an all-nighter means not having to get up to pee. I'm working on that problem myself. Remind me to tell you what I've found out."

"I got to figuring: what is an erection, anyway? Just a rush of blood to the spongy material in the penis. Your body only holds so much blood. Now if you were to give yourself a transfusion of blood in a greater amount than what was in your penis, the blood in your penis couldn't get back into your body because it would be full. Q.E.D., you could maintain an erection for a long time."

Phil was a good straight man. "Interesting theory. Did you try it out?"

"Yeah, I did."

"What happened?"

"I got a big blood blister on the back of my head and I lost the woodie."

"So much for the scientific approach. That reminds me of the one about this woman who went into a record shop looking for a Christmas record..."

"How far back do we have to go for this joke?" Mike beamed with warm approval.

"To the days of vinyl records. Don't interrupt. The woman asks, 'Do you have Jingle Bells on a seven inch?' The proprietor replies, 'No, but I've got dangling balls on an eight inch.' The lady says, 'Is that a record?' And the store owner says, 'Well, the girls around here seem to think so!' "

"Not bad for this early in the day, but you can do better. Personally, I don't know whether to go bowling or kill myself. There's not much action around these days."

"National orgasm week just ended. I only pretended to celebrate," said Phil. "But enough of this pecker bonding. I'm going to see a doctor up-Island in Parksville as soon as I'm up to driving, and I could use your help. I need the company, and I'd like you along to observe when I meet this guy."

"Who's the doc?"

"Robert Madigan. He's got enough of a beef against Poindexter to be a likely suspect in the murder. The College of Physicians and Surgeons sued him for practicing chelation therapy, and Poindexter was one of the members who instigated the lawsuit. But I also want to ask him about this chelation stuff. I might try it myself."

"How do you know about the lawsuit?" Mike wanted to know.

"Mary Podalchuk used to be Poindexter's office manager, she told me some of it. Then I went to the courthouse and looked up the case. So I thought I'd check him out, and I'd like to get your reaction to him, too."

"Okay by me, just let me know when you're ready to go."

Phil got up from the chesterfield and picked his way toward the door around stacks of books and magazines, video and audio equipment, a cluttered dining room table and a massive stuffed moose.

When he reached the door, he spun around. "Mike, I know we joke a lot about sex, I mean who doesn't? Sometimes it's like joking is about all we can do about it these days. But I found out about something called the Testoderm Potency Patch. Here, a friend of mine's a pharmacist, he did an Internet search for me." Rooting through his breast-pocket filing system, Phil found the piece of paper he was looking for and handed it to his buddy.

Mike's glasses hung on an idiot string around his neck. He perched them on the end of his nose and scanned the read-out.

"For patients who are mildly hypogonadal. Hypogonadal? Is that a word?"

"Your gonads. Just read on," Phil urged.

"Hypo—big, gonads—balls. Hypo as in not enough, and gonads as in balls. I get it. Like the word rhinoceros. Rhino meaning thick skin. Sore ass meaning piles."

Mike stumbled over some of the medical terminology as he continued to read aloud. *"The Testoderm Scrotum Patch reproduces a normal level of secretion of testosterone in the gonads. Absorption delivers a smoother, higher level of testosterone in the morning, lower levels in the evening—"*

Mike stopped reading and glanced over at Phil. "So your chances of scoring are better in the morning. That jibes with my vague recollection of how it used to work."

He scanned the rest silently, then said, "This doctor says he was surprised that his patients were willing to shave their balls and slap a patch on there. It's applied with a polymer, for Chrissakes—you're supposed to glue the damn thing on. Says here you heat the patch with a blow dryer and stick it on. Great balls of fire, they've gotta be jockstrapping it! Oh, I see, it says, *This tends to be well tolerated.* Easy for him to say, huh? There's more, but it's getting hyper-technical."

"If I can locate some of these patches, you want to give them a try?" Phil asked. "Never be afraid to try something new. Remember, amateurs built the ark."

"Yes," Mike replied, "but professionals built the Titanic."

"So, do you want some or not?"

"Well, I guess so. I've been low on candle-power for a good many years. I thought it was inevitable. Is declining libido reversible? I don't know. Ordinarily you've got to love it, but at my age do I have the time or the patience to do all that missionary work? The wining and the dining you have to do to get laid!"

"Remember, never up, never in. You don't have to worry about that anymore, look." Phil grabbed a copy of *Monday* from a pile of magazines on the cluttered floor. *Monday* was a news and entertainment magazine offering several pages of ads for escort services. It came out on Wednesdays, a freebie publication which everyone in town took home. "Look at all these ads for Sex Ranch, and Seduction Unlimited." Phil did a quick count. "Ninety-nine. Now that's a lot of available help."

Mike's face did a fan dance as he formulated another thought. "Our high school system probably taught these girls how to fornicate, but I'll bet nobody ever gave them lessons in how to shave a scrotum."

"Well, if this Potency Patch catches on, a new trade will be created—the scrotum shaver, and some of them could become specialists in it."

"They could have poetry readings included with the shave," said Mike solemnly, "but I've still got my doubts about this treatment. There's something you're not taking into consideration."

"What's that?"

"The great amount of energy which one has to expend in the continual search for a piece of tail."

"Do I take it, then, that you don't want any patches?"

"*Au contraire*, put me down for a dozen. Better make that two dozen."

Christmas had produced, as the *Times-Colonist* put it, the Blizzard of a Lifetime, the Snowstorm of the Century, in which one hundred and twenty-four centimetres of snow had fallen in just over a week, thirty-four of it in one day, blowing away all previous storm records. But then the rains had come and warm winds had blown, and within a week, except for the biggest piles and drifts, all the snow was gone, and the crows were picking over green lawns dappled by gentle sunlight.

Phil was soon back to regular walks, enjoying the hint of spring in the air as he strolled along the Inner Harbour. He glanced across the street at a line of cabs hoping for tourist business.

When his gaze came to rest on the third taxi in line, Phil suddenly yelled, "Son of a bitch! It's him!" So loudly as to alarm a couple of old biddies seated on a nearby bench. He sat down with them to think the matter over. They quickly got up and moved away. What to do? Got it!

His mind made up, Phil crossed the street to the row of cabs and approached the driver of the cab that was first in line. "How much would you charge me to go out to the Stonehouse Pub in Sidney?" he asked.

"Forty-five dollars." the Sikh-Canadian driver replied.

Phil pretended to consider the price. "Not

on. Hmm, tell you what. I'll give you a hundred dollars to take me there, on the condition that we make love when we get there, or somewhere along the route. You know, anal and oral sex."

"Get away from me, you old pervert. I don't want anything to do with you. Go away or I'll call the police," the cabbie spat at him.

Phil moved along to the second cab in line. Leaning into the window, he said, "How much is the fare to the Stonehouse Pub in Sidney?"

"Forty-five dollars would be about right."

"That's a lot. But I'll tell you what I'll do. I'll give you a hundred dollars if you'll take me there and we make love to each other, have oral and anal sex when we get there, or somewhere off the highway along the way."

"You miserable old fart, you fucking pervert. You make me sick. Get the hell away from me before I get violent," said the driver.

Phil approached the driver of the third cab, the jerk who'd left him stranded in the snowstorm just before Christmas. He smiled and asked again, "How much would you charge to drive me to the Stonehouse Pub in Sidney?"

"Fare's forty-five dollars," the driver replied, barely looking up from his newspaper.

"Good," said Phil, "I'll keep that in mind for the future." Phil hopped into the passenger side of the front seat. "Now take me down to the Bay on Douglas. Let's go."

Putting the cab in gear, the driver circled past the first two taxis. As they passed, Phil, grinning from ear to ear, leaned out the window, and flashed two big thumbs up at the other drivers.

Eleven

"We're off in a cloud of date pits and camel dung," said Mike, climbing into Phil's car.

A bright early February sun shafted over the surrounding hills from a faultless blue sky, reflecting off the ocean. They were traveling north on the Malahat highway, slightly over the speed limit, in light traffic.

Opened in 1911, the Malahat Highway was immediately hailed as a scenic wonder, though it was barely passable. Since then a continuous process of straightening, widening and paving had turned it into Vancouver Island's most picturesque and famous drive. The road connects the giant cedars and firs of Goldstream Park to Mill Bay, while soaring above sea, river, farm and mountain valley along the eastern coast of Vancouver Island. Named after a tribe of Indians who lived on the northwestern shore of Saanich Inlet, the Indian name means "plenty bait."

There were still lengthy stretches of natural splendour along the Malahat, undisturbed by commercialism.

Mike reclined in the passenger seat, enjoying the passing vistas and the warmth of the sun through the windshield. "I don't want to doze off, so fill me in again, why are we taking this little jaunt? Apart from being a pleasant way to spend the day."

"Are you losing your memory?" Phil demanded, glancing at his friend.

"I don't think so, but I do sometimes stand in front of the refrigerator door wondering what I was looking for in there."

"We're going to see the chelation doctor, Madigan. He just might be connected to Doctor Dick's death, so I want to have a few words with him. I'd like to get your impressions, too."

"Doctor Dick was his moniker?" Mike asked, chuckling.

"Well, yes, and it was apropos for a number of reasons, apparently."

"Liked the ladies, did he?"

"So I'm told."

"Why does his murder matter so much to you?"

"His father wasn't just my doctor, he was one of my best friends. We had some good times together. Dick was my godson. I've told you that before, haven't I?"

"Yeah, you have, but now that we're on our way, I'm paying stricter attention." Mike glanced around the car's interior. "A different jalopy now, is it? Not too shabby, but a far cry from that big '78 Lincoln. What happened?"

"Had to trade the Lincoln; it was a gas guzzler. Too hard to park, too old. New working parts were difficult to get."

"Sounds like us." They both laughed.

Phil turned the conversation back to the murder. "Why does someone become a psychopathic killer?"

"Beats me. You're the lawyer, aren't you supposed to know stuff like that? I'm still trying to figure out why kamikaze pilots wore helmets."

"Maybe I don't need to know why the murderer's a psychopath to solve the case, but it might help. Anyway, about all I can do is keep looking and hope somewhere down the line some small thing will trip the killer up—a lie, strange behaviour, something."

"Any money matters involved? Follow the money and you'll find the answer to most crime. Money or sex."

"Point taken. Thank you, Watson."

"You're welcome. If you need help, just ask."

An RV with two sea kayaks on top pulled out to pass them. Mike gazed after them. "I wouldn't mind trying kayaking, maybe we should take some lessons."

"Yeah, sure. If we drowned, I wouldn't have to worry about this case anymore."

Mike went back to taking in the passing scenery as the kilometers slipped by. "Didn't you say you wanted to have a serious conversation on this trip? What's serious enough to talk about these days?"

"How about monetary reform?"

"Okay. I just said that money matters matter. We could try it for a while, but I told you I didn't want to doze off."

"It's an important subject, but nobody seems to want to talk about it. People spend weeks learning how to program their VCRs or run their computer, but simply refuse to study issues that seriously impact their lives and welfare."

And Phil was off and running. As he warmed to his argument about interest payments being the source of Canada's accumulated debt, he shifted into lower gear to help the late-model Aries take a steep grade. It was Phil's opinion that all the social benefits that had been built up in Canada since the war shouldn't go down the drain because governments since 1974 had bought into neo-conservative economic theory. Parliaments were elected to fight for the people, not for their own self-interest, the banks and big corporations, NAFTA, the MAI, the WTO and globalization.

"Our accumulated debt now primarily consists of interest, since we paid the banks back more than the borrowed principal long ago. This is because most of Canada's money is created by private banks as interest-ridden private debt, rather than being created by the nation itself as debt-free public money. If most of the money supply needed to run our country was created and spent into circulation directly by Parliament itself, then our taxes could be greatly reduced."

"I'm still listening," said Mike.

"Thank you. Few people nowadays ever study or learn from past history, or they wouldn't be in such reverence of investment bankers; they'd stone them to death. The problem isn't ignorance in government, but the illusion of knowledge."

"What you're basically saying, then, is that ninety-nine percent of bankers give the rest a bad name."

"Right! Well put."

"Doesn't Canada have to go through the bankers?" Mike asked.

"No, not at all, but stunned governments now borrow vast amounts of money from the private banking institutions, at compound interest. Why should they? They have the primary right to create money themselves. They're the government, for Christ's sake. Their mints already print the cash that's used in everyday business transactions, our paper bills, our loonies and toonies."

"Hey, I know that—weren't those coins a great invention?" Mike interrupted. "They call the toonie 'the queen with the bear behind!' And we do have a loonie-tune government."

Phil had by now worked up a head of steam, and was pulling at his goatee with some agitation as he expostulated.

"Both hands on the wheel, if you don't mind," said Mike casually, "this *is* the Malahat."

"Sorry," Phil replied, conscious of his dereliction of driving duties.

Mike had lots of time for his buddy, but

couldn't help his reaction whenever Figg embarked on a political rant. As Phil went on and on, Mike's eyes began to glaze over and his head drifted ever closer to his chest. He suddenly snapped awake and noticed that the car's speed seemed to be increasing in direct proportion to the vehemence of his friend's diatribe.

"Figg, for God's sake. I'm telling you—give me the gnat's ass of your argument or shut up."

"Deal. The economist Hixson said nothing's dumber than a government that can create money for itself allowing banks to create money that the government then borrows and pays interest on. This is simply too illogical and outrageous a procedure to be countenanced. If the feds exercised their right to create money, our taxes could be reduced, and we wouldn't be paying compound interest to private banks and helping them make billions in profits every year."

"Sounds pretty jammy for the banks. How do they get away with a bamboozle like that?"

"Because of laws made in years past, on the advice of bankers, mind you. The Mulroney Conservatives were worse than the Trudeau Liberals, but the stand-pat Chretien Liberals are going along with it. Canada was in the driver's seat once, but those bozos sold the car."

Mike responded with a touch of impatience. "I was taught at my grandmother's knee—not a pretty sight, incidentally—that the Liberals were a consummate bunch of bastards. Grannie actually pasted a picture of Mackenzie King in the bottom of the old thunder mug under her bed in her Saskatchewan farmhouse. Every time she had to go, she went all over him." Mike chuckled at the memory, then added, "And when you gotta go, you gotta go, and I gotta go a lot lately. We're near the summit and just about here somewhere is a tourist viewpoint. I think they've installed composting toilets by now."

"Those ones with the solar panels that run circulating fans and lighting? Good cans, should be more of them." Phil wheeled the car into the lookout and braked to a halt. "I might as well go, too. As the Duke of Wellington once said, never lose an opportunity to pump ship."

A salt-laden breeze bent the branches of the trees adjacent to a row of portable johns situated along the embankment. The grey plastic structures marred the view of the white-capped blue waters of the inlet far below and the cloud-decorated mountains rising from the opposite shore.

Phil was just emerging from one of the privies when a terrible string of curses erupted from next door. Phil rapped on the door and shouted, "Are you okay in there?"

"You're not going to believe this." Mike's voice was more subdued now. "I've....I've got my shorts on backwards."

Phil erupted in laughter. "Don't you know by now that the brown side goes to the rear?"

"This isn't funny, Phil. These are those long-legged boxers, and I can't get my tool out the bottom or over the top with my pants on. I've had to undress just to take a piss." Mike began to curse again. Phil stood guard, grinning as he listened to the maledictions emanating from the portable can.

Water sports finally over, Mike sheepishly got back in the car, eager to change the subject as they descended toward Mill Bay. "You gave a good summation on monetary reform, counselor. Just remember, the public don't know shit from Shinola, and doesn't seem to care what the present bunch of lobbyists, bean counters and fart catchers in Ottawa are doing."

"Fart catchers? Mike, I haven't heard that

term since–when–maybe the Thirties. Wouldn't it be better if you'd said that their nexus with reality is so tenuous that those who inhabit the kingdom of the wilfully blind are by comparison heralded as clairvoyants?"

"That's what I meant," was Mike's reply.

A few miles further, Phil broke the companionable silence. "There's another reason why I wanted you along on this trip."

"Other than checking out this Madigan joker? What is it?"

"I'm driving on a learner's licence and I need another driver in the car."

"What? How come an old bastard like you only has a learner's permit?"

"I guess it's my turn to be embarrassed. I was supposed to renew my licence before I was seventy-five. The Motor Vehicle Branch didn't send me an expiry notice, at least I don't remember getting one, so I drove for months before I noticed my licence was expired."

"So what'd you do when you found out?"

"I talked to the Branch, but they didn't buy my song and dance routine."

"So then what?" asked Mike.

"This Eldridge guy failed me on the road test. He bushwhacked me. On a completely deserted street, he got me for not checking my blind spot before I backed up. Did it in the mirror but not a physical shoulder check. Hit me for an improper left-hand turn, too, and said I didn't read a right-of-way situation correctly."

Although Phil had stayed calm at the time of the test, the memory of his failure was anathema to him, and he got worked up again as he told the tale to Mike. "There's only one word to describe Eldridge: infreaking-credible! May he struggle through life like a one-legged cat trying to bury a turd on a frozen pond!"

This outburst shocked even Mike. "For Chrissake, calm down, and slow down on the curves!" Mike stared at Phil, astonished at his unusual lack of control. "Don't get so steamed! You should know we can't control ninety percent of what happens to us."

"Yes, but we have a lot of control over the other ten."

"Watch out for this guy coming out of that driveway!" Mike roared.

Phil swerved just in time. Mike swallowed hard. When his heartbeat had returned to normal, he sought to reassure Figgwiggin. "You know they have to fail you at least once to demonstrate their superiority and show they're on the ball. Power-mad pricks, they have you over a barrel and they know it. I'll get even with this Eldridge bum for you if you want. Do you know where he lives?"

"As a matter of fact, I've seen his house. We drove past it on the test." Phil glanced over at Mike, uncertain whether his friend was joking. Fowler had pulled some classic pranks in his day, and Phil wasn't sure he wanted to encourage him.

"Does he have a nice lawn?

"Yes. Big one, looked nice. Why do you ask?"

"Okay, we buy multi large boxes of corn flakes. I mean a lot of corn flakes. We go over there some night when it's raining hard and spread the stuff on his lawn. It's real hard to remove. We can throw in some green liquid detergent, too, which will bubble up all over the place. When our boy gets up in the morning he'll find his lawn a soggy, green, bubbly, bad-smelling, mushy mess. If the weather stays bad, the stuff'll rot the grass. And if the sun comes out and it's hot enough, it'll bake hard. Either way, you get revenge."

"Right now I like the idea, but let's wait to see if they fail me again. Maybe I'll just send him a post card. It's the Christian thing to do."

"What kind of card?"

"I saw one that'd be perfect. On the front

page is a picture of Jesus Christ—robe, halo and all—and it says Jesus Loves You. You open it up and it says, Everyone else thinks you're an asshole. Mike slapped the dashboard and roared.

"Anyway, I'm glad you came along for the ride, particularly as I need a qualified driver in the car."

Mike suddenly sobered. "Hate to tell you this, Figg, but I don't have a licence, either. I let mine expire when I sold my car a while back."

"The hell you say. Damn it! And I thought by having you with me I'd be covered in case a highway cop showed up."

"Don't look now, but the blue and reds are flashing behind you as we speak."

"Holy scrotum! I wasn't speeding, what the hell does he want?"

"Maybe he's got a quota to make."

The police siren wailed and the cop car pulled them over to the side of the road.

Phil preferred not to wait in the car for the cop to talk down to him. He leapt out of his vehicle, closed the door and stood waiting for the cop's approach. Don't let him get in the dominant position. Mike got out more slowly on the passenger side.

"What's the problem, Officer?" Phil asked politely.

The policeman rubbed his chin as he looked Phil over, then said, "I'm going to give you a ticket for failing to do up your seat belt."

"How do you propose to prove I wasn't wearing it? You were behind me."

"When the buckle hits the pavement and drags along the road, the sparks tend to give you away," replied the cop with a grin. "May I see your driver's licence and registration, please?"

Momentarily taken aback but keeping his mouth shut, Phil got out his wallet. Which licence should he produce, the one which had expired or the learner's permit? He decided on the latter, handed it over and hoped the cop wouldn't ask to see Mike's licence.

The officer extracted a ticket pad from one breast pocket and dug a pencil from the other. Mike abruptly stepped up and engaged him in conversation. "Officer, if there's going to be a fine, is there a discount for seniors who also happen to be veterans?"

The ticket writing stopped and the cop shifted his scrutiny from the licence to the two senior citizens. "No. Don't suppose they've thought of that. Sorry about this," he said as he finished scrawling, "just doing my job." He tore off the ticket and handed it and the licence to Phil, and returned to his cruiser.

"That was close," Phil said as he watched the cop drive off before he pulled back into traffic. "Thanks for the diversion."

Phil parked in front of the Parksville residence of Dr. Robert Madigan, and the two men approached the house. The wood and stone edifice, grey with white trim, was set well back on a one-acre lot, with a profusion of oak, cedar and plum trees gracing the grounds. A rock wall ran along the front property line, broken by an iron gate bearing the sign *Do you believe in life after death? Trespass here and your belief will be tested.*

Opening the gate must have tripped a motion detector, because a recorded announcement came from somewhere ahead of them: *You are being monitored by a guard station.*

"I bet lights would come on if we were here after dark," said Mike. "This guy sure isn't taking any chances, is he?"

As they neared the house, Mike pointed out the camera, sitting high above the front door. A .357 magnum was painted above it, pointing straight at them. Another sign underneath read: *Anyone found on this property at night will also be found here in the morning.*

"What's going on here?" Mike asked

Phil shook his head. "I wouldn't hazard a guess at this point." He rapped on the door, noting its solid construction and the absence of visible hinges. A steel plate ran the length of the door on the lock side, no doubt covering a heavy-duty deadbolt. There was a peephole in the centre of the door.

A dog began to bark deep inside the house, the noise getting louder until keys were turned in the lock. A double-key system for extra security. The door opened and they were confronted by a stone-faced man with eyes like dark agates, and a massive, snarling Rottweiler straining at the leash held firmly in the man's grasp. Phil's heart performed a backflip and he and Mike jumped back.

At a hand signal from the owner, the dog's barking ceased. It sat back on its haunches, content to fix the visitors with an unwavering, almost eerie stare. Phil noticed that the animal was a female. A smart thief couldn't buy this baby off with a bitch in heat.

"Don't mind Barkley," the man said, his voice clipped and precise. "She won't attack unless you directly threaten me. But I don't let strangers into my house unless they thoroughly identify themselves."

"Never mind the dog," Mike interjected.

"I'm more worried about that sawed-off shotgun you're sporting. Who were you expecting?"

"Who knows? You two could be from Revenue Canada, the College of Physicians and Surgeons, scuzzball lawyers, burglars, psychos—"

"I guess scuzzball lawyer comes closest, Dr. Madigan," said Phil, "although if it weren't for your pooch, I might debate your choice of adjectives. I'm Philip Figgwiggin."

"If you'll recall, I told you on the phone that I wasn't particularly interested in seeing you," Madigan shot back.

"But you did say you didn't care one way or the other, and that I could come if I wanted to."

Madigan waved the shotgun in Mike's direction. "I guess I did at that. Who's your friend?"

Mike introduced himself. "Dr. Robert Madigan, I presume."

"You old farts don't look too dangerous," said Madigan with more than a touch of impatience. "I suppose you want to come in?"

"If it isn't too much trouble, and if we could dispense with the killer dog and the gun," said Phil.

"All right, follow me." Madigan locked the door behind them, told Barkley to stay, and led the way into the house. Phil noticed that the dog had taken up a position by the front door, effectively cutting off that avenue of escape.

Phil and Mike trailed their reluctant host into a spacious living room modestly furnished with a large sofa and matching easy chairs in a nondescript brown.

Madigan's bearing, trimmed moustache and salt-and-pepper crewcut suggested a military background. He started to replace the gun in a small case lying open on the mantle above a gas fireplace.

Changing both his mind and his manner, he held the shotgun out to Phil. "Ever see one of these? Two barrels and two interchangeable butts, standard and pistol grip, which screw on and off. It all packs neatly into this little case."

"Do much hunting?" Mike asked, hoping to encourage the man's friendlier attitude.

"Not really. I bought this for personal security. It's standard procedure once you decide to stop being a victim. The shotgun's cheaper than a handgun and it's the most easily available close-range firearm in the world. You don't have to be a crack shot, but it has awesome stopping power. And the lighter buckshot loads won't pass through the body and hit an unintended target."

"What size shot do you use?" asked Phil calmly, slowing turning the gun over in his hands, then handing it to Mike for inspection.

"I prefer number one shot, but you could go as light as four."

"I like a stun gun myself," Mike chimed in. "I have one like the taser that cops use. Touch any part of the attacker's body and he'll start some form of high-speed dancing. His muscles will spasm and he can't threaten you anymore, but the gun doesn't cause permanent injury or death, which usually causes more problems."

"Good point, Mr. Fowler. I'll keep that in mind," said Madigan. He invited them to take a seat in front of the fireplace. "Now, Mr. Figgwiggin, what do you need from me?"

"I wanted to make your acquaintance, since you've had dealings with Richard Poindexter over the past few years."

Madigan interrupted. "None of them pleasant, but I'm sure you know that."

"I do. I've even read the pleadings in the lawsuit involving your chelation. We'd appreciate hearing your version, Doctor."

"My version," said Madigan bitterly, collapsing into an armchair. "To begin with, the College thinks I'm a greedy opportunist. It's to laugh. I'm way down on the income list, compared to cardiologists, neurosurgeons, obstetricians, gynecologists, dermatologists, pediatricians, even proctologists. It's the heart surgeons who make the big money. Almost four hundred grand on average. That doesn't count the kickbacks from pacemaker manufacturers, investments in CAT scan equipment and Magnetic Resonance Imaging centres or profits from doctor-owned pharmacies."

Madigan leaned forward in his chair. "I was pulling in maybe a hundred and fifty thousand, and I certainly paid out a substantial amount of that in legal fees trying to defend myself against their malicious charges. I got too stressed to continue, and was being bled to death. I decided to sell and get out."

"Some say chelation's dangerous," Phil said, "and that it's caused some deaths."

"Lies. There has not been a single death from the procedure in thirty years. We could probably double the dosage and still not have a problem. The safety margin's huge. Whenever my patients were too far gone to respond to chelation, I urged them to opt for bypass surgery."

"But some of them must have complained, or you wouldn't have run into trouble with the College."

Madigan rose and began pacing the handsome Persian rug. "Only doctors complained, the bastards. My competitors. My patients were happy, because the treatment has a high rate of success. What the College won't admit is that about eighty percent of conventional medicine isn't based on strict scientific principles, either. And they sometimes use far more dangerous therapies than the alternative practitioners they try to discourage." He stopped in front of the teak bookcase that ran the length of one wall.

Phil regarded the doctor. "I would have thought that given the positive anecdotal history, the medical establishment would've embraced well-designed clinical trials."

"No, quite the contrary," replied Madigan. "In Denmark, in fact, a medical association study concluded that chelation was useless for treating claudication due to atherosclerosis. The study was so flawed that ten concerned Danish physicians lodged a complaint with the country's council against scientific fraud. The cardiovascular surgeons who wrote the paper are now facing legal action themselves."

Mike was having trouble following the medical lingo. He'd been considering using a bathroom trip as a pretext for checking out the rest of the house, but the thought of Barkley out in the hall discouraged the idea. It was unlikely he'd find the murder weapon on the premises, anyway. In frustration he burst out, "What language are we speaking? Qu'est-ce say le cat's cut ass, as the French would say. What the hell's claudication?"

"A pain in the legs," Madigan replied, glaring at Mike, "as opposed to a pain in the ass."

"Should I take that personally?" Mike asked, with a faint smile.

"If you like. Try not to become part of the overall aggravation. I resent the double standard; tens of thousands of people are killed each year by reactions to prescription drugs. How many die from chelation or megadoses of vitamins? None, that's how many."

Madigan walked to the picture window and gazed out over the lawn, his hands clasped behind his stiffly held back. "Where do they get off with this harassment?" he said, as if to himself. "Damned Poindexter was one of the worst."

He turned back to his guests. "It wouldn't surprise me if Tricky Dick planted the idea for RevCan to pull that last audit on me. But he's probably sorry now. May his soul rot in hell, the son of a bitch!"

The last was delivered with clenched fists

and purpling cheeks, and Phil grew uneasy. "Shutting down your practice must have been traumatic," he said.

Madigan frowned. "My patients were extremely distraught and disappointed. No more than I was myself."

Mike spoke up again. "My friend here knows something about this chelation stuff, but I don't. Maybe you could explain the process for me."

The doctor stared at Mike for several seconds as if he were studying a cadaver, then he returned to the fireplace and stood facing Fowler. "Patients receive an intravenous drip of EDTA, or ethylene diamine tetraacetic acid, once or twice a week. EDTA is a synthetic amino acid that was traditionally used to counteract lead poisoning. It has long been thought to remove calcium deposits found within arterial atherosclerotic plaque, thereby breaking down the plaque and unclogging the artery. Plaque and heavy metals can lead to cardiovascular disease, glaucoma, poor circulation or arteriosclerosis."

Mike noted that the man's rage seemed to be spent. The mercurial mood swings had to be a sign of something, he thought. Mike returned to contemplating the large print over the fireplace, depicting life in miniature in an old English seaside village. A cheerful world full of cottages, gardens, pubs, village shops, everyday pastimes and special events, the picture's vitality and clarity seemed sharply at odds with the dejected manner of its owner.

"So you closed down your practice voluntarily?" Phil asked.

Madigan plopped back down into the armchair. "It was my decision, but the College might just as well have shut me down. This is no get-rich-quick scheme. When the College maintains there is no proof that chelation treatments are effective, deny it works at all, in fact, and says the placebo effect deserves the credit, they're simply exhibiting their hostile bias against alternative medical practice. I'd been battling them too long and my health was starting to suffer."

"What started the lawsuit?"

"Poindexter instigated it. I'm still trying to get over the psychological and emotional effects of the harassment they've subjected me to. I've found that an aggressive attitude is the best approach."

He paused. "I know why you're here. I can't say that I'm sorry Dick the Prick is dead. He cost me my practice and my peace of mind, and he's deprived a lot of people of a legitimate alternative to surgery. I may have hated him, but I didn't kill him. Does that satisfy you, Mr. Figgwiggin?"

"I suppose it has to. So if you didn't do it, can you shed any light on who might have?"

"That's where you and the police have a big problem. Poindexter was an arrogant, duplicitous bastard, the suspects are legion and I can only wish you luck."

Madigan rose. The interview was over. "Good day to you, gentlemen. I can't say it's been grand meeting you, because it hasn't."

He ushered them to the front door with Barkley snuffling uncomfortably close to their heels.

Twelve

Harry Muldoon was more frustrated than ever. Nothing the Victoria police force had done to date had turned up any new evidence in the Poindexter case. That afternoon, he'd been cornered by the media on his way in to headquarters after lunch. To the reporters' pointed questions about whether the cops were making any progress, why had no one been arrested after all this time and would the case ever be solved, Muldoon had quipped, "Working this case is like looking in a box of Grape Nuts—there are no grapes and there are no nuts."

The pizza he'd had for lunch wasn't sitting well on his stomach, either.

Muldoon was grilling Wade Cavanaugh, who had Annie Chance under surveillance as often as manpower could be spared for a rapidly cooling case. Muldoon wanted a progress report.

"We have a forensic psychiatrist working up a personality profile on the killer," said Wade, "and we're feeding him any information that comes in—which isn't much.

He shifted in his chair. "Chance has other businesses on the side, under separate numbers. The phone sex service is interesting. I've been checking it out myself. But you've gotta use your credit card when you call their number. You know, Sarge, at three-thirty in the morning, when you're so horny you can't sleep, a woman will come on the line and talk dirty to you. It's not always Annie Chance."

"Now that's ridiculous, to pay for that. Call *anyone* at three-thirty in the morning and they'll talk dirty to you. The question is, did you learn anything on the sex line?"

"I learned they charge thirty-five dollars for five minutes, for one thing."

"My God," Muldoon said, shaking his head. "They say you can feed a starving person in a Third World country for a couple of dollars a day. Why don't we just get women in those countries to call North American men and talk dirty to them? It could solve the world hunger problem."

"If you say so, Sarge," Wade replied, trying to keep any hint of insolence below the surface. It was best to agree with the Sarge when he was in a foul mood.

"Who's paying for these fucking calls, may I ask? You say you're checking out this business of hers yourself?"

"You did say to keep Chance under surveillance, Sarge. I try to get her on the line and ask leading questions, like about kinky stuff, sado-machoism, whether she likes to hurt people, things like that."

"Who's paying?"

"I'm billing the calls to the case, but I had to use a friend's phone. I'm paying his bill. If a call came from the police station or from me, she could check that out on her answering service and she'd be suspicious. But I'm not figuring on paying for the calls myself."

Harry took his pepperoni pizza heartburn out on Wade. "Don't be too sure. I'd have to explain an item like that to the accounting department. I can tell you now, they aren't going to like it."

"Ahh, that wouldn't be fair."

"I'll try to charge it to the Policeman's Ball fund, but damn it man, jerk yourself off that sex line. What else have you uncovered?"

"Chance talked to that old fart defence

lawyer again, you know, Philip Figgwiggin."

"No shit! That devious old dork. He came sidling in here a while back saying he wanted to help us solve the case. I gave him short shrift. Is he Chance's mouthpiece now?"

"I thought he was retired."

"I'd love to know what they talked about, but I doubt we'd be able to get a phone tap warrant on him. Tell you what, have a plainclothes keep watch on his apartment. When Figgpudding heads downtown, I want to be radioed so I can arrange to run into him accidentally on purpose."

"You got it." Wade rose from his chair. "Anything else?"

"We can raid the Chance joint again."

"On what grounds?" Wade asked.

"Running a bawdy house," Muldoon smirked. "Section 210 (1) of the Criminal Code. We'll pick her up on that first, which'll give us a chance to go over her place one more time. Also, it'll spring this Figgnewton out of the weeds for sure."

"You figure she's running a cat house and not just a massage parlour? We're not sure what actually goes on there."

"Wade, someone's always selling sex, someone's always buying sex, someone's always pimping. All kinds of sex, all the time, it's as old as history. They've found a five-thousand-year-old Siberian rock engraving of a Stone Age man on skis trying to have sex with an elk."

"You're puttin' me on!"

"No."

"I find the skis part a little hard to believe."

"True story. And another true story is the mess we got here in Victoria with prostitution. Makes it tough for us to get a conviction on a bawdy house rap. Check it out with that prosecutor, Thorndyke. And be sure and tell him whatever he needs to know to get you a search warrant. Round up the usual suspects. You know the routine."

Wade had serious doubts about Muldoon's strategy. "When should we pull the raid?"

"Get the warrant, then wait till the place is full of johns and the joint's jumpin'. Make sure Chance is on the premises. Book her and we'll ransack the place later."

"You complained the last time this method was used!"

"That got fouled up and besides, that was then, this is now."

Wade continued to protest. "Even if she's convicted, it'll probably just be a fine. The courts are too smart to come down on consensual sex between adults."

"Sometimes you can be a real pain in the tuckus, Cavanaugh. Do you want to get ahead in this business, or not? Now stop fornicating the canine and get busy."

While Muldoon and Cavanaugh were bad-mouthing him down at police headquarters, Phil's driving adventures continued to cause him problems. Phil's friends had never completely shared the his confidence in his driving skills. One figured Phil had invented the "eventual turn" signal—you signaled a left turn when you come out of the garage and eventually, sometime later in the day, you actually made the turn. A legitimate question in Victoria was—what age are you when you back out of your driveway and don't bother looking behind you for the rest of the day?

Despite the backlog of failures at the Motor Vehicles, Phil's re-scheduled test notice arrived. He'd read the driving manual and felt success was certain this time around. He'd refuse to be distracted by conversations, he'd check his blind spot before changing lanes and watch out for lane straddling and school zones.

For this test Phil was assigned to a different examiner. They drove a similar route and the examiner asked him to perform the same manoeuvres. He thought he had passed, but discovered he was five points over the allowable demerits. The civil servant congratulated him on progress he didn't feel he was making against bureaucracy.

Phil perused the test results, looking for loopholes. "What's this ten-point penalty for?" he asked, contemplating the examiner with disgust.

"You drove an entire block with only one hand on the wheel."

"Was that when I took the peppermints out of my pocket and gave you one? Or was it when I blew my nose? I'm perfectly capable of driving with one hand."

"It doesn't matter. You're supposed to have both hands on the wheel at all times."

"You'll pardon me for saying you're doing a good job but you're doing it wrong."

"I don't expect you to be happy, sir. But you're getting close."

On that sour note they parted company. This was getting serious—three failures and you were shit out of luck. Phil booked a third test, then rejoined the friend who'd accompanied him this time and got a lift home.

Later that day, unwilling to operate without wheels, he decided, as nearly always, to take a chance. He drove over the lift bridge

on Johnson Street, heading for Spinnaker's
and a plate of Oysters Rockefeller. He was in
a line of cars travelling at the same speed and
his tires hummed as they rolled over the steel
mesh of the bridge.

A couple of hundred yards past the west
end of the bridge, the road made a ninety
degree right turn under the Via Rail over-
pass. This was a blind spot for Victoria
motorists, who made sure they stayed in the
right lane coming around the curve.

Just past the turn, a cop stood in the middle of the road directing all traffic onto
Harbour Road, a quiet side street. There
were three cruisers and several motorcycle
cops, all busy writing out tickets.

Sons of bitches! The infamous Johnson
Street Bridge speed trap! As he pulled over,
Phil prayed they wouldn't notice that his old
licence had expired. He rolled down the window to find an officer already standing by
the door with his charge book in his hand.

"Were you aware you were speeding, sir?"

"No," said Phil, trying to keep any hint of
petulance out of his voice.

"The speed limit's thirty on the bridge. You
were doing forty-two."

"So was everybody else."

"That's not the point," the cop replied.

"May I see Your driver's licence and registration, please?"

"Where's your radar operator?"

"The radar is on a building on the other side of the bridge," the cop replied, beginning to lose patience because he was in a hurry.

"And he can tell who's doing what in all this activity?"

"Certainly."

"How'd he get the information to you so fast? You're just standing in the road stopping everybody."

No reaction from the cop. "Let's see your driver's licence and registration, please." Phil reached into his glove compartment and handed over the documents.

Moving faster than bubble dancers working with ping pong balls, the police were only interested in writing speeding tickets for as many motorists as possible, not in checking for any other offences. They were also causing a dangerous traffic jam, so some drivers managed to get away. At over a hundred dollars a pop, you couldn't blame them.

No use arguing with this guy. Phil was steaming but decided to say nothing more, to take the ticket and blow the ranch.

He was all set to dispute the charge in court, and debated whether to challenge the notoriously glitch-prone radar equipment or try for a defence under some provision of the Charter of Rights and Freedoms. It irked him that speed traps were set up for the sole purpose of raising money for the police and municipal and provincial governments.

In B.C. alone, photo radar grossed fifty-two million a year, making the program a prima facie cash cow that governments were milking for all they were worth. But Phil knew that you always had to give the cops their chance to foul up in court, which they did with astonishing regularity, which was why lawyers had to master the tiny technicalities.

Changing his mind about where to eat, Phil drove back into town to have the bottomless bowl of soup at Pagliacci's, then around the corner to the Motor Vehicle Driver's Service Centre on Broughton Street to register a dispute note. That would hold the bastards till after he got his licence renewal. Experience told him that it would be six months before he got a hearing, and he had a good shot at beating the charge to boot. In fact he was looking forward to having a day in court again.

Of course, there was that seat belt charge coming up, too. Phil recalled he was wearing a raincoat at the time, the one with the heavy metal buckle on the belt. He'd wear that to court. Undoubtedly that was what had been making the sparks on the pavement.

Phil spotted the single parking space from across the street as he drove west along Broughton. No oncoming traffic, no one behind him and no cruisers in sight. A smart U-turn pulled him level with the parking space, where he parked and got out, locking the door.

Turning, he started to cross the road, stepping over a flattened dog turd as he did so. Damn, he'd have to check out the canine litter law. Too many dogs are fouling the footpaths, their owners aren't carrying pooper-scoopers, and no one seems to be stopping this shit, Phil thought. I'm going to take it up with the mayor, Phil thought. There should be a fine of a hundred bucks per offence, or rub their noses in it.

Suddenly he became aware of violent shouting and cursing from up the street. another distraught city dweller must be losing it.

Life was becoming overly complex and there were a lot of angry, grumpy people walking and driving the streets these days, what with electronic voice messages, cell phones, ignorant pet owners, panhandlers and all the other prices to be paid for living in the city. Most of us don't lose our marbles, thought Phil, we just soldier on, resolutely ignoring the broken promises of life, determined to maintain an inner sanctum of relative calm against a million irritants.

Looking up the street, Phil spotted the origin of the commotion. It was a guy in the cab of a panel truck on the side of Broughton street from which Phil had made the U-turn. This apoplectic victim of urban anger was obviously shouting at him.

Wondering what was afoot, other than the dog turd, Phil walked over to the man in the truck, smiling broadly all the while. Maybe he knew the guy, who was about his own age, florid of face and obviously very unhappy about something.

"What the hell kind of driving is that?"the guy shouted at Phil as he came close and stood beside the open truck window. "We're trying to teach our kids the principles of good driving and to drive responsibly and then an old fart like you, who should know better, pulls an asinine stunt like that."

"What's the problem?" asked Phil, staying with the big grin.

"That U-turn. You should be ashamed of yourself. Worst bit of driving I've ever seen. Completely illegal."

"Is that so? Well, if it is, then it's partially

your fault," Phil announced. "You caused me to do it, you know."

The panel truck driver blew his stack. "What are you talking about? How am I to blame for your lousy driving?" he shouted.

"Well, ordinarily when I come down this street I park right where you've got your truck. You were occupying my parking spot, so what did you expect me to do? I had to take that other one across the street. You made me do it."

Having said this, Phil didn't linger further. Still smiling broadly, he turned on his heel and sauntered off down the pedestrian walkway leading to Fort Street.

The truck driver was still fuming and cursing as Phil departed. "Who let you out of the old folk's home?" were the last words he heard as he turned the corner.

It couldn't have been my driving, thought Phil, he's likely got some metabolic disorder resulting from eating too many Oh Henry chocolate bars. The Twinkie dysfunction, they called it. It's a social disease. That self-righteous nosey parker is probably the type of person who gets out of the shower to take a piss.

When Phil dropped in on Mike Fowler, he was shocked to find him on crutches, with his right ankle taped up. "What the hell happened to you?"

Mike sniffed. "You find me in this condition not from chasing pussy, but from trying to avoid it."

"That doesn't sound like your style, Mike. Not that you could get it up, in any case."

"Yeah, right, they're making condoms with suspenders for us old guys now." Mike hobbled over to his couch and dropped into it, leaning his crutches against the armrest.

"Go on, elucidate,"urged Phil, taking a seat beside his friend.

"I was visiting one of my daughters again, the one out in Sidney this time. She keeps cats in the house. Goddamn cats all over the place, hawking up hairballs, whizzing on your leg or yowling in the backyard in the middle of the night. They keep turning up where you least expect them to be. Now, let me ask you this, if you were to give a lot of cats a lot of beer to lap from their saucers, what would you have? I'm serious."

"Okay, I'll bite, what would you have?"

Mike delivered the punchline. "A pissed pussy posse!"

"Oh, God! You can do better than that. Must be too early in the day. I'm sorry I asked about your foot."

"Okay, okay. Let me explain. I was having a few beers and I thought it'd be funny to give some to the cats. So I poured a bit into a saucer and they just lapped it up. Then I decided to have a bath and I didn't close the bathroom door. When I finished, I hoisted myself up and went to step over the edge of the tub with one foot. I was about to step on one of the bloody cats, which was flaked out drunk beside the tub, so I tried to lengthen my stride to miss the cat, but just then it came out of its boozy haze and tried to get out of the way. So my foot came down on the cat anyway and I did the splits over the edge of the tub and sprained my ankle. Lucky I didn't break my stupid neck!"

"That must have been an altogether wrenching experience," Phil interjected, a comment that earned him a glare from Mike.

"Can you get around okay?"

"Yeah, but the ankle's gonna be sore for a couple of weeks and I have to use these crutches. Maybe I'll try a cane."

"Hard luck," said Phil. "That'll teach you to try to be a clean old man. It's not your style. You're too old to turn over a new leaf."

"I'll have you know," Mike shot back, "that the phrase turning over a new leaf can be traced back to Adam's hygiene habits."

Thirteen

Phil waited to be called into Dr. Charlie Scotland's office to get the results of tests for his heart condition. He distracted himself with good-news-bad-news jokes. In one, the doctor tells his patient his leg has to be amputated to save his life. The guy wakes up after the operation and the surgeon tells him, "There's good news and bad news."

"Give me the bad news first," says the patient.

"We cut off the wrong leg."

"Oh, my God," wails the patient. "What's the good news?"

"Your other leg's getting better!"

The way Phil figured it, you can't win them all, but you'd like to win a few. So what was Dr. Scotland going to tell him? Phil didn't have to wait long to find out. A nurse ushered him into the inner sanctum and he sat down opposite the cardiologist, trying hard not to regard the man as his nemesis.

They exchanged greetings, but both felt this wasn't the time for extended pleasantries. Scotland was a busy man, and Phil, who knew he was well past the seventh-inning stretch in this ball game, just wanted to know the score.

"First, the angiogram results," said Scotland. Plucking a sheaf of papers from the file on his desk, he read aloud from the report. *"The right coronary artery was occluded in the mid portion, as was the proximal LAD and proximal circumflex. There was a large patent ramus. There was also a patent right coronary artery graft with a fifty-percent stenosis in the distal portion of the graft and a ninety-percent stenosis in the native distal right coronary after the take-off."*

"Is that the bad news or the good?" Phil tried to keep his cool, but the medico-babble had lost him after the first few words.

"The latter stenosis is bad because it's around a bend, as it were; hard to get at. And you have three blocked arteries, which doesn't help the overall situation."

"I knew that. So what about the angiography? Any good news from that?"

Scotland nodded. "Yes, there is." He read again from another report. *"Only the right coronary artery graft was injected, and this again showed the ninety-percent stenosis in the distal right coronary artery after the take-off of the posterior descending branch. This did undergo angioplasty, with the stenosis being reduced to about forty to fifty percent."*

"Any reduction of blockage sounds good, doctor, but can you give me the prognosis in lay language? What are my chances?"

Scotland removed his reading glasses and looked Phil in the eye for the first time. "The permanent stent we installed was your second one. With luck, the stents will keep those arteries open for a reasonable length of time."

"Ah, yes, time! Regardless of the details, the essence of the matter is time."

"For all of us, of course."

"Well, in my case," Phil's voice shook slightly, "what time frame am I looking at?"

"Before you got a myocardial infarction?"

"Come again?"

"A heart attack. That's one possibility. Plaque may break loose and completely block the artery, or a blood clot might plug an already narrowed vessel."

"Let's deal in terms of longevity, Doc. How long do you think I have to live?"

"Right. Well, averaging similar situations, I'd bet you have four years, tops. A twenty-five-percent chance of dying within the year."

It was a sucker punch to the gut. Phil sank a little lower in his seat. He didn't speak for several seconds. His right hand, trembling slightly, began an involuntary stroking of his goatee. When he found his voice, he asked, "Are those odds cumulative?"

"If you don't die this year, you'll have a fifty-percent chance of dying next year. But remember, I'm no oracle."

"I'll consider your opinion an expert guesstimate."

"You've been taking blood thinners for some time. I want you to keep doing so. In addition, I'm prescribing one type of medication to help prevent blood clots and another to prevent angina. Just hope for the best."

"But expect the worst. Thanks, Doc, I think."

As Phil blindly found his way back out of the office, he mentally added, "Life's a play and we're all unrehearsed."

Walking in a fog, Phil didn't notice the police cruiser parked on the street outside the medical building, nor did he notice when it followed him slowly down the street.

The last chill of winter rippled the surface of the puddles left from two days of steady rain. Phil was barely aware of the overcast skies and biting ocean wind, but out of habit, he pulled his wool cap down more firmly over his ears and buttoned the collar of his coat. By instinct, he wandered into the Mocambo coffee shop and placed an order.

The officer in the cruiser radioed his boss. Muldoon tore out of the office, into his car and down Blanshard. He screeched to a halt around the corner and short-assed it into Mocambo's. Phil was the only customer. He was sitting by the right-hand wall under some colourful abstracts by local artists, dunking a biscotti into his latte and perusing the *Times-Colonist*.

Muldoon stood in front of him. "Mind if I join you, Counselor? I'll just get myself a cuppa," said Harry. He proceeded to the counter without waiting for a reply.

I'll be jiggered, thought Phil, observing Harry from the rear. Those legs are badly bowed, if I'm not mistaken. Phil chanted under his breath, "What manner of men are these, who wear their balls in parentheses?"

Harry returned with his java and sat.

" I don't remember inviting you to sit down," Phil said acidly.

"Our paths have unexpectedly crossed again, Figgwiggin, so there's no use getting your shorts in a tangle. Our last meeting was unfortunate, I'll admit. As I recall, we lost our collective tempers."

"And as I recall, you immediately took an offensive attitude."

"You must have known I had a hangover. Maybe not," he added when Phil simply stared at him. "Anyway, it's my nature, my job at times, to be offensive."

"Including nose hairs?" Phil couldn't resist.

"Now who's being snarky? Do you still want to talk about the Poindexter murder and help us with the investigation, or not?"

"To what do I owe this sudden volte face? I'm not sure you and I could ever work together, Muldoon."

"Maybe not. But I don't believe you're through amateur detecting. I know you've been talking to people connected with Poindexter."

"Have you got me under surveillance, Harry? Because if you have, I'm going to be mighty pissed off with you."

"Don't be so touchy. We both want to know who killed Dick the Prick, don't we?"

"The difference is, I think you've made up your mind and I haven't."

"So who do you think did it?"

" I wish I knew, but it wasn't Annie Chance.

So why don't you guys try another tack?"

"So you do have some other ideas."

"Perhaps. Which I would tell you only when I'm damned good and ready."

"Do you have any other suspects I should know about?" Muldoon pressed.

"I may have. Seems my godson had more enemies than I would have expected."

"The point is, are you going to tell us who they are?"

"Why should I?" Phil snapped.

"Because maybe if you don't, you'll be obstructing justice."

"And you'd love to charge me with that, wouldn't you, Harry?"

"Now why did you have to go and say a thing like that, when all I'm trying to do is make some progress on the case?"

Neither man was paying any attention to their drinks, which were growing cold on the table between them. They leaned toward each other like two pugilists looking for an opening to land the first blow.

"Before I agree to help you," Phil said, "you'll have to convince me you're taking a hard look in some other direction than Annie Chance."

"Is that because you're her lawyer, Figgwiggin, you sly dog? Trying to work some angles to get her off the hook, eh?"

"Who says I'm her lawyer?"

"I think you are, and I think you're trying to set me up to plea-bargain that bimbo. Look, I know the force didn't handle her right in the first place. But if you're looking for a deal, then why not start right now? She knows more than she's telling us, maybe more than she's telling you. Maybe she didn't do it, but I'll bet my puny pension she knows who did."

"I'm not her lawyer, Harry, and we can end this conversation right now."

Muldoon couldn't hack polite any longer. His frustration boiled over and his fist smashed the tabletop so hard the coffee sloshed over the rims of both mugs. "Damn you, Figgwiggin! You can't say I didn't try this time."

"No, I can't. But I can ask you a question. Did you come here alone, or is the front half of the horse outside in the street?"

"I'm warning you, Counselor, if you're not playing fair ball with me, I'll shove the bat up your ass!"

"There is one thing I can do for you, Harry," said Phil, his mouth twitching.

"And just what might that be?"

"Post signs all up and down the main streets for the tourists: Warning—our local police are armed and dangerous."

Fourteen

Phil channel-surfed, but found only the fringes of his mind paying attention to the television. Commercials on almost every station, most of them aimed at the ballooning elderly population. Modern snake-oil salesmen offered cures for the sundry ailments of old crockhood—nostrums for constipation, diapers for incontinence, adhesives for dentures, remedies for heartburn and gastrointestinal disorders.

In between, the programs were all of the dumbed-down variety. Phil agreed with Murray Dobbin, who had described the media best, as a daily barrage of propaganda aimed at trashing people's values, making them apathetic and helping them accept the new corporate reality.

Phil hit the off button, and with a small crackle, the set died.

Scotland's opinion as to his longevity prospects was worrisome. He'd have to keep his mind off the spectre of his own imminent death, which wasn't going to be an easy mental exercise. Phil realized that underneath his reasonably sound exterior appearance, his sewer system was wearing out, his pump was slowing down and his tubes were clogging up. Couldn't we just have a minute of flatulence in memory of the better health of our youth?

A problem kept nagging at the back of Phil's mind. How to check out Poindexter's proclivity for vicious practical jokes, as alleged by Annie Chance. Where to start? It had to be the beating of an unknown victim by unknown assailants, who were set up by Poindexter.

Okay, Phil mused. You know something happened and you know where. You don't need to know who did the beating, but you do need to know the identity of the beating victim. If you had that bit of knowledge and could link that party to Poindexter in some way, it would produce a suspect in his murder.

A long shot, but he might as well give it a try. He recalled reading somewhere that the police had a new computer system that categorized, checked out and tracked related crimes. He wondered how he could access that system to help narrow his search.

In the meantime, Don Shivagitz was probably back from wherever his perambulation in the Middle East had taken him, and at least Phil knew where to find him, since there was only one Shivagitz D., Dr. in the phone book.

Shivagitz answered in person when Phil called to request an appointment regarding a medical problem.

"I no longer practice western medicine," Shivagitz stated cautiously. "Sometimes the ancient remedies are the best. We use many traditional methods of healing at my complementary care clinic. We treat the whole person, not just the disease. If you're interested in that approach, I might be able to help."

"I want to hear about anything that will prolong my life," said Phil. "I'd rather have a cure that isn't worse than the disease."

"Good attitude," Shivagitz said approvingly. "People can heal by using their mind as much as by treating their body. If you came to the clinic, we'd spend a fair amount of time talking. I'd want to know all about you: your lifestyle, what you eat, your temperament and a host of other things. It's the only way to come up with remedies that will relieve your condition."

"There's something else," Phil said. "I'm working on the estate of Richard Poindexter and I wanted to talk to you about that."

No response. The phone might as well have gone dead.

"Are you still there, Doctor?"

Shivagitz showed less enthusiasm for the subject than a cat for swimming lessons. His reply was slow and distinct. "I have no desire to talk about that individual. Especially not to someone I don't know, so—"

"I should explain," Phil interrupted. "I was a friend of the family. Poindexter's father was a buddy of mine. I came across an odd bit of information in the estate records, something which made me think—"

"That I might not like the man," interjected Shivagitz, his voice rising slightly. "Well, that's certainly true, but I don't see what that has to do with anything, or why I should talk to you about it. So, if you don't mind..." Make up something, Phil thought, keep talking.

"It's strictly estate business, because of the medical claim you brought against him. I just want to make sure the matter's been settled properly. Also, I'm trying to get some insight into a side of Poindexter I wasn't aware of. I thought since you've known him for some time, you might remember something that could help me."

Another pause at the other end of the line. "That lawsuit was a long time ago." Shivagitz's voice brightened as he added, "But I *can* see you about your health problem, and if you have any other questions, well, we'll see. Perhaps I can give you some advice, Mr. Figgwiggin, that could help you live a little longer. In fact, I'm sure I can."

"Traditional doctors aren't giving me much hope, so why not? How soon can I get an appointment?

"How about three-thirty tomorrow? I work out of my home, close to Spinnaker's." Shivagitz gave him directions to a Dundas Street address.

"Sounds easy to find, said Phil. "I'll see you tomorrow."

A narrow lawn separated Shivagitz's house from the street. Phil passed a lilac hedge and climbed the wooden stairs of a wide veranda heavily laden with leafless Virginia creeper vine. A wall sign said *Open* and invited him to enter. A bell jingled as he pushed open the door. The small waiting room off the vestibule was empty except for the chairs and sofa arranged along its walls. The coffee table was piled with *National Geographic*, *Equinox* and other magazines.

A young woman carrying a clipboard emerged from the adjoining room to inform him that Dr. Shivagitz would see him shortly. Phil picked up a humour magazine called *Stitches*. After a brief wait, he was ushered into the office, which contained some familiar medical apparatus, including scales and an examination table against one wall.

Shivagitz was a pleasant-looking, balding man of medium height and abundant belly encased in an expensively tailored three-piece suit. He rose from behind his desk and shook Phil's hand, then waved him to a chair.

As he sat, Phil noticed something peculiar about Shivagitz's eyes, but he put it down to thick contact lenses. "Where should we start, Doctor? I have atherosclerosis. I'm also working on the Poindexter estate file and I have to assure myself that there are no outstanding claims against the estate. Specifically, that *you* have no further claims." It was a flimsy story, since Phil knew a quit claim agreement had been signed.

Shivagitz opted to get the Poindexter matter out of the way first.

"Can you tell me what happened with your operation?" Phil asked. "It must have been horrific for you."

"It was. Dr. McCarthy, the senior surgeon who did the appendectomy with Poindexter assisting, had some kind of a mental breakdown right in the middle of the operation and slashed my stomach up every which way. It was a godawful mess."

"But it wasn't Poindexter who did the slashing."

"No, but he should have seen that McCarthy wasn't fit to perform his surgery. They'd worked together often enough that Poindexter should have known the man was in a chronic state of rage and was barely keeping the lid on. I found that out after the fact, of course, or I'd never have allowed McCarthy near me."

"So you resented anyone connected with the botched operation?"

"Wouldn't you?"Shivagitz demanded, his eyes glinting. "It took me a long time to forgive them, but I can't say I can ever forget. But I'm curious about you. It's strange that you should think I killed him."

"I didn't say that!" Phil exclaimed.

"No. But let's face it, you're considering the possibility, or we wouldn't be talking. Well, I'm not the culprit, so you can drop that line of conjecture. It is odd, though, that you're the only person who's questioned me. Why haven't the police come by?"

Phil didn't answer immediately. "Because they aren't aware of the connection between you and Poindexter."

"But you are. You must also know, then, that I settled out of court and that I received considerable compensation from McCarthy's and Poindexter's malpractice insurance, as well as from the insurer representing the hospital."

"In my experience as a lawyer, Dr. Shivagitz, monetary compensation doesn't ease physical pain and mental anguish, nor long-term suffering and reduced quality of life."

"McCarthy's still in a mental institution, and they tell me that these days he couldn't even run a piss-up in a brewery. He'll never get out. Besides, as a naturopath and a homeopath, Mr. Figgwiggin, I recognize that prolonged anger isn't healthy. I've been able to control any impulse toward revenge I may occasionally feel in the wee hours of the night. I try not to wallow in negative emotion. Unless of course I were to resent your intrusion into my privacy. Surely you should let the police handle the search for Poindexter's murderer."

"The police think they know who committed the crime. When that happens, they usually don't look much further."

Shivagitz shifted in his large chair. "Ah, yes, the masseuse. And you don't think she killed him?"

"No, I don't. But I have no idea who did. I am curious, though."

"That begs the old cliché about the cat, so be careful."

"You don't happen to know her, by any chance?" Phil asked, the pun deliberate.

Don smiled. "Annie Chance used to be a nurse. I'd see her at the Royal Jubilee Hospital from time to time. To be frank with you, Mr. Figgwiggin, I'd hate to see her or anyone else falsely accused of Poindexter's murder."

"Do you know anyone who disliked Poindexter enough to kill him?"

"Well, he had his friends, he had his enemies," Don replied, "but you may as well know that I'm a member of an organization called Citizens for Choice in Health Care. We believe doctors practising non-mainstream medicine are being targeted by the College of

Physicians and Surgeons. As such, we're usually at loggerheads with that august body."

"And Poindexter was on their disciplinary committee." Phil watched Shivagitz carefully.

"Yes, and I clashed directly with him on a number of occasions. I believe in the mind-body connection. I feel that people can recover from life-threatening disease, severe trauma and chronic pain through a combination of diet, exercise and a positive attitude. The College doesn't buy that philosophy, so they're constantly harassing me and others like me."

Shivagitz adopted his best bedside manner. "Now, I think I've said enough about Poindexter. Let's talk about you. You seem to be in good shape; you should live to be at least seventy-five."

"I am seventy-five."

Both men grinned. "See—what did I just tell you? Already we're making progress. Why don't you tell me what's wrong, and give me your medical history."

"Sure," Phil replied. "I brought some medical records. I can leave them with you."

"Fine. I'll look them over, but not right now." Shivagitz checked his watch. "Look, it's late afternoon, and I'll bet we could both use a pick-me-up. Why don't we go to

Spinnaker's? We can just as easily discuss your health over a pint of beer."

Phil found himself liking both Shivagitz and his approach to medicine. "That's the best offer I've had all day."

"I've got a couple of quick calls to make, so I'll meet you there."

Fifteen

Spinnaker's, Canada's first and most famous brew pub, was located in a handsome old estate house on Victoria's Inner Harbour. Hand pumps linked the cellars and the brewhouse to the pub and restaurant, delivering lagers, pale, brown and Scottish ales, cask-conditioned bitters, porter, stout, and a nine-point-five-percent Christmas Ale. Beer was a featured ingredient in many dishes on the restaurant's menu.

On entering the pub, Phil read the foyer sign that greeted all customers:

Weak Men
Suffering the Effect of Youthful Errors,
Loss of Appetite, Disturbed Sleep, Brewer's Droop,

Depression of Spirits, Loss of Manhood and Memory,

Loss of Hair and Hearing, general lack of Vitality and Purpose,

Should Drink our Sparkling Ales

Sold Here in Glass, Jug or Bottle.

A friendly young waiter ushered Phil to a window seat overlooking the harbour.

Don Shivagitz arrived a few minutes later.

"I've just ordered the Scottish ale," Phil said, handing Shivagitz the beer list. "What's your pleasure?" He gave the high sign to the waiter, who hustled back to the table.

Shivagitz ordered a pale ale, the Fogg Fighter, prompting Phil to remark, "I trust you took note of the eight-point-five-percent alcohol content."

Shivagitz grinned and replied, "Part of the pleasure of these pubs is being able to know precisely what you're drinking."

When the beers arrived, the two men took several healthy gulps, agreeing that the first beer always tasted the best.

As he neared the bottom of his mug, Shivagitz fixed Figgwiggin with a stare. Suddenly, he dug into his left eye socket, plucked out a glass eye and dropped it into his large-handled, scalloped beer mug. Phil sat transfixed, staring at the glass eye rolling about in the dregs of the Fogg Fighter ale. That was no contact lens.

Shivagitz tipped the mug sideways, reached in with his thumb and forefinger and gave the eye a good rinse. Then he popped the eye back into its socket and gazed quietly at Phil as a beery tear rolled down his cheek.

"Bet you have a lot of fun with that eye," Phil ventured.

"Sure do. In fact, before we start arguing about who's going to pay, let's see if we can get these beers for free."

"How do you propose to arrange that?"

Shivagitz swung around in his chair and beckoned to their friendly and loquacious waiter, who came down the several steps to the main floor and stood by their table.

"Are you a betting man, barkeep?" asked Shivagitz in a comradely tone.

"I've been known to take wagers," the waiter replied. "What'd you have in mind?"

"I'll bet you these beers that I can bite myself in my own eye."

The waiter thought for a moment. "This I gotta see," he said.

Don took his glass eye from the left socket, placed it between his teeth and bit down.

"Wow, a glass eye! Why didn't I think of

that? Okay, this round's free. Can I get you another?"

"Of a certainty," answered Don. "The same for you, Mr. Figgwiggin?"

Phil, spotting an ad for Red Ass above the fireplace—*You'll get a kick out of this one*—ordered a half-pint of the ale.

"I'd better have something a lot weaker," said Don, choosing the Honey Blonde Ale. "Mustn't open the clinic with a hangover tomorrow, sets a bad example for the patients."

When the waiter deposited their order on the table and swept up their empties, Shivagitz asked him, "Game for another bet?"

"I don't know," said the waiter hesitantly.

"I'll bet you, double or nothing for another round, that I can bite myself in the right eye."

The waiter's mouth dropped open slightly and his brow wrinkled as he worked the puzzle. He couldn't resist a chance to recoup his previous loss. The guy can't be blind, he thought, he walked into the bar all by himself. No white cane, no seeing eye dog. Took out his left eye and was now betting on the right. Couldn't have two glass eyes, could he? Maybe he planned to lose the bet so the waiter wouldn't be out any money. The waiter decided to humour his customer in hopes of a large tip at least. "I'll probably regret this," he said, "but okay, you're on!"

Shivagitz removed his false teeth and bit himself in the right eye with the dentures.

"Holy Toledo," exclaimed Phil in admiration. Another practical joker, but one whose gags were pretty tame compared to those attributed to Poindexter by Annie Chance. Shivagitz was so affable it was hard to cast him in the role of murderer.

"Oh, damn it! Why didn't I think of that!" the waiter yelped. He slunk away, resigned to eating the cost of four beers.

As the men sipped leisurely, Phil acquainted the doctor with the details of his heart ailment, the major events in his life over the past several years and his daily routine.

Shivagitz listened intently. "As Hippocrates said, 'Your food shall be your medicine and your medicine shall be your food.' That's a good start, and I can give you a couple of preliminary recommendations. First, you should take red cayenne pepper. Not the low-powered stuff you cook with, but the little capsules of Birdseye pepper from Africa. It has more than a hundred thousand heat units per capsule. Also, you need to drink purple grape juice, seven to ten milligrams per kilo of your body weight per day."

"I like to know why I'm taking a remedy, Doctor, so what's the benefit of the ones you're suggesting?"

"Okay." Shivagitz was in his element. He rested his elbows on the table and clasped his hands, leaning toward Phil as he spoke. "Red cayenne pepper jump-starts your heart with a jolt of strengthening energy. It opens your arteries so your body gets the circulation it needs without straining your heart. You can feel the surge of energy, but cayenne doesn't raise your heart rate or your blood pressure. It's nature's most powerful stimulant, but unlike caffeine, it's good for you."

"What's the purple grape juice for?"

"It delays oxidation of LDL cholesterol—that's the bad kind. The oxidation is a key contributor to the development of atherosclerosis, or plaque buildup in your coronary arteries. The two remedies should also improve your digestion, elimination, energy level, sex drive, attitude, complexion, respiration, sleep, ambition, stamina, eyesight, ulcers and headaches. You name it, red pepper and purple grape juice will do something for it."

"Let's hope I'm not too far gone," said Phil. "I'm starting to feel better already, just talking about it."

"Hope in itself can be a real tonic, but I've never seen the placebo effect kick in quite so quickly, Mr. Figgwiggin. Are you sure it isn't the beer?"

"If it is, I'd say it's working all too well. Excuse me, would you?" Phil rose and headed for the men's room.

While relieving himself he read the blackboard above the urinals, specifically placed so that witty graffiti artists could chalk up their bons mots on the board rather than write them on the lavatory walls. *Virginity is a social disease, but there is a cure*, and *A husband is someone who takes out the trash and gives the impression he just cleaned the whole house* were among the offerings. What were women's jokes doing in the men's can? The item he liked best was a poem, a classic, he thought:

With heaving breast
The Dean undressed,
The Bishop's wife to lie on,
He felt it rude to do it nude,
So he put the Old School Tie on!

Turning to leave, Phil took note of a machine that dispensed flavoured condoms. The selection included Lager & Lime, Chocolate, Whiskey, Vanilla, Banana, and Custard & Rhubarb. Marketing was surely getting strange. It occurred to Phil that if he'd still been in the market, he would have bought the Lager and Lime.

He returned to his table, where Shivagitz gave him another prescription. "Try a strict brown rice diet, at least for a while. And stay off prescription drugs as much as possible. They'll kill you quicker than curiosity. I hope you'll take my warning to heart."

"Well, more surgery will probably kill me, but I think my doctor's given me up for dead, anyway. Not that I'm eager to go under the knife again, in any case."

"You know," Shivagitz said, staring into his beer, "I used to believe in surgery and pills as much as any conventional physician. But I didn't realize how dangerous and debilitating they can be."

He looked up at Phil then, his glass eye glittering with reflected flame from the fireplace. "I've had to act as my own doctor since my unfortunate operation, and I think I've done a pretty good job. I learned all about herbal medicine, which is the safest, most effective treatment of all. Now, the suggestions I've made to you are just preliminary recommendations. I'd need to study your records in detail, combined with what you've already told me. But you should know all your options and take charge of your own health."

"Purple grape juice, red cayenne pepper and brown rice? Good colour scheme, at least," Phil joked.

"Doctors don't always know what's right," Shivagitz emphasized. "You can't trust drug companies, whose highest priority is turning a profit, and why rush into surgery when you know that the referring doctors get paid for every 'sale.' "

"We certainly have one thing in common, Doctor," said Phil. "We're both iconoclasts."

"I'll send you some literature on a macrobiotic diet as well."

"Thanks. But now it's suppertime, and I plan to feast right here. Care to join me?" Shivagitz agreed and they placed their orders.

Shivagitz pondered Phil for a moment. "Do you have any problems with impotence? It's not unusual as we get older."

"If sex is like a five-mile walk, then I haven't crossed the street in two years. What do you suggest?"

"There's a foundation in Chicago doing research on perfumes. Perfumes have been used to elicit sexual arousal for centuries, but this is the first scientific study of why they work so well. They've discovered that combinations of lavender and black licorice cause a significant increase in blood flow to the penis of males exposed to the scent. They're testing a host of other substances as well."

The waiter arrived with their orders, for Shivagitz a pumpkin pie made with pale ale and honey, topped with an apricot glaze over dark chocolate and dipped whole pecans, served with whipped cream. As he took his second bite, he commented, "Too bad they're not testing this stuff."

As he ate, Phil wondered what credence to give to any of Shivagitz's revelations. Was he dealing from a full deck? Lavender and black licorice as aphrodisiacs? He's got to be putting me on, Phil thought, deciding he would just keep looking for some of those potency patches.

Sixteen

Mike Fowler studied his countenance in the bathroom mirror. Muscle comes and goes, flab lasts. Only in his eighties and losing his looks. He put on his glasses to get a better look at his kisser, searching for signs of deterioration. When he smiled, the face in the mirror grimaced back, reminding him to insert his dentures. With a forehead that high, he didn't need to worry about going bald. He finally decided he looked better from a distance.

A faint sound kept impinging, bothering him. He put in his hearing aid and finally heard the loud pounding on his apartment door. Mike forsook both bathroom and introspection to go see who was calling.

Phil stood before him. "I tried calling, but all I got was your damn answering machine. Mike, I need your help."

"What's so important that you have to disturb a man's ablutions this early in the day? Well, come on in." He ushered his friend in with an exaggerated wave of his arm.

Phil followed Mike down the hall to the jumbled living room and plunked himself onto the sofa. "I had a bad night," he complained. "Took me hours to fall asleep, then I woke up early because of a bad dream."

"What did you dream?"

"That Dolly Parton was my mother."

"What's so bad about that?" Mike wanted to know.

"I was a bottle baby!" Phil pretended to cry.

"You've got a bullshit problem as well as insomnia. Maybe you need professional help."

"Like what?" Phil asked, genuinely interested.

"Well, you could try a sleep lab. It's costly, upwards of a couple of hundred dollars, and there's a long wait list. There's one at the Jubilee Hospital. Or you could try a private one, where they hook you up to a computer that tracks things while you're asleep."

"Like what things?"

"Like air flow out of the nose and mouth, blood oxygen levels, heart rate, that kind of thing. They can even rent you the equipment so you can do the tests at home, then bring the stuff back in the morning. They download the info, analyze it and tell you what they've found."

"Okay, you've convinced me to look into it," said Phil. "Say, is that coffee I smell?"

"It is, and you do. Do you want a cup?" When Phil nodded, Mike fetched two mugs of java from the kitchen. Phil cleared magazines and other clutter from the coffee table to make room on one corner, and Mike took the armchair across from him.

"You said you needed my help. What for?"

"I'd like you to check out Annie Chance's massage business, find out exactly what goes on down there. Is it legit, kinky, crazy or what? I'm inclined to believe her version of events, but I don't want to miss anything. Otherwise, any other deductions I make could be wrong."

Only slight hesitation on Mike's part. "What do I have to do?"

"I want you to pose as a customer, maybe a john. You've been around. Just go down there, get a massage or whatever else they offer. Talk to them, check out the equipment." Phil took a sip from his mug. Too hot. He set it back down.

"Let me get this straight," Mike sounded surprised. "You're asking me to frequent a whorehouse?"

"It's not a whorehouse, it's a massage parlour."

Mike shot Phil a quizzical look. "That's what she says, but you don't sound so sure about that. Those places go by lots of names: sensitivity meeting centre, co-ed wrestling studio, horizontal hustle parlour, nude encounter centre or sex-therapy clinic. Cops call it a disorderly house. I knew one in Boston that sported a well-stocked library, complete with 'librarians to better serve you.'"

Mike paused. "Am I supposed to just talk and look around, or do you want me to get laid?"

"Only if you feel it's necessary. You could just start with a massage."

"And you're going to pay for whatever charges I ring up at this house of...whatever it is?"

"Yes, and try to keep your pecker up."

"That reminds me, have you got a line on those patches yet? I may just need one for this job."

Phil shook his head. "Unfortunately not."

"Too bad, since I haven't had a better offer since I don't know when. Maybe this decade!"

"So you'll do it?" Phil pressed.

"Only because it's for a good cause. A research project, an investigative procedure which might help you in this case you've been trying to solve. Otherwise I'd refuse out of a deep-seated aversion to anything immoral."

"I can understand that. I don't believe it, but I understand it."

"And you're paying?"

"Of course." Phil reiterated, now finding his coffee cool enough to drink.

"So why don't you go yourself?"

"Annie Chance will be there and I don't want her to think I'm investigating her. So you're the man for the job, no experience necessary. My murder investigation has come to a dead end, if you'll pardon the pun, possibly aided and abetted by my recent heart problems. Haven't felt up to it, and maybe I'm no good at it. I've travelled the mental hypotenuse of many an isosceles triangle I've come across in my lifetime, and found out shortcuts don't often work."

"Muldoon and his cops haven't come up with anything, either, have they?"

"That's true," Phil replied, brightening a bit. "So all I can do is stay on the job. It's a matter of honour, isn't it?"

"Yup. Like I always said—there's only two types of honour—get honour and stay honour."

"How about," said Phil, getting into the act, "she offered her honour, he honoured her offer, and all night long it was honour and offer!"

"Nowadays I'd find that impossible," said Mike. "You know, this caper could be entertaining. Reminds me of when I was a kid, fourteen or fifteen, and I went out to the midway at the Winnipeg Exhibition. Royal American Shows always had a girlie revue there. Good one too, black jazz band, chorus line, hootchy-kootchy girls and a headliner—on this occasion, Sally Rand, the famous fan dancer. I was too young to go in, but I snuck in anyway. Was I ever excited! My first chance to see some skin."

"Did you?"

"No, it was a gyp, really. In her main performance you didn't get to see a damn thing. She was supposed to be dancing in the nude, but all the titillating bits were always covered with her bloody big fans. After her act the emcee said for fifty cents you could stay for a special performance where Miss Rand revealed all."

"And?" Phil asked.

"I spent my last four bits. Sally did the exact same dance, but at the end, just before she ran offstage, she dropped the fans for about one second —the quickest flash I've ever seen. And do you know what?"

"What?"

"I swear to God she was wearing a flesh-coloured body stocking. I haven't trusted women ever since. Suckered! If females didn't have a particular brand of plumbing, there'd be a bounty on them. The experience made me feel a few feathers short of a whole duck, I can tell you."

"I can understand your frustration, Mike. Now, I hate to bug you about it, but will you do the Chance thing for me?"

"Okay, I'll go to this massage parlour, but I gotta tell you, I'm pretty rusty."

Phil stayed for lunch.

Mike booked a massage, got an appointment for later that same day and turned up in a taxi at the appointed hour. He got out in front of 1073 Seaquay Crescent in Vic West, paid the fare and, leaning heavily on his cane, limped up the curved driveway. The black trim on the white turn-of-the-century Edwardian stucco was begging for a retouch. The steep shingled roof, showing areas of mottled green moss, covered what was likely a large attic. The flowerbeds hadn't seen a gardener for some time, but would still provide bright colour in season. It was a handyman's dream, but if the price was right and you were into reno, some money could be made on the place.

Arriving at the heavy wooden door, Mike pressed the bell and heard chimes sound inside. A broad-beamed woman answered. Her dyed and frizzled hair stood well out from her head, and the distressingly heavy application of mascara reminded Mike of Tammy Faye Bakker. She wore a black cloth jacket nearly unbuttoned to the waist, which revealed a black underwire bra supporting drooping breasts of considerable amplitude. Mike pegged her in her late forties, but couldn't be sure.

She cordially invited Mike into a large entrance hall that opened onto spacious rooms on either side. A broad staircase to the right went to the upper rooms and a hallway going past the stairs to the left led to the rear. Soft music emanated from the room on the left, which contained a grouping of lounge chairs and a huge coffee table. An oak-veneered bar and a stone fireplace were in evidence, but no customers.

"My name is Beatrice Wild," said the woman. "And you are?"

"Mike Fowler. Just call me Mike," he said cheerily.

"And I'm Bea. What service did you require, Mike?"

"I called earlier for an appointment."

Bea checked a leather-bound ledger lying on the corner desk. "Ah, yes, for a massage, correct?"

"That's it."

"Would you like one of our girls to give you a hot, foamy bath and an oil rub first? Many of our clients find that interesting." Mike thought he caught a wink, but wasn't sure.

"Ordinarily yes, you gotta love that, but I think I'll have to pass." Mike pointed to his bandaged foot.

"Ah, too bad," Ms. Wild commiserated. "Well, there are other things you might try after your massage. I'm sure Annie will tell you all about them during your treatment."

Bea led the way upstairs, Mike hobbling behind her with the aid of the handrail and his cane. They entered one of the rooms off the L-shaped hallway.

"Just strip to the buff, Mike," said Bea, indicating the massage table, "and lie face down under the sheet. Annie will be in shortly." With that, Bea Wild turned on her heel and left him alone.

Mike damned all cats to hell as he sat on the edge of the table, his feet and other body parts dangling over the edge. The bath and oil rub had sounded good. Plus, it was a missed opportunity to explore the establishment's operations. He climbed under the linen sheet and lay with his face through the padded doughnut hole.

Ample Annie entered in a white cotton dress cut to look like a sexy nurse's outfit. Mike turned his head and they exchanged greetings.

"Any particular area of your body that needs working on?" Annie asked, her voice low and warm.

"Not really, I just like massages. They relax me, make me feel good."

"Yes, they do, don't they, Mike? Wish everyone felt that way. Now, do you like your massage soft or hard?"

Mike thought this over and figured he might throw out a verbal feeler. "Don't use that word 'hard,' please. It has sexual connotations that I may not be up to."

Annie laughed. "That could be taken care of, Mike, but not here and not by me. This is strictly massage. Unfortunately, some of us get a bad reputation. We do provide other therapeutic services you might like to try, depending on your lifestyle, of course. We can discuss that later if you like, but let's get started on relaxing these tense muscles in your shoulders. You've got a lot of knots here." Annie worked on his back with strong, competent fingers.

Mike gradually relaxed into a state of torpor. Annie told him to roll over, then began working on his legs and one good foot.

"What other services does your establishment offer?" Mike asked.

"Well, one's called Northern Exposure Domestic Services. It's an affiliate of an Edmonton group. Do you need your house cleaned?"

"I live in a small condo and I've been told it could stand some housekeeping."

"We send men and women to perform housework in the nude."

"Ho, I haven't heard of that before," said Mike. "Okay, I'll sign up on condition you send a female, and that she does a stint in the apartment of a friend of mine in the same building."

"No problem. Just understand, she'll only do cleaning. No hanky-panky. People may think the service is borderline, but it's all legitimate. We also help people find work. It's good pay and all you have to do is lie on your stomach on a table like this one. Interested?"

"Sounds dead easy. What's it pay?"

"Thirty-five dollars an hour."

"Not bad at all," Mike said. "Who's hiring?"

"The medical school at the University."

"What would I have to do?"

"You'd act as a practice patient for medical students, who'd be doing rectal exams."

"Ahhh." Mike lay in silent surprise for a second or two. "Well, no, I think not. Some of those students have awfully big fingers. So how about other therapies right here on the premises?"

"Do you want me to hurt you?" asked Annie. "Would you enjoy that?"

"Right now?" Mike yelped in alarm, bolting upright on the table.

"No, silly, not unless you wanted me to."

"Ah, can't say that I would," Mike said. Would *you* like to hurt *me*?"

"Only if you wanted me to," Annie reassured him as she gently pushed him back down. "It gives me a rush to create whatever sensation a person wants, whether it's pain or pleasure."

"Well, you've certainly given me pleasure, but I don't think I want to try for pain. By the way, can you shave a scrotum? And if so, would it be painful?"

Annie had heard it all, from penile probes to piercing needles, from nipple clamps to butt plugs, but this question surprised her. Was this some new kind of kinky sexual turn-on? "Yeah, I could do that. When I was a nurse I could shave a peach without cutting the skin, but you have to use a special razor. Why do you ask?"

As her hands continued to knead his muscles, Mike explained the search for the potency patch.

"Pain can be a prelude to sex, you know, Mike, have you tried that?"

"That's as may be, but I've never considered it as an alternative."

"Would you like to be invited to an S & M party, a fetish night? You might like to try it out. It's completely consensual and it gives some people an outlet for their repressed sexual fantasies. Don't tell me you don't have any of those," she said, chuckling.

Mike searched desperately for a reply. "Well, sometimes. I had a sex dream last night that was so vivid that when I woke up, my wallet was gone. Also, I used to pretend that I was Lash LaRue, the silent movie western star. And it's a fact I was pretty good with a bullwhip, back when I was a cowboy in Alberta. Does that qualify?"

"Lash LaRue? Way before my time, I'm afraid. Were you the flogger or the floggee?"

"I'd rather be handling the whip. A bullwhip is actually too dangerous for use by anyone but an expert. I always thought there were people in Victoria who oughta be bullwhipped, but you're telling me there are some who ask for it?"

"There are, sure, but only a few of them come out of the closet. And we don't hurt people who don't want to be hurt. Mostly we get voyeurs who come to see a show. But bondage and discipline, sadomasochism and domination and submission in their various forms appeal to a lot of educated professionals.

"At our meetings we get a cross-section of business people, service-industry workers, sailors, police officers, politicians, bureaucrats, some retirees like yourself, even mental health professionals. If I thought they'd go for bullwhips, I'd get some in. If you're somewhat of an expert on whips, maybe you could help me."

"Could be, but I'd have thought you'd be heavily into whipping anyway, if you have all these BDSM clients."

"We use wooden flogging paddles, actually, small braided whips and riding crops. Only a real sadist would go for a sound thrashing with a bullwhip."

"So what happens at your parties?"

"A planned and prearranged show, mostly, theatrical games presenting scenes of bondage and humiliation. We've got a bondage ladder, a whipping horse, stocks, crosses and spanking benches. There are intimacy areas for couples or customers who might want privacy for a role reversal.

As if the idea had just occurred to her, Annie said, "There's a party tonight. "Why don't you come? It could be an invigorating liberation for you, Mike, cerebral sex. Twenty dollars gets you in, plus two free drinks."

"What time does the action start?" Mike asked, mustering as much enthusiasm as he could.

"Show up around eight or whenever you like. You could even rent a slave on a per evening or per diem basis, if you need one. Play dog-and-master."

"Do what?"

"Rent a slave. You can be a master with a

sexual servant. Your slave has to do whatever you want—play your French maid, massage your feet, lick your boots, kiss your ass, clean your toilet—you name it, they do it."

"I'll think about it," said Mike, sitting upright now that the massage was over. "I've got some ashes I might need hauled."

Seventeen

After he left Mike, Phil ended up at the Mocambo again, listlessly reading the paper and sucking a steamed milk at a window table. He hadn't slept much the previous night and now the inside of his skull felt like an empty ballroom, with a single saxophone playing with light piano backup, lending a haunting echo chamber effect to the slow melancholy tune in his head. Who am I saving the last dance for? Phil wondered.

Big band oldies but goldies were one reason he frequented the establishment, rather than the Starbucks across the street. Another was the owner, Claire, who always made him feel welcome. His goatee reflected white in the window glass as he watched the slanting drizzle of early spring rain gusting up Blanshard Street.

The best thing about getting old, Phil mused, is that you didn't die young. Also, you could finally speak your mind. After all, what could anyone do to you, kill you? What did even that matter if you didn't give a damn? Dr. Scotland had tried to appear hopeful, but it was as obvious as a hernia at a weightlifters' convention that he didn't think much of Phil's chances of survival. Spring would mark his seventy-sixth birthday. He'd had a pretty good run, but what now?

Gophers dig holes for protection against predators, but they never figured on humans. Kids poured water down their holes to force the gophers to the surface, where they were clubbed to death. If the gopher stayed down the hole it drowned in slough water. If it came to the surface it got a sawed-off axe handle across the noggin. Someday, somewhere, something is going to do the same to each of us, Phil thought.

Dr. Scotland had handed him a six-month minimum death sentence. What was he supposed to do? Hope the joker reading the goat's entrails was wrong, and when he did die, that someone would sing over his grave,

Phil Figgwiggin's body
Lies a mouldering in the grass,
Blackbirds and beetles
Playing checkers up his ass...

Like all oldsters, Phil had mourned for a lot of friends with whom he could no longer break bread. There weren't many left, nor family for that matter, who would mourn for him. He wasn't ecstatic about his prospects, but was determined to carry on as long as he could and finish any project in which he was engaged.

That included the Poindexter murder, but there were too many questions to which he had no answers, too many unknown factors, and not enough clues. Richard Poindexter had bought the farm, but Phil didn't know what kid had drowned him out of his gopher hole and clubbed him with the sawed-off axe handle. Harry Muldoon wasn't doing any better. You could actually sympathize with Muldoon if it weren't for the cop's fixation on Annie Chance.

To make things more difficult, Phil's heart condition kept intruding on both his thoughts and his physical ability. He knew it was going to do him in, leaving only the matter of when, and whether the end would be quick whether a stroke would leave him a vegetable.

There was nothing sacred about dying in

agony. More than anything, he feared a lingering death. Mainstream medicine was trying to make use of increasingly sophisticated palliative-care skills to bring comfort to dying patients, to alleviate their pain, sadness, regret, anger and fear. But the medical professional still had a way to go.

Phil figured the terminally ill would seize the debate on the right to die from doctors, ethicists, and lawyers. Self-deliverance for the dying was certainly a problem, but Phil knew how to go about it, had been a member of the Hemlock Society for several years.

All this thinking about his own health made Phil remember a strange place he had once visited: the Peak of the Love of Life, a gloriously bright granite cusp on China's holiest mountain, Taishan. You climbed up more than seven thousand steps. If that didn't kill you, you arrived at a spectacular drop-off into a blue-white infinity of clouds and air. If you flung yourself off the cliff into this panoply of light, you'd fall well over a thousand feet before you hit the distant earth. Taking one's life in a leap over the yawning chasm at Taishan has been a tradition in eastern China for centuries.

The Love-Life Peak was actually the opposite of the purpose it so often served, and had reverted to its primitive religious purposes. Couples hoping for a boy child would go there to pray and to place red ribbons and booties on altars in the Temple of Azure Clouds. Phil could afford a ticket to China, but did he have the guts to leap into space? Maybe he should try naked bungy jumping in Nanaimo as a warm-up.

His drink had gone cold, so Phil walked over to the counter to ask for a straight coffee top-up. Re-seated, he stroked his goatee as he watched the passing parade of umbrellas through the rain-streaked window pane, his mind reverting to his review of euthanasia as a viable modus operandum in shuffling off the mortal coil. As a lawyer, Phil knew the sizeable risk doctors took in aiding and abetting euthanasia. They had their own ethical problems to consider, along with the risk of criminal code charges and lawsuits.

Lawyers sued on almost any cockamamie pretext these days, whatever the facts of the case. It was an inevitable development, given the number of the pettifogging profession trying to make a living from the population. Things weren't so bad in Phil's day and he was glad he wasn't in the game anymore. Lawyers were becoming a barnacle on the ass of progress.

Phil looked around as the lunch crowd began to arrive. You never knew what they would serve at the Mocambo, but it would always be varied and tasty. He looked at the menu, debating having lunch himself. The daily special, lambs' fries, didn't fool Phil—the dish was creamed curry of thinly sliced lamb's testicles. The "fries" combined the texture of scallops with the taste of gamey liver. Daisy would certainly have refused to let him order such a savoury dish. Bad for his cholesterol, she'd have said.

At the thought of Daisy, his heart suddenly did a backflip, landing hard against his rib cage. Daisy's death had been one of the most sudden shocks of his life, and the memory came rushing back.

"You've got all the leisure time you want now," Daisy had said. "Let's take advantage of it and do the things we've always wanted to do. Buy that recreational trailer and hitch it to the car. We can go wherever we want and do whatever we want. Get some well-earned rest and recreation."

So when Phil retired, that was the first thing he did. They were going to have some fun and games. All systems were go. He and Daisy started out early on a bright, sunny day that seemed full of promise. They had figured to get their kicks on Route 66. In the afternoon, they saw a sign for a recently constructed tourist attraction, Wild Animal Park which they had always meant to visit. See some deer, buffalo, elk and moose. They still weren't too far from home, but felt they should put their plan into effect immediately —stop when they wanted to and do what ever pleased them.

They had entered the park, Phil remembered, noting the sign which told them to stay in the car for their own safety, as some of the animals were unpredictable. The animals were unpredictably absent that day. The rolling hills and meadows were bare at first, and no game emerged from the wooded areas they encountered later on in the park. So when Phil and Daisy spotted some creatures at a watering hole, they got out of the car and wandered over to take some pictures.

When they got back to the car a short time later, a large bull buffalo was leaning against the front fender. Buffalo are heavy and they do that—lean against anything handy in order to take the weight off their feet. The Figgwiggins had to wait until the animal left, but they were excited and they took pictures of the beast reclining against their vehicle. When the buffalo departed, they saw the big dent in the fender and the broken headlight.

"Golly Moses," Phil swore, "damn disappointing thing to happen just at the start of our trip. What will we do now?"

"We're still close to home," Daisy had replied helpfully. "Why not go back, get the damage fixed at our own garage and make a fresh start as soon as the car's fixed?"

"Good idea," Phil decided.

Even though he stepped on the gas on the way home, night soon fell upon them. Phil was doing five to ten miles over the speed limit when the motorcycle cop pulled him over and flashed his badge. Jam tomorrow and jam yesterday, but never jam today, Phil thought as the policeman harangued him about his speeding at night, to which he had been attracted by the broken headlight.

"Officer, there is a good reason for that," Phil said condescendingly, "a big bull buffalo leaned on my car and smashed in the front fender and headlight, as you can see."

"Get out of the car," said the cop tersely, "I want you to take a sobriety test, and right now. Let's see you walk that white line."

Phil walked the line, and managed with protestations of innocence to get by with just a warning and a ticket for the missing headlight.

"I want your wife to drive," said the patrolman, "and you get that light fixed immediately when you get home." The cop jumped on his motorcycle and took off, leaving the Figgwiggins standing in the middle of the road.

Phil had, at that point, been just a little disillusioned with his first efforts at retirement, and hoped it was not an omen for the future. His head ached and he told Daisy he might just as well get in the back of the trailer and sleep the rest of the way home, since she had to drive anyway. Daisy got behind the wheel while Phil proceeded to the rear.

As he entered the trailer, whose doorway was new to him and very low, he bumped his head on the door sill and his hat was knocked off backward onto the pavement. Letting out a curse, he jumped back onto the roadway, slamming the trailer door in disgust and anger as he did so. Daisy heard him say something and the trailer door shut with a bang, so she put the car into gear and drove smartly off down the highway as Phil picked up his hat.

"My shattered, tattered ass," yelled Phil into the night as he watched the tail lights disappear into the darkness. "What the hell do I do now?" He threw down his hat and stomped on it in a red rage. He decided to hitchhike and for once, he got lucky.

Phil refrained from telling the truck driver about the buffalo; he'd learned his lesson from the cop. Instead, he convinced the man that he'd been inadvertently left on the highway by his wife. The trucker volunteered to try to catch up with Daisy and the trailer so Phil could stop her and reboard his own transportation.

As it turned out, he would have needed grappling hooks to do so, because although they managed to come up alongside Daisy for brief periods and Phil waved frantically to her from the truck's cab, they could never stay abreast of her long enough for Daisy to get the message. Also, it was dark and the cab of the truck was much higher up than the driver's seat of the car. Daisy kept her eyes steadfastly on the road, trying to ignore the crazy truck driver who wouldn't pass and seemed to be determined to run her off the road. She paid strict attention to her own driving since, after all, she only had one headlight.

"Well, anyway," Phil said to the driver, aiming for a bit of macho humour, "she's had a lot of experience handling one-eyed monsters. She'll drive it home all right."

So they passed Daisy and carried on down the highway. The trucker graciously said it wasn't out of his way and he'd drive Phil right to his house in town.

After thanking the driver profusely, Phil went up the steps of his home, turned on the front porch lights and was unlocking the door when he saw Daisy, the car and the trailer coming down the street. She turned into the driveway as Phil turned from the door and stood waiting for her, the pool of light from the house and street lamps illuminating his face.

Terrified to see her husband before her and not asleep in the trailer, Daisy let out a shriek. Her eyes wide with fear, hands frozen to the steering wheel as she looked at Phil, she drove the whole contraption right through the garage door and halfway through the back wall.

She died in the accident, sprawled across the front seat, stone cold dead from a broken neck.

Was it Phil's fault or fate—the purblind doomsters at work? Phil remembered the many sessions of counselling he'd needed to contend with his guilt.

He still couldn't believe he had joined the ranks of seniors who were left with few old friends to talk to, drifting inexorably into the "why bother?" stage. Another thought popped into Phil's mind. You knew things were getting worse, while politicians told you they were getting better. Politicians and diapers have one thing in common, Phil told himself. They should both be changed regularly and for the same reason.

Phil found himself looking for people with an interesting story, who could tell it well. Good bullshit was better than sober reflection on the problems of the world and the vicissitudes and brevity of life. That's what Phil appreciated about Mike Fowler; he could always count on his buddy for the non sequitur, along with exaggeration, satire, spoof and weird old jokes. It often descended into juvenile humour, but they both felt younger in each other's company.

Everything in life held the potential for bounty or disaster, but you couldn't shy away from the risks. He'd chosen to do certain things and not to do others. He'd never worked in a factory making tin assholes for Teddy bears, so there were still a few things left to do—like giving the Doctor Dick case one more shot.

The rain had stopped. A good thing, too, because Phil had forgotten his umbrella. He pushed the newspapers aside, put on his padded Mackinaw jacket, picked up his old fedora. The hat, purchased for ten bucks at Value Village, was still in good shape. The sweat band read The Mallory Ten and the inscription on the silk lining said, *For Youthful Smartness — Premium Quality*. That was as good a motto as any he'd ever heard. It was time to get off his duff and get cracking.

He idly watched as a panhandler set up shop across the street. Phil talked to a good many street people. He pitied the ones who were down on their luck and deserved a break, but others who had levelled with him had said they could make upwards of a hundred dollars a day in a good location. Some panhandlers were merely trying to bring their living standard up to subsistence level. Others resorted to beggary to feed a booze habit — in which case they were really only begging for the government, because liquor taxes constituted such a high percentage of the cost of a bottle of spirits that alcoholics paid higher taxes as a percentage of income than any other Canadians.

The homeless youth wore a torn windbreaker; his head was covered by a bandana with a Union Jack print, and he was accompanied by a large, smooth-coated dog with powerful jaws, a mutt of the Mexican Careless breed, likely sired by a committee. The derelict sat in an alcove between adjacent buildings, further protected from the weather by shop awnings. Producing an old workman's cloth cap from inside his tattered jacket, he dumped in some chump change to encourage the largesse of prospective donors.

Phil made his way across the thoroughfare and ducked under the awnings. "Do you mind if we discuss business for a bit?" he asked with a twinkle in his eye.

"What kind of business?"

Phil squatted down beside the surprised youth. "I'd like to give you some advice on how to improve your box office take on this operation."

"I guess I can listen, mister."

"Leave the dog alone on his mat here, next to your knapsack and begging cap. Attach some signs to the wall above the dog, saying something like, Am working my way through veterinary college, I'm saving up to buy a cat, or Will work for dog food."

The dog's ears perked up and he wagged his tail. Phil reached over to pat the mutt, then continued, "You buy stiff wires and attach a harmonica to the dog's collar so the instrument sits out in front of the dog's

mouth. You could probably get a gizmo like that from a music store. You want it to look like the dog is playing the harmonica. Then you hide a tape recorder in the knapsack right next to the dog."

"I don't have a tape recorder," the young beggar said.

"Well, we could probably dig one up for you. Anyway, then you turn on a tape of mouth organ music. Some tune like *Brother, Can You Spare a Dime?* from the Depression. Then all you have to do is step back and keep an eye on things."

"What's this supposed to do for me?" A note of complaint had entered the panhandler's voice.

"It will appear to the passing chumpery that the dog is the beggar. People going by will love it, which will cause them to contribute mightily. They'll appreciate your business acumen."

"I don't have one of those, either. Sounds like a lot of work for some sort of gag."

Phil really wanted to see whether the idea would work, so he offered to help the guy do it. They talked a while longer until it became clear that the junior beggar didn't want to make the effort. Maybe he couldn't find any humour in his situation, maybe it wouldn't be funny after all, or maybe they were both whiners, the dog with perhaps the better reason.

I'd have better luck persuading Rover, thought Phil. He at least looks interested, or maybe he wants to learn to play the mouth organ. With a final rub behind the dog's ears, Phil headed off toward the Eaton Centre mall. He'd finally cheered himself up.

As he neared his destination, he entered the turf of dozens of ladies of the evening in all sizes and ages, from soiled sixteens to social security types reaping a last harvest from undiscriminating tourists. A dark-eyed burlap sister of easy virtue, her best-before date long expired, sidled up to him and said, "For a hundred bucks, do you want to go to bed with me?"

Phil figured she'd probably waved good-bye to the Canadian navy when it left port in World War II. Pausing for a moment to think the proposition over, he replied, "Well, I don't know, I'd have to see the money up front, of course." She spat on his shoe before turning away.

On his way through the mall, Phil picked up a bubble-jet ink cartridge for his printer. He stopped at a pay phone to look up the address of the Upper Room, a soup kitchen he'd heard about, where staff sold meal tickets for a dollar that could be handed out to street people. The tickets could be redeemed for a meal, but not turned in for cash. The program helped the Upper Room defray the heavy cost of feeding the needy, a task the government had dumped onto the backs of charities and the private sector.

As Phil walked north down Douglas, he passed several more panhandlers. He knew he was part of the endemic problem, but he had neither the time, money nor inclination to do anything about it.

He was certainly trying not to become blasé about the outstretched hands of the homeless, but admitted to himself that they could get on his nerves. They invaded your privacy and made you feel empathy, guilt, frustration and anger. In any case, they were now a fact of life in Canadian cities, and in Phil's opinion, lousy and incompetent governments were doing nothing to alleviate the problem.

Mike Fowler's take on the homeless was, "Ducklings are born with the ability to waddle immediately into the nearest pond. Humans are slower at developing their ability to cope in life. We all work our own system, our own way of dealing with the economics of our times. All these beggars are doing is playing the game of survival of the unfittest, using whatever brains they were either born with or have developed during their formative years while being lied to by the educational system. After all, they're only imitating what they've observed in politicians—waste, bribes, bid rigging, fraud, patronage and kickbacks."

The Upper Room turned out to be on the main floor of a decrepit building on Pandora. The front door was locked, but a smoker told him he had to go through the back entrance during meal hours.

Just then the door opened, and as a man departed, Phil slipped through into a long hallway. Offices and lavatories lined the passage. He walked back into a large dining room complete with long cafeteria-style tables, which seated a kaleidoscope of diners, men and women of all manner of dress and demeanour.

To his right, a young woman emerged from the open kitchen doorway, carrying bowls of vegetables. Phil asked to speak to someone in charge, and she directed him to a small, dark-visaged cook, who was frying something on top of a large stove against the wall. When he spotted Phil, the cook beckoned to a kitchen helper to take over, then motioned to Phil to follow him out of the combined clatter of kitchen and dining room to one of the cramped offices off the main passageway.

"I'd like to buy some meals," said Phil.

"Fine," said the cook-cum-official. "We charge a dollar a meal if you can afford it. How many do you want? What's your name, by the way?"

"Figgwiggin."

"Your initial?"

"P."

The cook wrote this information on a green numbered card as Phil put twenty-five dollars on the desk.

"Now, when you come here for meals, the routine is that you come in through the back entrance at the times posted and identify yourself by presenting this card."

Phil was more that mildly surprised. He checked his clothing, looking around for a mirror. He remembered he needed a haircut; his white hair sticking out at the sides made him look like an Einstein clone, and he certainly wasn't dressed for the Union Club dining room. No tie.

After a longish pause, Phil explained that he wanted the tickets to hand out to street people. The cook tore up the admission voucher and sold Phil twenty-five small plastic squares, each one marked

Good for 1 Meal
Upper Room
919 Pandora
No Cash Value

Exiting the premises, Phil headed for Prosecutor Thorndyke's office, which was on his way home. As he walked, he sang softly to himself. It was a ditty from his youth, but it seemed to fit the day's adventures with the homeless:

It's the same the whole world over
It's the poor what gets the blame;
While the rich has all the pleasures,
Now, ain't that a fucking shame?

Justin Thorndyke rose to greet Phil as he stepped into the prosecutor's courthouse office. He shook Phil's hand warmly and waved him to a seat.

Phil was beginning to appreciate how frustrating the private dick business could be. All he was getting so far was the thin end of nothing, sharpened to a point and then broken off. He was beginning to think he couldn't run a wheelbarrow if they wrote the instructions on the handles. Not yet willing to give up, Phil decided he'd follow up on all leads before turning the information over to the authorities.

Phil began to explain his suspect X theory to Justin, the possible connection between Poindexter and a man he'd set up to take a beating. Thorndyke listened attentively for a few moments, then asked, "Why don't you get the cops to check it out for you?"

Phil shook his head sorrowfully. "The cops don't like me, especially Muldoon. We had another scrap. He'd probably find out the request came from me and refuse to approve it. A waste of time and effort, would be his opinion."

"Is it?"

"That's just it, I don't know. I'm only playing a hunch."

"Which is?"

"That somewhere out there lurking in the boondocks is a victim of a vicious assault and battery, and although he doesn't know the identity of the thugs who beat him up, he might have found out who was responsible for setting it up," said Phil firmly.

"Dick Poindexter?"

"Yes. If we could get a list of possible victims and could link one of them to Dick, then we'd have a murder suspect with a strong motive."

"Pretty tenuous. What makes you think this arranged beating took place at all?" Justin asked.

"Talking to Annie Chance, who I guess you could call my client. She says Dick told her something to the effect that he'd managed to have someone in Vancouver beaten up by some strong-arm types, because this victim had screwed him around financially, caused him to lose a lot of money. I understand there may be a system that can name such a person. Read something about it recently. Seems the police forces in this province put a lot of work into the program."

"Yes. It's called ViCLAS," said Thorndyke, explaining that the acronym stood for Violent Crime Linkage Analysis System.

"We've got access to it, so I might be able to help you. I've always felt there should be a free flow of this kind of information, across the country and with the Americans, too."

"I'm only interested in B.C. at the moment. How does this ViCLAS work?"

"It tracks all solved or unsolved homicides, attempted murders, sex crimes and assaults of a sexual or predatory nature, whether apparently random or suspected of being part of serial crimes. The system keeps track of murders and assaults arising from domestic incidents or barroom brawls, all types of foul play, date rape, pedophilia, child sex rings—any kind of violence involving heavy assault and battery."

"Great! That fits the bill," Phil said, excited now. "Could you do a search covering a certain time frame in a specific area, see if it turns up the names and vital stats of guys who were badly beaten for no apparent reason? If it spits out anything useful, you could let me know. Then I could check out the list to see if any of them had some business or other connection with Richard Poindexter. If I found anything, I'd get back to you, and you could suggest to Muldoon that he'd better look into it."

"That's exactly what the system was designed to do," said Justin. "Okay, I'll do it. For you, and because bringing criminals to justice is my job, after all. I'll be in touch. But, you know, I still don't understand why you've involved yourself in all this, especially when you're not practicing law anymore."

"The common perception of Victoria is that it's a cemetery with street lamps where they don't bury their dead, they just wander the streets. I may be retired, Justin, but I need something to do to keep busy, keep the brain cells firing."

"Are you getting paid for this?"

"No...er...not so far," Phil admitted, noting the disapproving look that crossed Thorndyke's face. "But listen, I'd like to spring for a shot of painkiller. Let's go across the street to the Cherry Bank. You still look stressed out to me."

To his surprise, this time Thorndyke accepted eagerly. "You're on. I'm so busy I hardly know which case to start on next, so it might as well be a case of beer. Anyway, it's four o'clock, so fuck the Attorney General for today. Let's go." Justin grabbed his cap and jacket off the rack. Phil donned his raincoat and they walked out the door.

The Cherry Bank Hotel Rib House was once a family manor in a large cherry orchard, then a boarding house. The current incarnation, a quirky Victorian hotel in the heart of downtown with an old world atmosphere, sported a famous rib house and Roaring Twenties lounge complete with rotating glass ball chandeliers and a glassed-in mezzanine. In times past, the local wags claimed it was the only hotel in Victoria where they stored maidenheads.

The two lawyers ensconced themselves in a corner of the lounge on the padded black banquette, and Phil ordered a round.

"You really should be getting paid for your efforts, Phil. Otherwise, it's a flagrant violation of the legal ethics code."

Dodging the query, Phil asked, "You've heard the old story about the public's basic opinion of lawyers, right?"

"Well, I've heard a lot of them. The last one was: What's the difference between an angry chicken and the average lawyer?"

"I'll bite," said Phil.

"The chicken clucks defiance!" Justin chuckled at his own joke. "But I interrupted you. Maybe your story goes back a ways and I haven't heard it. Go ahead." Just then, the waiter thumped two mugs of ale down in front of them and scurried off to the next table.

"Okay, there was this poker game with four players in it: a high-priced lawyer, the Tooth Fairy, a low-priced lawyer, and Santa Claus. The pot was huge and was about to be won, when suddenly the lights in the gambling establishment went out. Pitch darkness. When the lights came on again, the pile of cash on the table was missing. Now the question is, to be deduced from those facts alone, can you tell which one—the high-priced lawyer, the Tooth Fairy, the low-priced lawyer, or Santa Claus—stole the pot?

"Okay, I'll bite, which one?"

"The high-priced lawyer."

"Why?"

"Because the other three are figments of your imagination."

The punchline earned a genuine guffaw from Justin. "I'll have to remember that one. Good thing we can still laugh at the jokes."

"How many lawyer jokes are there, do you think?"

"Oh, must be thousands," Justin answered, taking a deep draught of his beer.

"Nope. Only two."

"Two?"

"Yeah, all the rest are authentic case histories."

Justin broke up. When he stopped laughing, he said, "I have my own theory as to why only about ten percent of the population likes lawyers."

"Is the percentage that high? Let me guess. Is it because the courts have become overbooked, slow, confusing, intimidating, expensive, non-user friendly, pretentious, overbearing and insensitive?"

"No."

Phil began stroking his goatee as he warmed to the subject. "Is it because behind every child molester there's a bottom-feeding lawyer arguing about constitutional rights? Or because multiple murderers are getting lenient sentences thanks to trendy defence strategies that fool judges and juries?"

"Neither, but I know what you mean. The standard tactics now, when speaking to sentence, are things like, 'My client just wants to put this thing behind him and start the healing process for his family,' or 'My client didn't really mean to do it, he's very sorry and he won't do it again, so why don't we just forget about these charges and let him go free so that he can get on with his life?'"

Phil picked up on the theme, "Yeah, it's doublespeak. Stuff like 'I know you believe you understand what you think I said, but I'm not sure you realize that what you heard or thought you heard is not what I meant.' So, Justin, is the public cynical, then, because of all these idiot TV shows and novels about grasping, soulless lawyers?"

"That's not it, either. It's because Canada's in a mess and lawyers are to blame. Since Confederation in 1867, we've been governed by lawyers for ninety-five of the past hundred and thirty-five years. That's well over seventy percent of all that time. The debts we owe, the whole mess, was created when lawyers were in charge."

"Point well taken," Phil agreed. Personally, I'm going to plead *de minimus non curat lex*."

"The law doesn't concern itself with trifles," Thorndyke translated.

"Or, no matter how thin you slice it, it's still baloney."

"Which is why we should only tell lawyer jokes among ourselves. We may think they're funny, but ordinary Canadians are deadly serious in their distaste for law firms like Welsh, Robb, Steel, Whine, Wheedle and Begg."

"Or Crocker-Schmidt," Phil interjected. "Or how about Sucks & Bloess?"

"Enough of this *non compos mentis* bullshit,"Thorndyke said abruptly, "Drink up. Look, Figg, I'm happy to check out your theory out on ViCLAS, but please, be careful. I don't want to end up prosecuting you for violating someone's privacy."

Phil threw Thorndyke a look of gratitude and admiration. "Thanks, Justin. I really appreciate your help."

Eighteen

A bouncer wearing a dirty white sweatshirt with the slogan $2Q + 2Q = 4Q$ crudely lettered on the front greeted Mike at the door of Annie Chance's S & M party at eight that evening. The back of the man's shirt said *Red Rum*. A big truck-driver type, his legs encased in blue jeans and heavy work boots. Shoulder-length yellow hair hung below an orange construction worker's helmet. As his big paw closed the door, Mike noted the black swastika tattooed on his left arm. A muffled rhythmic beat came from inside the building. Bea Wild sat at the lobby desk, this time with lightning flashes on her cheeks. She wanted twenty bucks before he went any further.

"Two beers with the cover," she told Mike, handing him a couple of tickets.

The bouncer guided him past the stairs to the back of the house and opened the door to the basement. Mike's ears and nerves were assaulted by the rock music blasting up the stairwell.

The music lover in him was appalled. Judas Priest, he thought. This stuff's about as bad as you'd expect anything to get. He wondered what the odds were that they'd switch to big-band jazz at his request.

The basement, rigged out like a dungeon, appeared to run the length and breadth of the house. The walls were covered with grey and black Styrofoam faked to look like rocks. Dim lighting was relieved by several small ceiling spots shining down on assorted instruments of torture. In one of the partitioned booths at the end, several people were taking turns whacking at each other with paddles provided for their pleasure. Mike couldn't judge the severity of the blows.

There was a motley crowd in the basement, but the joint wasn't packed. Some of the guests had not been blessed by nature when it came to looks, so they needed little adornment to achieve a menacing effect. Black leather and latex were much in evidence, and for many of the players, S & M dress was clearly an affectation; token fetish concessions to the scene, like dark glasses, turtlenecks, body piercing.

This wasn't going to be a spiritual experience, Mike figured. The whole thing seemed pretty lame, the guests desperately looking for some kind of good time.

In the centre of the room, a ladder rose from floor to ceiling, with ropes and chains hanging from it, and a padded gym horse stood beside it. Mike pictured someone draped over the horse, getting a good whipping. Most of the guests stood around in groups, drinking, waiting for something to happen.

Mike was heading for the bar when a heavy-duty lady in black leather jacket and gloves sidled past him. She looked like she was chewing tobacco with the seat of her pants. As her buttocks swayed by, Mike muttered under his breath, "If a sheep is a ram and a donkey is an ass, why is a ram in the ass a goose?"

Acting on impulse and figuring to get right into the action, Mike goosed her. She turned slowly to see who had done her the dirty, looked him up and down as he leaned on his cane, smiled, then kicked the cane out from under his weight. He hit the floor with a thud.

"I thought you were trying to pick me up," she said as she grabbed his arm and hauled him back to his feet, "so the least I can do is the same for you. I like your style, old man, you don't waste any time. Now come on over to the bar and let's have a drink."

A shaken Mike followed her. He knew he had a live one, but what the hell was he going to do with her? All that meat and no potatoes. He felt like an astronaut who'd just farted into his space suit.

They sat on stools at one end of the bar. The bar man produced two bottles of beer with alacrity.

"What's your name, honey?" his buxom companion asked. "Aren't you kinda old for this scene? You look like you were a waiter at the Last Supper."

"Thanks for nothing. Just call me Mike. What's your name?"

"I go by my pen name," she replied. "From when I was in the pen. Annabelle Wrang."

"I hope it doesn't toll for me," Mike mumbled, taking a long pull at his beer.

The assembled throng looked up when a fat, white, middle-aged man appeared at the top of the stairs. A black leather mask covered his entire head. He was stark naked except for the chrome studded collar, with chain attached, that encircled his neck. The other end of the chain was held firmly by Annie Chance.

Annie jerked the man down the stairs and over to the whipping horse, then ordered Anonymous to lie spread-eagle across it. When he complied, she proceeded to whack his bare derriere with a wooden paddle.

Mike thought she was pulling her punches, that this joker was not getting a real beating, even though he was all humped over like a dog shitting thumbtacks. He took the whipping in silence.

The watching crowd was restive but hushed until the man, ass in the air with his cheeks spread apart, let out a tremendous fart. The watchers howled with laughter. Annie backed off and waved the paddle to and fro while holding her nose.

To punish her victim for this breach of good taste, she placed him on the ladder, tied him up with some chains, and offered the paddle to any onlooker who wanted to take a few whacks. A couple of people tried but seemed afraid to hit the silly bugger very hard.

Mike idly wondered what the guy was getting paid for this gig. Not that he intended on applying for the job himself. Annie, meanwhile, had retreated to the bar, where she knocked back a scotch. She returned to hand out some more humiliation.

Taking the masked man off the ladder, she made him get down on his hands and knees and bark like a dog.

Then the bouncer turned up with a young woman of considerable pulchritude and began ripping off her clothes. Shrugging off their apparent boredom, the audience gave this action a standing ovation and gathered around the new scene.

Annie and the bouncer abandoned the fat doughhead. They placed the naked lady on the ladder and tied her with thongs. The fat man in the mask went to the bar and came back with a banana.

The background music died and an amplified voice boomed, "Ladies and gentlemen, we pause for an old commercial." A tinny soprano sang,

I'm Conchita la Banana and I've come to say,
That bananas should be eaten in a certain way,
When they are flecked with brown and have that golden hue,
Bananas are the best, they are the best for you.
You can eat them in a salad, you can eat them in a pi-eye,
But no matter how you eat them, be sure you never keep them,

In a...re...fridg...erator!... Olay!

While the song played, lardass slowly peeled the banana. This done, he inserted one end into the woman's vagina, and after glancing around the room, commenced to eat the banana. The resulting roar of approval from the crowd almost drowned out the sound of the basement door crashing open.

A shitstorm ensued. Shrill bursts of police whistles cut through the din as Wade Cavanaugh and two other constables charged down the steps, followed by an officer taking flash photos at lightning speed.

A convulsive shudder ran through the pack of voyeurs and a split second later, they scattered. There was nowhere to go, and they were met by more police at the only other exit, a curtained door that led up some outside stairs onto the side lawn.

Laissez le bon temps roulez! thought Mike as he moved quickly behind the bar to avoid the stampeding crowd and observe the action. "May the skin of your backside never cover a banjo," he said to the barman. "There's going to be a hot time in the old town tonight."

"This is a raid!" Cavanaugh announced through a bullhorn, as if this information would come as a surprise to the assemblage.

"Give your names and vital stats to the officers at the door and then leave; the party's over."

"No shit, Sherlock!" someone shouted amid a chorus of boos and catcalls. Several derogatory remarks were hurled at the cops, in keeping with Shakespeare's advice in Henry IV, Part 2, 1600: *Tis needful that the most immodest word, Be looked upon and learned.*

Wade advanced on Chance, his main target. Standing at attention before her, he announced, "Annie Chance, I'm placing you under arrest and taking you into custody. Please be advised that anything you say will be taken down and may be used as evidence at your trial."

"I'm calling you an asshole."

"I'll make a note of that, ma'am."

"Let's hope they use that information in court. It shouldn't be hard to prove. What am I charged with?"

"Keeping a common bawdy house, ma'am," Cavanaugh replied politely, as he cuffed her and jerked his head toward the stairs. The other cops took charge of the bouncer, the cunnilingating fat fool and the naked woman, sans banana. Wade used his bullhorn again to order the house cleared of occupants. He briefly entertained the idea of searching everyone for drugs, certain it would've yielded results, but the raid had only one object in mind.

"What the hell can they charge us with?" Ms. Wrang asked Mike. "We weren't doing a damn thing except watching."

"Nothing, in my opinion," said Mike, "unless it's a crime to look mean, dress outrageously, talk dirty, watch some phony crap-can sadists, and be one of the suckers getting jerked off around here."

"Yeah, there's a lot of shit going down. Wanna come up to my place?" she asked.

"Don't say 'come up' to me, honey. My prostate may preclude it."

"I wanted to be a dominatrix tonight," she said wistfully. "I could just beat the living shit out of you if that's what you're here for. Or you could lick my boots."

Mike blanched at the thought. "And you could kiss my ass! Figuratively speaking, of course. No offence, but this is goodbye, Annabelle, my dear. I don't think I'm into this sado-machoism. I'm outta here and you should scram, too." Mike navigated the stairs as quickly as he could with his cane, and was off like a dirty shirt.

Nineteen

Harry Muldoon was seething. He had picked up the latest *Frank* magazine at the Yates Street newsstand on his way to work. The issue contained yet another article on prostitution in Victoria, aimed at ripping the veil of propriety from the face of the fair city. Muldoon's blood pressure rose steadily, spiking at every suggestion that the cops were to blame for the existence and extent of the problem.

The story didn't sit well with Harry, who was only too well aware that these birds of the evening, or any other time of the day, flocked to Victoria because of the climate. And who could blame them?

B.C.'s Internet hookers was the heading of the article.

Back in the Sixties, hype artists for the B.C. tourism industry came up with the now-forgotten slogan, "Follow the birds to Victoria." What vision they had.

According to the new Internet hand guide for American sex tourists, the southern tip of Vancouver Island has become the pants-down wind-surfing capital of Canada.

Desiree's Worldwide Guide to Sex describes Victoria as a corn-utopia for johns, a friendly one-stop shopping zone at bargain basement prices. All aided and abetted by local authorities intent on looking the other way.

Muldoon regarded this as a personal affront. He kicked the desk in anger, then slumped back into his office chair and read on.

Desiree's field report touts the City of Gardens as one of the best places in North America to meet accommodating service workers who specialize in fulfilling domination fantasies. One Victoria agency bills itself as a "playhouse" with fully equipped dungeon and offers a variety of services catering both to regular chaps and chaps who like chaps.

"Damn it," Muldoon reacted, "that's gotta be Annie Chance's place."

Enterprising Victoria city councillors have tried

to cash in on this trade by charging both escort services, and the women themselves, annual licensing fees to ply their trade. The net effect, however, has been a tax flight to less hypocritical precincts nearby, especially the city's low-rent western suburb of Esquimalt, West Coast headquarters of the Canadian navy.

Desiree argues that there's no better place in Canada for a certain class of visitor to meet interesting new people in their home or apartment for an hour. Or by the hour.

As generations of stout-hearted young Victoria lads know, one of the best places to get laid on the West Coast if ye be a lusty young man is to try your luck in the taverns of Esquimalt several weeks after the fleet is out of port, and desperate young wives are at the end of their tether. (Ever been blown ashore, Billy?)

The article included a Web site address where interested parties could obtain Desiree's Guide, which contained a wealth of travel information for visitors to Victoria, including handy advice for out-of-towners looking to pick up teen street hookers, a how-to guide for stickhandling through the welter of escort services the city had to offer, and bargaining suggestions. It ended with a caveat: *Desiree's Guide hastens to point out that the information it provides constitutes a fictionalized document.* But of course, thought Muldoon. Why else would there be precise information on how to avoid getting nailed by the cops in an embarrassing sting operation?

Harry had to admit to himself that the article might help him head off trouble before a crime was committed, and he pencilled himself a note to check out both the Internet and this guide. He noted from the price list that a special eight-hour session with a pair of young lasses would set you back a mere thirteen hundred dollars. House calls from Vancouver to the U.S. were one thousand dollars a day per companion plus airfare.

What really got his goat, however, was that the article ended by stating: *Of course, if the police were ever to hear about any of this, it would no doubt be stopped immediately.*

"They are dipping me in shit!" Harry exploded. "The nerve of those fucking bastards!"

Muldoon tossed the tabloid onto his desk and got up to pace his office floor. Escort services were too well treated in Greater Victoria, in his opinion. In one municipality, a resident police expert on prostitution kept a close eye on escort agencies that set up shop in the area. He interviewed the new owners, checked the age of escorts, ensured the agencies were properly licenced and that they obeyed all the bylaws. Muldoon had briefly toyed with the open, cooperative approach, but it wasn't his style. He just wanted to run them out of town.

Over in Vancouver, twenty prostitutes had disappeared in a relatively short period of time and even the *Globe and Mail* had taken notice of the problem on the West Coast. *Why not legalize the trade?* One columnist wrote. *Prostitution is as much a part of reality as death and taxes. It has flourished as a supply-demand, buyer-seller business throughout recorded history and even in today's free-sex society still flourishes. Perhaps it is time for cities to accept this reality, license some brothels and set some health and safety standards.*

The region's various city councils occasionally debated the issue. Hooking was a dangerous, not a glamourous job, despite the more than seven hundred dollars a day some of the women earned. Some councillors felt police should get the independent hookers off the street and into agencies, where their money wouldn't go directly into the pockets of their pimps.

Most escort agencies only took twenty-five percent. They screened the johns, confirming names and addresses and even trying to make sure the men turned up alone. They installed safety procedures and had call display and 911 on speed dial.

Muldoon didn't want to start babysitting the hooker trade. When the council had asked his opinion, he'd recommended that the force should stick to tracking down the bad, useless animals—the pimps. Sweep some of that dirt so far under the rug they'd never crawl out; kick their butts so hard they'd start to smell shoe polish on their breath.

Constable Cavanaugh entered the office. Muldoon passed a weary hand across his brow and demanded, "Okay, what'd you find out at Annie's?"

Wade's face cracked into a smile. "There's a lot of kinky sex going on. They were having what you might call a fetish night. Closet perverts were everywhere, cavorting around in a dungeon. Mostly S & M types. We pissed a lot of people off, got a lot of names. Only arrested the main characters, just like you said, Sarge."

"Did you catch anybody actually fucking anybody?"

"No. But we got some pictures and seized whatever paperwork we could find."

"Weapons?"

"Knives, no guns, a whole raft of whips

and paddles and stuff you could certainly use to assault someone, but mostly sex-oriented. Weird costumes; some looked like they were bloodstained."

"No medical instruments, things she might have used on Poindexter?"

"We're running the knives and some clothes through the lab. I'll bring you the reports as soon as I get them."

"Good. You'll make detective yet," said Muldoon approvingly.

"Well, I'd appreciate any advice you can give me, Sarge."

"Today's tip, Cavanaugh: never hide in a closet after eating Mexican food." He grinned at his own joke.

"Thanks, Sarge, you're all heart. Chance's hearing is this afternoon, before Magistrate Horrigan. She'll probably make bail."

Muldoon nodded. "Yeah. Don't they all."

The surreptitious phone call tipping him off to the previous evening's raid on Annie Chance's establishment startled Phil. Not because Annie was in custody again, since he'd received Mike's report over a cup of spiked coffee that morning, and seen an item on the TV news shortly after. But he was sure he recognized the caller's voice. The TV reporters had questioned the cop who conducted the raid and identified him as Wade Cavanaugh. There were clips of his voice on tape. Phil had an excellent memory for the timbre and rhythms of people's speech, and although the voice was muffled as if the caller were speaking through a handkerchief, he was certain he recognized Cavanaugh's inflections.

If he was right, it meant there was a difference of opinion at headquarters as to Annie's guilt. The caller had kept it fairly short, but he made sure Phil knew what time to be at the courthouse later that day.

Phil sat in the back pew in the provincial courtroom listening to the case in progress and waiting for the court officers to bring Annie Chance up from the cells for her plea and bail application.

The current case being heard by the magistrate was one of attempted robbery, assault causing bodily harm and wearing a mask with the intent to commit an offence.

The female complainant stated that she had been sitting on a bench in Beacon Hill Park about two a.m., listening to the waves, when a man suddenly appeared in front of her, wearing a white goaltender's mask and clutching a knife with a long blade.

"I asked him who he was, but he didn't say anything. So I screamed and kicked him in the groin. But that didn't stop him and he lunged at my chest with the knife. I fended him off and we fell to the ground. We struggled and I got him in a headlock with one arm and grabbed the wrist of his knife hand. I was using all my adrenalin at that point, let me tell you. I asked him what he wanted, and he said money. I told him I'd give him some if he dropped the knife. Then he said, 'I've got a gun, too, and you're gonna die.' "

"Please go on," Horrigan said when she paused.

"That's when I knew I was dealing with some kind of nut case," the woman continued. He got out of the headlock and we both jumped up. I thought if I ran he'd chase me, maybe kill me. So as a last resort, I asked him if what he really wanted was sex, and that he could have some if he threw the knife away and didn't hurt me."

"What happened next?" asked the crown prosecutor.

"The guy threw the knife and mask over the cliff and I told him we'd be more comfortable if we could walk over to my house rather than do it in the park. We took a roundabout way through James Bay and when we got to my building, I went in the front door and told him to go around to the back and I'd let him in. I said I didn't want the neighbours to see me bringing a man home at that time of the morning. When I got inside, I called the police. He was still waiting at the back when they got there, so they arrested him."

The accused took the stand and related his own version of events. "I had no intention of robbing or hurting that woman," he said. "I was just trying to get away from her, but I couldn't. I was in Beacon Hill Park to rob faggots, I, I mean, homosexuals, Your Honour."

"Is that why you were wearing the mask and carrying a knife?" the prosecutor asked.

"Yes, I like that movie *Friday the 13th* and that guy Jason who's in it. I was stalking a guy I figured was gay when I came across this woman sitting on a park bench. What was she doing there at two in the morning?

"When she saw me she screamed and kicked me in the nuts. I wasn't trying to hurt her. I had no time to get away because she grabbed me in a headlock. That is one tough baby. I would never use a knife on a woman."

"But you were going to use it to rob gays, weren't you?" the prosecutor asked.

"Yes, I wanted to rob homosexuals, not girls."

"And that, I take it, is why you entered a not guilty plea?"

"Yes. Not guilty as charged."

"Have you got anything else to say in your defence?" This question came from the magistrate.

The accused hung his head and mumbled "Fuck all."

"What did he say?" Judge Horrigan asked the court reporter.

"He said 'Fuck all,' Your Honour," the reporter said.

"That's funny," said the magistrate, "I would've sworn he said something!"

Rolling his eyes and shaking his head, Horrigan intoned his decision. "Guilty! And I wish to compliment the complainant on her cleverness and creativity in helping apprehend the accused, who is remanded for sentence till May twelfth." Horrigan banged his gavel. "Take him away. Next case, please."

A bailiff entered the courtroom with Annie in tow. The Clerk of the Court read from the court list, "Annie Chance, charged under section 210 (1) of the Criminal Code of Canada. Everyone who keeps a common bawdy house is guilty of an indictable offence and liable to imprisonment for a term not exceeding two years."

Phil came forward from the spectator section as the charge was being read out. He stood beside Annie at the counsel table and motioned her to sit. He did likewise.

Annie just stared at him. He whispered, "You seem to need legal representation, Ms. Chance, but you have to ask me to provide it. This is a freebie; we can talk business later. The bottom line is, we've got to get you out of here. I got a full report of what went on last night from a friend."

Annie, only somewhat subdued, eyeballed Phil for a few more seconds. "Okay, be my guest," she finally said.

Phil stood up. "Your Honour, I am representing Ms. Chance at this hearing. I am Philip Figgwiggin, Q.C., a former B.C. barrister who retired before your time on the bench."

"A long time before, I think," Horrigan observed. "I was wondering who you might be. All right, first let's hear what our young whipper-snapper from the Crown, Mr. Sheldon Snively, has to say," and the judge nodded to the prosecutor. "Please proceed."

The newly minted prosecutor obliged, reciting the pertinent details of what the police had encountered at No Lipschtick Traces the previous evening.

"Does your client understand the charge, Mr. Figgwiggin?" the judge asked.

"She might, Your Honour, but I do not. I am not referring to the factual matters as related by my learned friend, to which we would actually agree, at least in part. As to the illegality or criminal nature of the alleged offence, we would not."

"How does your client plead to these charges?"

"Not guilty, Your Honour."

"We do try to speed justice as much as possible," the judge said, leaning forward from on high. "Do you wish a short adjournment in order to talk to crown counsel?"

"No, Your Honour. The Crown has failed to specify how they think Ms. Chance has broken the law, since no one has said, and has certainly not proven, that she acted as an agent in the sale of sexual intercourse and took money for such an alleged service. Even if they have implied such an offence, they have not, and cannot, demonstrate any proof."

"Perhaps you would care to explain further, Mr. Figgwiggin," said Horrigan.

"Certainly. I also have no need nor use for a lengthy legal process, unless the Crown insists. What we have heard in the recital of facts clearly indicates that an S & M party took place, at which Ms. Chance acted as a dominatrix for the pleasure and entertainment of those parties gathered there to view such a performance. Now, this may be considered kinky by some people who do not share the sadomasochistic sexual lifestyle, but that form of adult-only show does not fit the charge of running a bawdy house, Your Honour. By analogy, the Crown would have to lay the same charge against movie theatres for showing *Boogie Nights*."

"Interesting argument, Mr. Figgwiggin, although you may be swimming against a strong tide in this bailiwick. What have you to say in this regard, Mr. Snively?"

The scrawny young prosecutor leaped eagerly to his feet. "I don't agree with my learned friend, Your Honour. The accused knowingly allowed the premises to be used as a place to which men and women resorted for the purpose of illicit sexual intercourse."

Phil rose and vehemently objected. "What intercourse? There was no intercourse!"

"A common bawdy house is one resorted to by persons for the purposes of prostitution," Snively hastily replied, "or to practice acts of indecency and related illicit activities."

Snively warmed to his topic. "The Crown does not have to prove specifically that acts of sexual intercourse took place on the premises. Practicing prostitution does not require actual fornication, nor need there be physical contact between the customer and the performer. If, in return for payment, a woman offers her body for lewdness or for the purposes of an unlawful act, or as a participant in acts of indecency for the sexual gratification of another, then that is sufficient."

Phil leapt to his feet again. "What prostitution? What indecent acts? What payment? The bawdy house law is a bad law per se, but regardless of that opinion, our contention is that it does not apply in these circumstances, and therefore the charge should be thrown out. Ms. Chance is an entertainer and a producer of shows. A cover charge for such shows does not constitute payment for prostitution, nor for alleged indecent acts. There is no evidence of that."

"We will produce some," Snively said, still on his feet. "And in determining whether an act is indecent, the community standard-of-tolerance test should apply."

Horrigan interjected. "What the community will tolerate will vary with the place in which the acts take place and the composition of the audience."

"Your Honour," said Phil, "although I have other legal arguments and grounds for dismissal, may I point out that the community in question and the house, although jurisdictionally in Victoria, is right on the border of the community of Esquimalt, a naval base of long standing."

This last was greeted with general merriment in the courtroom. Horrigan rapped his gavel for order.

Even Snively smiled, but he stated, "Sir, there is evidence of continual and habitual use, evidence of a reputation as a bawdy house in the neighbourhood, and of such circumstances as to allow the court to make a proper inference that the premises were resorted to habitually as a place of prostitution and indecent acts. Further, there is a mandatory presumption whereby the accused will need to call evidence to show otherwise."

"Now just a moment here," said Phil austerely, "that presumption on your part infringes the presumption of innocence as guaranteed by section 11 (d) of the Charter of Rights, and by the common law."

"Not necessarily," said Judge Horrigan. "Snively could be right under *Rex v. Downey*, which seems to impose a reasonable limit on that argument. But I'm not here to try this case today."

"Annie Chance is the proprietor of a legitimate, licensed massage parlour," Phil said fiercely, "with a phone sex component, none of which is against the law. She should not have been arrested. In fact, I'll ask Your Honour to consider an application for dismissal right now."

Horrigan turned his attention to the prosecution. "Mr. Snively, does the Crown want to go to trial? You've got a challenge here to the bawdy house law under the Code. Now there's a long drawn-out legal battle for you."

"We certainly wish this matter to proceed to trial forthwith," replied Snively.

"Your application is denied, Mr. Figgwiggin. This is not for me to decide at this juncture, gentlemen. Any further applications? Bail? I don't suppose your client," the judge directed a friendly smile at the blonde accused, "is so enamoured with the accommodations at Victoria police headquarters that she wishes to extend her stay there any longer than necessary."

"Indeed not, Milord," said Annie, smiling back as she promoted the judge to Supreme Court status. "If I'm going to be behind bars, I'd prefer it to be in the Old Bailey Pub across the street."

"Now, Ms. Chance, I wouldn't want to

think of you as a smartass," Horrigan chided.

Phil figured that Annie could likely tell the flavour of an ice cream cone by sitting on it, but kept that observation to himself.

He rose to address the court. "My submission, Your Honour, is that Ms. Chance be released on her own recognizance forthwith. She will not be leaving the province. We have pled not guilty and want to get to trial as soon as possible."

"Good," Horrigan said gruffly. "I don't want trial dates cluttering up my court unless it's been determined that a trial is indeed required. I want both of you," he warned, glaring at each lawyer in turn, "to examine the evidence carefully early in the proceedings. I want to see minimal overbooking and bumping of trial dates, and witnesses attending only when required. Have you got that, Mr. Snively, Mr. Figgwiggin?"

Both lawyers politely replied in the affirmative.

"Now what do you have to say about bail, Mr. Snively?"

"I am instructed to oppose bail, Your Honour," said the Crown.

This position did not sit well with Phil, who was on his feet immediately. "Does it make any sense to try to control consensual adult activities by spending inordinate sums of money on police, lawyers and courts? We're not talking about prostitution here."

"Then just what do you say we *are* talking about?" asked the judge.

"Perhaps my client could answer that, Your Honour," Phil offered.

"A little unusual, but all right, Ms. Chance. Would you care to describe what it is that you do? I'll take your statement into consideration in setting bail."

"Thank you, Your Honour," Annie said, flashing him a grateful smile. "It's like this: spanking and humiliation are my stock in trade. I run a legitimate massage business. I don't like prostitution and I don't practice it. When I stopped nursing, I started to work out of my home as a paid dominatrix. It makes me feel powerful and beautiful. Men exalt me as a goddess. I feel that sado-masochistic acts do not constitute sex, and my clients are not allowed to have sex in my house." Annie leaned toward the judge.

"The women I employ are called mistresses, and they're not allowed to have intercourse or oral sex with clients, or masturbate them. They can only touch a client's genitals in order to tie them up for a bondage ritual. They've been told never, ever to insert a dildo into a client. There's a theatrical element to S & M scenarios, and clients pay up to three hundred dollars an hour to participate."

Horrigan was hanging on Chance's every word. "Scenarios?" he queried.

"Yes, things like equestrian training. We dress clients up like little ponies and put a bit in their mouth, ride around on their back and make them jump over obstacles. Then there are courses in feminization for cross-dressers. You know, how to walk in high heels, serve tea and dust furniture. And we've got bondage videos that clients can watch at the house." Annie finished with another wide smile.

Phil was on his feet at once. "Like I said, we're not talking about prostitution."

"Oh, yes we are," Snively, also on his feet, shot back. "We have pictures of a sex toy being used by—"

Phil responded in a flash. "A sex toy. Just what kind of sex toy are you talking about? Be more explicit, please."

"A, a...banana actually," said Snively, his confidence slipping a bit, "used by a masked man upon a woman who's tied in bondage gear. This is a crime," he went on, his voice gaining strength, "and it must be dealt with. By the very nature of the sex trade, this kind of thing attracts the sort of people society pays police officers and courts to deal with—pimps, drug users and dealers."

Phil had remained standing, stroking his goatee, a dumbfounded expression on his face. "Do I take it the Crown's case depends upon proving that a banana is a sex toy? That should prove interesting."

Horrigan banged his gavel. "I think we've bandied this about quite enough, gentlemen. Let me check the trial list and set a date for trial as soon as possible. In the meantime, whether Ms. Chance runs a bawdy house or not, the premises are shut down until the trial. Ms. Chance can continue to provide massages, but nothing else. Ms. Chance is to be released upon posting a bail bond for five thousand dollars."

He rapped the gavel again and rose from the podium. The clerk closed the court. As the magistrate retired to his chambers, he decided to make sure he'd be the one to preside at Chance's trial. The case promised to attract a lot of publicity, and Figgwiggin's argument seemed right up his alley.

Sheldon Snively headed for the barrister's lounge. He hadn't expected to keep Annie Chance in the lock-up, but the bit about bawdy houses had him worried. He won-

dered if he should report Figgwiggin to the
Law Society for practicing without a license.
At the least, the retired lawyer would have to
pay the heavy membership fee to get himself
re-instated.

Annie, still sitting in the courtroom, turned
to Phil. "Thank you, kind sir," she said flirta-
tiously. "I was about to pull the panic zipper
when you rode up on your white steed.
Hardly anybody rides to my rescue these
days. Now, I'm not exactly broke, so we have
to talk about your fee.

She regarded Phil thoughtfully. "You
know, money isn't the only thing in this
world. You're really sexy when you get
feisty. Perhaps you'd like to take it out in
trade?"

"A tempting offer, Ms. Chance," Phil replied
politely, "but I have to decline for three reasons. I won't be requiring that many massages
in my remaining lifetime, it might cloud my
judgment and it might ruin your defence."

"What's our defence going to be?"she
asked, her manner serious as she crossed her
legs. Phil noted the coffee-coloured hose.

"You heard some of it just now," he replied,
"but I'm thinking we should go on the offensive. Paper-hang them. That always compli-
cates things, because the prosecution doesn't

expect it, plus it gives us a bargaining chip."

"Like what?"

"I'm thinking charges could be laid against the city of Victoria and/or city council under the pimping laws."

"Hoo boy! We can do that?"

Phil donned his fedora, then pushed it to the back of his head as he answered. "Yes, we can. Prostitution is legal in Canada, but it's impossible to practice it without running afoul of municipal bylaws. By using a fee structure for escort services, Victoria city council is trying to make prostitution illegal through the back door."

"I'm not quite following you. Would you run that by me again, please?"

"Municipalities who sell business licenses to escort agencies are living off the avails of prostitution. Victoria is directly involved in the licencing of prostitution. Under case law, the relationship has to be parasitic. The city takes money from prostitutes and gives nothing in return. Ergo, they're living off the avails, they're pimping. So charging the city with that crime turns your case into a *cause celebre*, and should make it a walk in the park."

"I like your style, Mr. Figgwiggin."

"Thank you."

"And the fees they charge!" Annie said. "Back in 1993 the business licence for an escort service was three thousand dollars, plus a thousand-dollar bond and five hundred for each employee. The excuse council used was that this covered policing costs."

"I've checked that out," Phil said. "The licence fee's been reduced to fifteen hundred, plus the bond and two hundred fifty per employee. But even at that, if an escort agency had fourteen employees, I figure they'd pay six grand a year, twice as much as they charge a big department store."

Annie uncrossed her legs, stretched, then crossed them the other way. She smoothed her skirt over her knees. Phil shuddered.

"The high fees Victoria charges are why only one agency's actually licenced in the city," Annie said. "The rest of them set up in Saanich, which only charges a fifty-three-dollar fee, and the women work out of apartments in Victoria. So, tell me, is Saanich screwing Victoria?"

"I see your point," Phil replied. "I'll check that out. But the amount of the fee doesn't matter, the principle's the same. We may as well sue them all."

"Hmm. Sounds good to me."

"There's also Section 213 of the Criminal

Code to consider. It says that in a public place you can't offer to sell sex to someone. It's known as the john law. It's another bad one, because it's not about prostitution at all, it's about creating a nuisance."

"I get it," Annie jumped in. "When the cops enforce the john law, they're protecting the prostitutes from being harassed by the johns, who are the ones creating the nuisance, not the hookers. The city charges the escort agency a big fee to run a business they already have a legal right to operate, so the city's living off the avails. The cops are in charge of enforcing both laws. They offer the prostitutes protection—from the johns, from the council and from the police force itself. So the cops can also be said to be running a protection racket, for which they should also be charged. That means the only innocent people here are the prostitutes."

"Maybe you don't need a lawyer. You're good at this game."

"Have you tried this type of tactic before?" Annie asked.

"Yes, in a civil matter, against a client of mine who was way behind in his mortgage payments. The bank tried to foreclose, but our defence was that the plaintiff bank hadn't lost any real money—just the money the gov-

ernment allows them to create with a stroke
of the pen out of thin air. A bank doesn't stand
to lose anything if you default on your payments. It's only when you pay them back in
cash that they're getting anything of real
value, with interest, to stuff in their coffers
and add to their profits."

"That sounds novel! How did it work out?"

"We lost the case, but at least we tried.
That's only a brief outline, but if you look
into monetary reform, the approach has
merit."

"Well, I'm willing to do whatever it takes,
because I'm sick of their song and dance rou-
tines. I'll get Bea Wild to come down with the
bail, so I'll see you later, Mr. Figgwiggin.
We'll talk more about Dex's murder."

"You're right, we do have things to discuss.
And soon. Give me a call when you're settled. It's been a while since I was in court. I'm
going up to the Y and relax."

Despite her cool exterior, Annie was mixed
up, confused and angry. A psychiatrist could
have told her that anger was certainly a normal reaction to the situation in which she
found herself. She was stressed out from the
complexity of her lifestyle and personal relationships. Annie felt tears forming behind
her eyes, but fought them back. Not here, she

admonished herself. Stiffen that backbone, don't let the hard bastards get you down. She could afford the luxury of a cry when she got home, if she still felt like it, and no one would ever know.

Phil exited the courthouse through the side entrance and jaywalked across Courtney Street, heading for the YM-YWCA. The shortcut was part of his new plan not to waste another instant of his life. He wanted to spend time on things he valued most, and right now, what he wanted was a wet steam and a hot jacuzzi.

As he cut across the street, Phil failed to notice the police officer walking in his direction through the parking lot opposite. What he did notice on the YMCA side was a parked car whose meter had expired. On impulse, he reached into his pocket, pulled out a quarter and plugged the meter.

The cop behind him shouted at him to hold up. Phil ignored him and continued walking up the street. That's when la merde hit le fan.

The policeman, a short, pigeon-chested man with a narrow face sporting a recently broken nose, caught up with him. "You realize you were jaywalking, sir?" the cop asked brusquely.

"Yes," Phil admitted.

"Is that your car?" The cop pointed at the vehicle whose meter Phil had fed.

"As a matter of fact, no, it isn't."

The cop got snarky. "Then I'm giving you a ticket."

"On what charge?" snapped Phil, now highly incensed himself.

"Jaywalking."

"You've got to be kidding!"

"How about obstructing official City of Victoria business?"

"It's to laugh! Under what chapter and verse?" said Phil as he turned away.

"And if you keep making trouble," said the cop, grasping Phil's elbow, "disorderly conduct."

"Unhand me, varlet," Phil protested, wondering which side of the bed this character had gotten out of. "If you want to make an issue of this and write me up on these scurrilous charges, I insist we go back into the courthouse and that it be done before witnesses."

"Fine by me."

"You'll find, my good man, that you're exceeding your authority by trying to curb my generosity."

"I'm not your good man and you can't put coins in other people's parking meters in this town—not on my beat."

"Out of deference to the fact that a premier of this province used to be a meter maid, I'll need a better explanation than that."

"Parking meters are for people who need to spend an hour or so in the city," the cop replied angrily. "This is a busy area, and if drivers are allowed to feed the meter all day, some people will never be able to find parking and do business downtown."

"That's just it," Phil jumped in. "The driver wasn't feeding the meter, it was me."

"No one's allowed to hog these spaces; if someone's going to be here for more than an hour, they should put their car in a parking lot and pay the going rate."

"The going rate, you dummy, in all the city operated parking arcades, is first hour free. What about that? All I did was extend the same privilege to this driver."

"Placement of money by third parties in an expired meter is against the law in Victoria. You were denying access to someone who has an equal right to this parking space."

"That makes no sense to me. I was just being a good Samaritan."

"Yeah, and you know what happened to him," said the cop with a smirk. "His can was kicked and he was left lying by the side of the road. Too bad I can't do that with you."

"You'd love that, wouldn't you?" Phil spluttered. They continued to argue and vilify each other as they entered the courthouse.

Annie was seated in the police office when Phil and the Keystone Cop came in.

"Tony LeBlanc!" Annie snarled, jumping to her feet. "Get away from me or I'll break your nose again, you little bastard. Ah! I see they've busted you back to walking the beat. Good!"

Tony responded by trying to simultaneously bare his teeth and grind them, which ended up as a shit-eating grin. There were worse jobs on the force than pounding a beat, and he knew Muldoon would see that he got one if he tangled with Annie Chance again or with anyone associated with her. Tony didn't want traffic and he didn't want to ride an administrative desk.

Backing away from Annie, Tony said to Phil, "Listen, mister, I've decided to just give you a warning this time! Don't do that crap again." He turned on his heel and retreated post-haste.

Phil sat down beside Annie and their hands involuntarily clasped. "What was that all about?" he asked.

"He's one of the cops that falsely arrested me that first time on a trumped-up drug search."

"That donkey," Phil said. "You sure put the fear of Muldoon into him. Thank you, I sure don't need any more tickets." Phil explained the jaywalking and other charges LeBlanc had been trying to pin on him, and how Tony was harassing citizens in the street. "But to hell with him, I'm not worried about it."

"Everything seems to be conspiring against us," Annie lamented.

"Right, but I have this philosophy that you should enjoy life while it lasts. So I tend to do things on the spur of the moment and hope they turn out for the best. As Caesar may've said, it's not these well-fed, long-haired men that I fear, but the pale and the hungry-looking, by whose conspiracy I may fall."

"You're talking about Brutus and Cassius, aren't you?" Annie queried. "Yeah, that's the type that gets you in the end, for sure. Something always does. Adam and Eve were never married, and you know what that makes all of us, right?

Annie dug into her purse and came up with some bills. "Now back to business. I don't know what your fee's going to be, but I've only got five hundred dollars with me. Here, take this as a retainer to seal our arrangement." She counted the money into his lap.

"You're now officially my lawyer, right?"

"If I put this in my pocket, yes."

"I'm waiting."

Phil pocketed the cash.

"Now whatever I tell you is confidential, right?"

"Right."

"I'm not geared for the confessional booth, but I have no family, and if anything happens to me, I want my lawyer to know where I keep certain things pertaining to my business. Stuff only I know about."

"Why should anything happen to you?"

"I'm in a lot of trouble," Annie said, her forehead creasing with worry. "Plus, I'm in a dangerous business. You should know that. Seriously, when all candles be out, all cats be grey, as they say, and I'm not the only feline mixed up in Dex's life."

"So what do you want to tell me?"

"A little more than I have already," Annie said in a low, precise voice. "Somebody paid me to help them play a practical joke on Dex."

"Who?"

"I don't know. The arrangements were all done by phone through a third party, who said the person he was calling for just wanted to embarrass Dex, leave him in a ridiculous position and make him a laughingstock when it came out. All I had to do was leave him strapped down on the table after his massage and take off. Well, I'd already decided that Dr. Richard Poindexter and I were through, so why not let someone pull a caper on him—he'd done it to others so many times, he deserved it—and line my own pocket at the same time. I swear, I had no idea that the real plan was to kill him. "

"Not too smart, Annie. Whoever did it was likely setting you up to take the rap at the same time," Phil interjected.

"Don't I know it now! Okay, so like I said, if things don't go right for me, then unlike the proverb, I want you to look a gift horse in the mouth."

"Meaning?"

"I'm talking about the one in the basement of my house. It's a gym horse. It's hollow and it doesn't contain Greeks. Among other things, you'll find my will. While I was waiting here, I started drafting a holograph will, in which I'm naming you as my executor. I'll have it properly drawn up and put it inside the horse with my other papers."

"Let's not get ahead of ourselves here. Think carefully, are you sure you don't have any idea who might've set Poindexter up?"

"It has to be someone who knew about us.

I'm frightened. Which is why I'm making a new will, giving you the power to name some charity to get the assets of my estate, maybe some kind of hooker rehab project."

"You're overreacting, Annie. You're not going to be convicted of murder, not even accessory to murder. I'll see to that."

"There's one other thing," Annie said.

"Yes?"

"Watch your own tail as well as mine. This game's more dangerous than I first thought."

Of that Phil was already convinced.

Bea Wild appeared and Annie was released when the paperwork was completed.

Back on the street, Phil grumbled as he rooted through the mess of papers in the portable filing cabinet in his jacket. He was going back to practising law like he had always done, so what difference did it make if he had six months or four years to live? He wondered who had penned the rhyme:

There was a young man named Clyde,
Who fell down a shithouse and died.
He had a brother,
Who fell down another,
And now they're interred side by side.

If Phil were a horse, the glue factory gates would have slammed shut behind him long ago. Insomnia and indigestion plagued him. All he was missing was incontinence, and the prospect of this final indignity nagged at him. When he'd asked his doctor's advice about it, all the medic had said was, "Get off my carpet."

Mulling over the various charges against him and the defence he might now have to prepare for Annie, Phil felt grateful for the reigning mediocrity among government agencies, politicians and the police force. If he could get enough adjournments in his own cases, he might not have to show up at all.

Screw them all but six and save them for pallbearers!

Twenty

Tale of two cities — what a contrast! the headline over the Vaughn Bostrum story read. Phil was relishing the misery of Canadian prairie dwellers grappling with the worst mid-March storm in a hundred and thirteen years. After the trouble Phil had had with Victoria's own storm, he was particularly happy to read that while Victoria was basking in glorious spring weather, Calgary and other cities had a sixty-centimetre snowfall in one day, with the usual result: cancelled flights, blocked roads, power failures and school and business closures. In other words, things were back to normal, with both places getting what they richly deserved.

Phil answered the insistent ringing of the telephone. "Mary-Mary Quite Contrary

Podalchuk! What a delight!" he crooned into the receiver after the caller identified herself.

Mary had continued to help him with the Poindexter case, providing him with details of the anti-chelation lawsuit against Dr. Madigan from Poindexter's private files.

He had a sneaking suspicion that Mary found him attractive, although his hunch could just be the remnants of his male ego.

Even if he had felt some attraction himself, Phil knew he was poor pickings in the hockey game of love. His goal-tending and defence were good, but his offence was woefully weak. Like most hockey players nowadays, he could only play dump and chase—shoot the puck into the enemy zone, chase it into the corners and hope for a break. Any game he played in was bound to end in a scoreless tie.

Mary inquired about Phil's health, then asked whether he was making any progress in his investigation.

"No, there's not much to tell," Phil admitted sadly, "partly due to my heart problems. Listen, I owe you for all the help you've given me. What say I take you to lunch and we can talk more about the case?"

They agreed Phil would pick her up that Sunday at eleven a.m.

As Phil walked to Mary's place on Moss Street, he reflected that Victoria was unbeatable for its spring botanical splendour. In February, the local shrubbery already struggled vigorously awake with a continual parade of primula, daffodils, tulips, crocuses and snowdrops.

Moss Street in March was a showcase of frothy plum blossoms, making it a dreamy experience to stroll along under the spreading arch of branches beneath the bright blue sky, watching the sunlight splash through the beautiful white and pink clouds of petals.

Mary ratified his choice of a dim sum brunch and they set out on foot for Chinatown. They cut over to Linden Avenue to admire its hawthorn and magnolia trees, then zigzagged their way downtown along streets lined with flowering crabapple and cherry trees.

"Is this God-given beauty or what?" Phil exclaimed. "A lot different from some of the devil's spawn that accounts for most of humanity, isn't it?"

Mary grabbed Phil's arm in a surprisingly forceful squeeze. "Don't knock the devil, Mr. Figgwiggin," she snapped, "he keeps the Church in business. And don't thank God," she added with a slightly diminished intensity as she released his arm.

"Why not?"

"He may have been originally responsible, but you have to give some credit to city council, who imported most of these flowering trees from Japan in the 1930s. Most of them aren't cherry trees, they're ornamental non-fruit-bearing plums. About twenty varieties were brought in."

"Lots of foresight on someone's part, certainly. You know, some ecologists figure Adam and Eve didn't steal the apple, they clear-cut the whole orchard. Not surprising, since that's how we do things in B.C."

"You joke around too much, Philip, you always have. You should try to be more circumspect. Walk while you have the light, lest darkness come upon you," Mary again remonstrated. Phil wondered whether that was a Bible quote.

They walked down Government Street, Victoria's main drag in the nineteenth century and the scene of much lingering period elegance. As they walked, they talked in generalities, progressing through Market Square, the heart of the Olde Towne. The area was the bohemian centre of the city, where locals came to enjoy a bowl of won-ton soup.

More than a century old, the historic centre was originally home to Oriental tailors, shoemakers and tradesmen of many another ilk. The square was a large open inner courtyard surrounded on all sides by three stories of shops and businesses.

Opium was legal in Canada before and after the turn of the century, and opium dens had once thrived in the area, together with saloons, pawnshops, legitimate brothels and small dark cribs.

Joy and sorrow had likely been equally unrefined, with the demon drink selling at two shots for two bits. The myriad bachelors from China who once lived here had long since moved out, and the second and third floors of Market Square were now artist's studios and offices.

Phil preceded Mary through Fan Tan Alley, Canada's narrowest street and former location of fan-tan gambling clubs and an opium factory. In its heyday, the Alley had been closed off at both ends by a series of doors with peepholes to keep out interlopers.

Now the crowded passageway was a tourist mecca, offering books, used CDs and record albums, retro clothing and musical instruments. Phil spotted a penny on the pavement and bent to retrieve it. His stooped walk meant his eyes were often on the sidewalk, although he tried to remember to walk more upright by humming the old jazz tune *Straighten Up and Fly Right*.

"Nobody picks up pennies anymore," Mary scoffed. "They aren't worth anything."

"It's obvious you didn't grow up in the Depression, Mary-Mary. Picking up a penny meant there were more to come."

They emerged from the alley onto Fisgard Street a few storefronts from the massive ceremonial archway called Tong Ji Men, the Gate of Harmonious Interest, then jaywalked over to the Pale Dragon restaurant. There was a lineup for the dining room, so they sat on straight-backed red chairs in the vestibule and watched the oversized fantail goldfish in the adjacent aquarium.

"So what's your opinion on Eldridge and Shivagitz?" Mary asked, regarding him sternly.

"To be precise, neither of them are overtly paranoid or officially nuts, but both are definitely on the far side of normal and suffering from stress or some kind of mental disorder. Just like the rest of us, I suppose."

"Do you really think so?"

"Maybe. I've given it some study, and according to the headshrinkers, there's no shortage of disorders to choose from these days: attention-deficit disorder, alcoholism, eating disorders, social anxiety, manic depression, panic disorders, you name it. Then there's borderline personality disorder, which is a tendency to split the world into heroes and villains, combined with an intense fear of abandonment. Another popular one is obsessive-compulsive disorder, or the most dangerous one, schizophrenic psychosis. Throw in alien abductees, road ragers, Internet addicts and politicians and you've got to conclude that everyone's unstable in some way. As a matter of interest, where do you fit into that list, Mary-Mary?"

"Where do you think?" she retorted, giving him a dark, brooding look.

Never ask a question to which you don't know the answer. Phil groped for a conciliatory reply. "I'd have to say sensitive-personality syndrome. You're quick to take offence and unable to tolerate criticism. Far be it for me to give any, though," Phil hastened to add.

He was only half joking, for she had always seemed brittle and awkward in his presence.

"You've certainly been boning up on the subject."

"I have. I no longer think a psychopath is a bicycle route. I've been trying to figure out two things: what kind of nut I am and what kind would be responsible for Dick Poindexter's murder."

"A fiend lies dormant within us all," Mary replied sententiously. "I've seen a lot of suffering in my time, Philip, and I've often asked myself why there's so much depravity, death and disaster on this earth."

"A lot of people are willing to kill, maim and torture in God's name," Phil replied, "and others are prepared to die for a cause or a faith. So I assume God must be alive and well and in charge of those things."

Mary was taken aback by his sarcasm, so he added, "I don't proselytize for any faith, I don't represent any religion. Lawyers deal only in facts."

"Actually, I agree that one could easily conclude there's no God and that the Devil runs things here on earth."

The maitre d' came to show them to a table next to a window view of the colourful Chinatown streetscape. Heated trolleys circled the room, loaded with covered bowls, bamboo steamers and small plates filled with shrimp dumplings, stuffed crab claws, spring rolls, preserved duck egg and pork congee, fried jellyfish in ginger sauce, rice and fried noodles. The variety seemed endless.

"Will you have some chicken's feet?" Phil asked.

"No, thanks, I'm adventurous when it

comes to food, but I've tried those, and I don't fancy them. I can't help thinking what they were walking around in."

"What about the squid cooked in its own ink? Or the marinated beef heart in mustard sauce? Exceptionally tangy, apparently."

"I do like heart. You know, that was a big part of the Aztec religion in Mexico. The priests would rip the beating hearts from live captives and devour them."

"Yes, gruesome practice wasn't it?"

"It was literally their form of communion."

Phil looked over the goodies passing their table. To hell with the diet today, he thought, and as they ordered, the table gradually filled up with gourmet delicacies. They dug into the repast with gusto, remaining silent until the first edge of their hunger was satiated.

Mary, staring thoughtfully out the window, said, "Maybe I should have been more forthcoming with the police. I knew Eldridge, Madigan and Shivagitz had quarrelled with Dick, and for good reason. Do you think one of them might have done it?"

"Who knows?" Phil replied, swallowing some pork congee. "There's no smoking gun. I'd like to pin it on the guy I dislike the most, except that I'd likely be wrong. I didn't like Eldridge, but I'm biased because of the driver's test. Madigan's hard to figure out. I wouldn't want him for an enemy, or a friend, for that matter. Shivagitz was a hail-fellow-well-met type, very entertaining. You picked well, Mary, when you pulled their files. They all have motive. But Muldoon seems adamant that Annie Chance is the culprit. Do you know her?"

Mary's smile faded to a frown. "Yes, I've met her, and I've known for some time that she and Dick were having an affair. So of course there could be a motive there, but I don't think she could kill anyone."

"The cops would probably say why not? She's in a strange business, sadism and sex. They'd probably even pin lesbianism on her if they weren't basing their suspicions on her affair with Poindexter."

"Yes, their ignorance about those subjects is staggering," Mary commented dryly. "They're so small-minded."

"Can you blame them? I have to admit, I'm no expert, either."

"Sadomasochism," Mary explained matter-of-factly, "is sex play involving the exchange of power using pain as a form of erotic excitement. For some women, a reversal of the usual power roles can create a highly charged sexual atmosphere. That's what Annie's into.

Ordinarily, S & M isn't dangerous, although the possibility is always there."

"Hmm, interesting. I'm just worried that if the police don't turn anything else up, or I don't do it for them, they're going to lay a murder charge against Annie."

"Really?" Mary seemed concerned. She leaned toward him across the table. "What has she told you?"

"She hasn't entirely confided in me. I think she knows something that could incriminate the killer, but either she doesn't want to reveal it, or she's afraid to."

"The poor woman. If that's the case, she may well be in danger herself. Unless, of course, she's guilty."

"I think she's innocent, but a murder charge might persuade her to reveal what else she knows about Poindexter and his activities."

"Has she said anything specific about that?" Mary asked while reaching for more beef heart.

"She said he had a really mean streak, that he often took vicious revenge on anyone he thought had wronged or slighted him. She called them pranks, but some of them were outright criminal acts. Also that he had a secret addiction to masochistic sex. You worked for him, Mary, what do you think?"

Mary concentrated on consuming some Chinese sausage and rice before replying. "Things aren't always what they seem to be. Dick could try your patience to the nth degree. There are people in this world..." Mary paused, watching Phil closely, then continued vehemently, "who will traumatize another person's forever, for their own sick gratification! Look at the cruel things done in the name of Christ by puritanical ministers and priests. Some of them say the devil made them do it. Maybe Dick deserved to be killed by someone he'd wronged. He was certainly no angel, but then neither are the born-again Christians."

"Calm down, Mary. So, if you're a born-again Christian, does that mean you have two bellybuttons?"

"There you go again, Philip, with the sharp remarks. You're incorrigible."

"How about Madigan?" Phil asked. "What's your take on him?"

"He really hated Poindexter. That lawsuit against him for providing chelation happened after I left Dick's clinic, but the suit was instigated by Dick."

"Madigan's a bitter man, all right. He's convinced chelation's a legit treatment for atherosclerosis. Or is it arteriosclerosis? I can never remember which is which."

"Same difference. One's the formation of fatty material, the other is hardening of the arteries." Mary reached into a bamboo steamer for a spring roll.

"What do you think about chelation?"

"I think it works for some people. Dick thought so, too, later on, but he wasn't a man to apologize for anything or admit he might've been wrong. He found out more about chelation when his sister was taking treatments."

"So it's true that Dick thought chelation was okay!" Phil exclaimed.

"Well, yes. It certainly cured his sister's problem."

"That's what Eldridge said," Phil acknowledged.

"I just found out myself, from talking to the sister. Do you think Madigan knows Dick reversed himself on the issue?"

Phil stroked his goatee. "Maybe. He told me chelation had never killed anyone, but I'm beginning to wonder whether it might be what got Poindexter killed."

Twenty-one

Phil poured himself another drink of grape juice as he spooned his puffed brown rice cereal. He washed down his aspirin, his halibut liver oil, his vitamin E and two pills for his heart condition. Once he had more food lining his stomach, he'd pop the East Indian and African Cayenne King hot-pepper pills with ginger root. You were well advised to take those 105,000 heat unit babies on a full stomach.

His breakfast over, Phil went into the bathroom, where he bent over the basin and used both hands to splash water onto his face. Son of a bitch! he cursed. Had he suddenly gone blind? No, just forgot to take off the glasses.

He descended to the lobby to check his mailbox. Along with the usual plethora of junk mail, there was a letter from Justin Thorndyke. Ripping open the envelope, he examined the contents. Thorndyke had sent him a single sheet of paper with three names on it, along with abbreviated personal histories and a ViCLAS record of each person.

The names were Drew Hollingsworth of Delta, Abdullah Muhammad of Vancouver, and the one that seemed the most likely candidate, Clarence Crepeau of Richmond. Crepeau's occupation, stockbroker, was the first clue. There was a cross-reference to a criminal record number.

Crepeau was attacked by two unknown assailants on May seventeenth the previous year. The assailants blackjacked Crepeau from behind and knocked him to the ground, then continued the vicious attack, stomping his head as he lay in the gutter.

Crepeau was in a coma for some time and required a lengthy convalescence in hospital. He suffered partial memory loss and serious internal injuries. His face swelled badly from nose and cheekbone fractures that required extensive reconstructive surgery. Crepeau hadn't recognized his attackers, the investigation went nowhere and the case was soon closed.

Phil would have to go to the Lower Mainland to check out all three suspects. He returned to his apartment, quickly inspected the contents of the bag he kept ready for short trips and looked up the schedule for Harbour Air, the seaplane company that provided harbour-to-harbour service between Victoria and Vancouver. His friend Gordie Haskins was always bugging him to spend a few days in the big smoke, and if he needed a car to get around, he could always borrow Gordie's old Volkswagen beater. He ran the risk of being asked to produce his licence, but he was resolved to do nothing to attract attention to his driving.

Phil's first stop in Vancouver was the Securities Fraud Office, ostensibly established to clean up the Vancouver Stock Exchange. Financed entirely by the B.C. Securities Commission, the Vancouver office was staffed by five Crown Attorneys and five RCMP market investigators. Been there, done that, thought Phil, and they could likely hire twenty-five more of each and still not catch up with the backlog of cases.

There were few deterrents to securities fraud, and sharp con artists were getting away with financial murder. Most victims were wealthy investors or corporate creeps, so there was no public sympathy factor. There were jurisdictional problems with the few cases in which a prosecution was launched, adding to the nightmare of trying to navigate a patchwork of securities regulators and industry associations.

Phil was referred to RCMP Corporal Ron Reynolds, a friendly, talkative type and the only officer still familiar with the Crepeau case.

Reynolds pulled the file and ushered Phil into a dark panelled ten-foot-square sitting room A utility table and several chairs were the only furniture. No windows, depressing atmosphere.

"Yeah, I remember Clarence," said Reynolds, tossing a thick sheaf of papers onto the table. "Not my favourite con artist."

Phil was sure he saw a little puff of dust rise from the file into the still air.

"Slick operator, likable on the surface, mind you, but a nasty piece of work."

"How come he eventually walked?" Phil asked.

"Because when Clarence's case came up, he was suddenly in no condition to stand trial and the money he'd embezzled was gone, so restitution was impossible. But I'll get to that."

"Good, some details about his case would be nice. If you don't mind."

"Glad to be of help," said Reynolds, waving Phil to a seat and folding his rangy frame into a chair opposite. "Crepeau had a partner, a lawyer named Homer Wilson from Toronto, who was also facing professional sanctions from the Law Society of Upper Canada."

"That figures," said Phil, who occasionally agreed with H.L. Mencken's opinion, at least about a few of his fellow legal practitioners, when Mencken said, "A lawyer is one who protects us against robbers by taking away the temptation."

"I guess. Well, anyway, these two culprits ran a scheme involving approximately three million dollars, six counts of fraud, and one of laundering the proceeds of a crime. The charges were laid following a two-year investigation by Revenue Canada. The Crown alleged that Crepeau and Wilson misappropriated the money from two companies, after taking over the firms in earlier controversial buyouts. According to the Crown, the money was channelled to another company in the Caymans, then funnelled it back here. They went on a spree, managed to spend a chunk of it on homes, ski chalets at

Whistler, sports cars and stocks. They were high rollers for a time, all right."

"Conspicuous spending attracts the attention of Revenue Canada every time," Phil remarked. The two crooks could've fleeced Poindexter, Phil thought. "Does the file have a sucker list?" he asked.

Reynolds checked. "Negative. Crepeau and Wilson owned Durham Mining and Resources Inc., aka Bull Durham. They were papering, using this company to manipulate the market price in the shares of two other companies, Golden Handshake Ltd. and Bottom Line Investments Ltd. Golden was a junior B.C. resource company and Bottom had diamond mining interests in the Northwest Territories. Both companies traded on the VSE.

Reynolds checked the file again. "The actual offences occurred between 1988 and 1990 when both men were licensed brokers in both Ontario and B.C. They used other brokerage firms to disguise a bid for control of Golden Handshake and Bottom Line. Once they established control, they jacked up the public market price of the two companies. They were frequently involved in the opening trade and in trades at or toward the close of trading. On a number of occasions their trades set a daily high and frequently set a new high."

"Certainly sounds like a slick operation," Phil interjected. "One of my ancestors was hung for manipulating stock—he put his brand on the neighbour's cattle."

Reynolds raised his eyebrows, smiled briefly, then continued his recital. "The case finally came to trial last spring. The Crown's contention was that Crepeau and Wilson had created an appearance of active public trading in the Golden and Bottom companies, which also falsely inflated their price on the Vancouver Exchange."

Reynolds played with the corner of the file folder as he added, "It was a complicated case. Even if the accused could prove otherwise, the money was taxable income, and none of it had been reported to Revenue Canada. If convicted, they faced sentences of up to ten years imprisonment. They were in the middle of the trial with everything pointing to conviction, when proceedings were delayed because Wilson, who was over sixty, went into hospital with kidney failure and fluid on his lungs. That's when Clarence was beaten nearly to death, so he ended up in hospital for a long stretch, too. To cut to the chase, the Crown agreed with Crepeau's and

Wilson's lawyers that a jail term amounted to a death sentence because of their physical condition. While these two fraud artists were in hospital, the lawyers plea-bargained a guilty plea and heavy fines. Also, they'd be banned from trading, and the Crown got a restitution order."

"Did the suckers got their money back?" Phil asked.

"No. The trial was never completed and the prosecution never succeeded in tracing the money to its final destination. It was stashed somewhere, probably out of the country. Anyway, it was never found."

"So what happened to the perps?" Phil wanted to know.

"Wilson got out of hospital first and promptly flew the coop, leaving Crepeau broke and holding the bag. Wilson probably spend the loot in South America, but I figure he's got to be dead already, given his condition last year. Crepeau's still around, but any money he might come by, honestly or otherwise, he'd owe to the government and all his creditors."

After a pause to digest what Reynolds had told him, Phil said, "Maybe not. He's likely smart enough to have gone into bankruptcy. Couple more questions if you've got the time." Reynolds nodded.

"Did Crepeau just walk away or did he fight back? And did he have a record before the Golden Bottom fiasco?"

"The beating he took screwed up his memory. He'd managed other people's money for a long time, ran some Ponzi schemes, that kind of thing, but nothing had stuck to him before that. Now he's a broken down con artist."

Phil decided he didn't need to look at his other two suspects until he checked out Crepeau. "So where would I find Crepeau, do you suppose?" he asked the Mountie.

"Try one of those fleabag hotels on East Hastings," Reynolds suggested, and provided Phil with a description of Crepeau as he might have looked once the plastic surgeons got through with him. "I hear he's drowning his sorrows these days."

Rising from the table, Phil shook Reynolds's hand, thanked him for his trouble and left.

Phil loved Vancouver's gorgeous setting, but the place wasn't immune to the stink, noise, ugliness and broken promises of any modern city. As he walked into the downtown core, Phil observed many changes from his earlier recollection of the metropolis. He passed cheap residential hotels, wondering whether those who lived in their single rooms could be termed homeless. They had a roof over their heads and maybe a hot plate (or maybe not), along with a common bathroom down the hall. But there was little personal security or privacy, and it sure wasn't much of a home life.

Years earlier, the hotels had provided reasonable accommodation for sailors and construction workers. Half the rooms were gone now, shut down by health inspectors, burned down in fires or demolished to make way for new office, retail and apartment buildings. The ones that remained, mostly on the Eastside, were crowded and run down and housed poverty-stricken women and children, childless young adults, destitute oldsters, pimps, hookers, ne'er-do-wells, alcoholics and dope addicts—the last stop before life or death on the street.

Lacking even the minimum housing offered by the hotels, other down-and-outers slept on the street in soiled sleeping bags or old mattresses, under bridges and in abandoned buildings. The city couldn't seem to choose between tearing down the more rickety buildings and forcibly evicting the derelicts, or letting them live in danger and squalor.

Phil headed up Hastings from the corner of Granville, the exact heart of the once beautiful old city. By now, hardening of her arteries had set in. She'd had a multiple bypass and her heart had moved elsewhere.

The epicentre of skid row was the 100 block of East Hastings, and it stretched several blocks to the east and west. Phil passed through Pigeon Park in the corridor connecting Gastown and Chinatown, observing several scurrilous characters, drug dealers no doubt, who eyed him with cold suspicion as he went past. He didn't stop to chat with the tough characters of mixed ethnicity, many of them with baggy designer jeans, Nike runners, soccer shirts and gold chains.

According to the cops, there were about a thousand dealers peddling narcotics in the area. Crack was the drug of choice, along with heroin and cocaine, as easy to obtain as a pizza, much of it sold by dangerous fake refugee members of Colombian drug cartels.

Phil had nearly sixty licenced premises to cover in his search for Crepeau. It would be hard to hit every tough beer hole here, but he could try. These were no doubt class hostelries when built. The old hotels along the street hadn't changed, only deteriorated. They still sported the beverage room, or beer parlour, where a glass of beer in his youth had cost ten cents, and two at a time constituted a round. Wives hated them, but men spent a lot of time in these emporiums in the old days.

Seeing the beer parlours again brought back a few memories. One was of a crazy game they used to play for rounds of beer.

Phil grinned at the recollection. Ten young guys bullshitting around a table. As the glasses gradually emptied, some one would yell "Dead Bug!" All ten would fall to the floor as fast as they could, raise their arms and legs upward, and fix their version of a dead insect look upon their faces. Whoever was deemed to have been the last to assume the position was the sucker who had to buy the next round. Made for lots of arguments and fun. Did they do that kind of stuff today? He supposed not—kid stuff.

The Penthouse Cabaret used to be along this way—locally and perhaps internationally renowned, particularly in the Fifties, Sixties and early Seventies as a notorious prostitution palace. Men, many of whom were tricks, sat and drank and arranged sexual encounters while being entertained by strip dancers on the stage at the back of the club. If women left the club with a customer, they would have to pay double the initial $2.95 admission charge to re-enter, tip the maitre d' and doorman two dollars each and pay another two bucks for a table.

Phil recalled the investigation and prosecution that had closed down the club in 1975. Charges of procuring and living off the avails of prostitution were laid against the owners of the club and three employees. They were initially found guilty, heavily fined and sentenced to sixty days in jail. But since it couldn't be established that any sex acts had ever ccurred on the premises of the Penthouse, they were all subsequently acquitted on appeal.

Crown counsel should have heeded a previous report on prostitution to the police commission, which stated that the *Penthouse owners seemed to abide by the law and little could be done to prove otherwise. Any attempt to show that they contribute to procuring, or directly procure and live off the avails of prostitution through direct cuts on the more expensive transactions are probably doomed to failure. As long as the owners continue to watch their step and the situation remains under control, the Penthouse provides a rather convenient channel for local activities.*

The Penthouse case would come in handy when it came time to argue the Chance bawdy house hearing in Victoria. It provided a telling example of the contradictory results of prostitution law enforcement.

At every bar he came to, Phil described Crepeau to the barkeeps and managers and asked whether they knew him. He put the same questions to the prostitutes working the street. At one point, he spotted several women crouched behind a dumpster, smoking crack or shooting up heroin. As he walked down the alley toward them a rat darted out from the accumulated litter of old towels, beer cans, rotting orange juice containers, dirty and discarded clothing, cigarette packages and the empty bottles of bleach the addicts used to disinfect their needles. The women faded away at his approach.

Phil trudged on, then circled back, covering ten hotels. The going was tough. He got little feedback and no positive reactions. It was like playing blindman's bluff.

He passed a Starvation Army hostel adjacent to the Patricia, a landmark hotel of some size. A crack dealer stood outside the run-down premises, the low-end product of the annual five-hundred-billion-dollar global drug trafficking industry that started in the steamy tropical Andean highlands of Colombia.

The sky had turned a dirty grey and a light
rain began to spit down. Phil pulled a light,
clear plastic rain poncho out of his coat pocket
and pulled it over his topcoat.

No question, this was a rough neighbourhood. In the narrow space between the two
buildings, a dishevelled man was trying to
stand up. As an old tomcat edged his way
past him, the drunk threw up all over the
animal. Looking down, the rubby mumbled,
"I can't remember eating that!"

Fighting nausea, Phil turned quickly away
and entered the Patricia Hotel. Feeling a little
weak and out of breath, he sat down at an
empty table. The place smelled of urine and
the clientele was an over-intoxicated but
somnolent crowd of misfits, many of them
native. He took two puffs under the tongue
from his nitro puffer, then ordered two half-
pints for four dollars and pretended it was
nineteen forty-two.

He shut his eyes, leaned back and reminisced. Which dance hall would he go to
tonight—the Cave, or the Palomar to hear
Dal Richards? The old son of a gun was still
playing. Were the Mills Brothers or the Ink
Spots appearing anywhere? Or would the
Four Skinner Sisters be featured, singing that
old favourite *I'm in the Nude for Love*?

Hearing movement near him, Phil opened his eyes. Three grungy-looking biker types had quietly seated themselves at his table. They stared at him and he stared back.

"You're too old to be either a bounty hunter or a cop," said the one with the enlarged, booze-reddened nose. "Maybe a narc, eh? We been followin' you."

If one old fart gets rubbed out in a sleazy bar on East Hastings, Phil wondered, does anyone hear his screams? He maintained eye contact with the burly specimen who'd spoken. His smiling scrutiny seemed to irritate the pachyderm.

"What're you smilin' at?" he asked Phil. The others shuffled their chairs closer.

Phil began to chuckle as hard as he could manage. Then he said, "No offence, mate, but you remind me of a guy I used to know in the merchant marines during the war. Big guy like you, from Poland I think. This guy could drink more booze, win more fights, kick more butt than anyone I ever knew. Liked Canadian rye whiskey—by the bottle. This one fight he got into? He threw a cop right over a police car." Phil prolonged the story, laughing often, trying to deflect the immediate threat to his person. "My name's Figgwiggin. What's yours, may I ask?"

The big biker grinned widely, enjoying the comparison with the fictitious Pole. "Name's Fawcett. But you can call me Tap." The other two weren't so friendly, but Tap told them to put a cork in it. Phil bought a round for everyone.

"So what're you doin' here, Fuggmiggin?" asked the leader.

"Figgwiggin. I'm looking for a buddy of a buddy, a guy who's hit hard times. He's on the booze somewhere in Vancouver. But I'm not having a whole lot of luck. His name's Clarence Crepeau."

"Clarence? Nobody's gonna use a name like that around here. But Crepeau? Creepo? That sounds familiar."

"So you think you know Crepeau?"

"Not by that name exactly. But there's this guy called the Creep. Used to be a gent, like you. So you're lookin' for him, eh?"

"Figure it'd be the same guy, eh?" Phil's attempt to establish rapport by aping Tap's speech patterns went over Fawcett's head.

"If it's the same guy, yeah, we know him. Comes in here sometimes, big spender when he's holdin', which ain't often, eh? Used to be a stockbroker, or so he says. Last name could be Crepeau, but down here he's called the Creep. You want to see him?"

"Can you arrange it?"

"Yeah, sure," Tap Fawcett said, "but I'm warnin' you, this better not turn out to be April Fool's Day. You'd better have a story the Creep likes, or you'll find out how tough you thought you used to be."

Unhappily pondering the thought that the Creep might very well not like the implications of his visit, Phil tried to come up with a spin that would work, then decided he'd play it by ear. "You wouldn't beat up an old fart like me, would you, Tap?"

"Maybe not, 'cause you're such a great friend of mine, eh? But these two boys would. I don't think they like you."

"Maybe if I bought another round?" Phil offered.

"Yeah, that might improve their bad attitude," Tap replied, "but for a bill or two, they might even get to like you."

Phil dug deep in his pocket.

Twenty-two

Clarence Crepeau had always been on the business end of psychopathic activity. Many of his qualities could have qualified him for high political office or the CEO of a large corporation. He bore no one allegiance, knew no loyalty, no guilt and no remorse. He lied easily and frequently, but could be utterly charming when he so desired. In those traits he was no different than Dr. Richard Poindexter, including the large ego, cool demeanour, glib manner, deceitful and manipulative conduct and shallow emotions. Both men brought enormous potential for destruction and ruin to whomever they met or to any organization for whom they worked. They were obergruppenfuhrers, whose enemies patiently waited in long queues to get a crack at them, but seldom succeeded.

Crepeau's beating had been the culminating act in the horrendous run of bad luck that had brought him to a cheap East Hastings hotel room. His plight had started long before the Bull Durham-Golden Handshake-Bottom Line deal. In fact, those organizations had been dreamed up to extract him from his other financial peccadillos, to distance himself from his far too many creditors.

The scheme might have succeeded, if his erstwhile partners hadn't double-crossed him. Then came the point when everything turned to rat shit, leaving him sitting in the rat trap, with no cheese. The Golden-Bottom bit blew up, and Crepeau and Wilson lost their broker's licences.

The Creep knew he still had a chance because he had been able to stash and secrete some of the loot where he thought it would be safe. But that kind of money never is, which Crepeau had found out in spades. Some bastards beat him up, damn near killed him, probably meant to.

If he had come out of that coma and out of the hospital before Wilson, then the Creep would have grabbed the cash and left town himself. If his brain hadn't been left in a mess, that is.

From out of that fiasco the Creep had arrived at his present condition, from dining at the Top of the Mark in San Francisco to holing up at the back of the Mac in Vancouver's MacNamara Hotel, two small rooms with a view of the back alley.

The sitting room off the hallway opened onto the bedroom, where a leaky faucet dripped into a chipped enamel sink. Undoubtedly the original owners of the Mac were Irish, but there were no longer any gnomes, leprechauns, goblins or other friendly little people on the premises. There were, however, many malcontented spirits, tricksters and assorted pests in residence.

That this was home pissed the Creep off no end, but there were two reasons why he wouldn't have to put up with it much longer. The first was his sincere hope that he would find the mooches, whackjacks and gearbox idiots who had the money to get him back into the game.

The second reason was more pressing. Tenants of the MacNamara Hotel in Vancouver's Downtown Eastside had been given one week's notice to find new accom-

modations. The city health inspector had
decided the building was unfit for human
occupancy. He cited resident cockroaches,
mice and a lack of working toilets. Broken
glass, cigarette butts, old sleeping bags, used
condoms, syringes, human waste and blood
covered the floors of some of the rooms,
many of which didn't even have a mattress
and were rented out on a daily and possibly
an hourly basis.

Crepeau sat nursing an unsanitary belt—
two fingers of cheap rye in a dirty glass. He
gazed past the seagull shit on the window
pane and down to the back alley below,
watching the dumpster-divers scour the lane
for returnable bottles and other cast-offs. Life
for them was one long alley full of ash cans.
The poor bastards might as well try to stuff
butter up an eel's ass with a hot poker as try
to make a decent living that way, he thought.

A heavy knock on the door interrupted the
Creep's reverie. He slid back the bolt and
peered out before unfastening the chain. Tap
Fawcett stood in the hall, accompanied by an
elderly stranger in a black fedora and raincoat.

Phil stared at the middle-aged balding man
in front of him. What hair Crepeau had left
was combed sideways over the top of his

head in an attempt to hide the lack thereof, a ploy which didn't work. Overall, his features seemed slightly askew, and Phil wondered whether his plastic surgeon had been a trainee. A wide, slack mouth and a drinker's ruddy complexion didn't help.

Crepeau wore a three-piece grey pinstripe suit, badly in need of a cleaning. The too-short vest flared over his potbelly and his shirt hung over his belt.

"To what do I owe this unexpected pleasure?" asked Clarence, his manner gallant. "You're here, you might as well come in." He pointed Figgwiggin to a broken-down sofa while motioning Fawcett to follow him into the bedroom. He closed the door.

"Why the fuck did you bring this old fart around?" he hissed. "Damn it, Tap, you couldn't pour piss out of a boot if they wrote instructions on the heel."

"He says he's somebody you might wanna know," Tap whined, his bravado evaporating in the face of Crepeau's outburst.

"Is that right? What's in it for you? You never do anything for nothing."

"Only a few beers so far. You're gonna hurt my feelings. I just thought this guy might have some information, you know? Just so's I get the usual cut, eh?"

The Creep thought for a moment, "Yeah, okay," he relented, "but you better know shit from putty." They went back to the outer room. "Please excuse my rudeness, I'm a bit out of practice," he said to Phil, faking a solicitous manner. "I may even have a drink left, but I doubt it."

"Thanks just the same, but I'll pass," Phil said hastily. He couldn't stomach the idea of touching anything in these surroundings. The only glass in evidence was filthy, and his tolerance for hard liquor was near zero, anyway.

Tap plunked his big frame down on a chair near the door, deciding to keep an eye on things. Besides, the Creep hadn't asked him to leave.

Phil extracted a card from his pocket and handed it to Crepeau. All it said was Philip Figgwiggin, Q.C. "I'm from Victoria, Mr. Crepeau," he said. "If you are indeed the Clarence Crepeau I was looking for when I so fortuitously ran into our large friend here."

"Yeah, that's my name," Clarence replied cautiously.

Tap interrupted. "He said he was tryin' to look you up for a friend of his, you know, who was a friend of yours."

"And just who the hell is this friend?" asked Crepeau, turning back to Phil.

"Dr. Richard Poindexter."

"Poindexter. A doctor, you say." Crepeau searched his damaged memory banks. He looked slowly around the dusty room, then his lips wrinkled into an expression of disgust. "Yeah, I remember the guy. How is he?"

"Perhaps we should refer to him as recently departed," Phil replied. "I'm surprised you haven't heard. He met with a fatal accident a while back. Murdered, actually."

"Is that so?" Clarence replied calmly. "I didn't know. But then, I haven't been reading the papers lately." He waved his arm around the room. "As you can see, this isn't exactly the Sheraton. I had a booze problem and I fell into straightened circumstances. But I've seen the error of my ways." A frown flickered across his twisted face as he asked, "How did he die?"

Nothing in the Creep's demeanour gave Phil the impression that he'd known about Poindexter's death, but then Phil knew that Crepeau would rather lie on credit than tell the truth for cash. He filled Crepeau in on the details of the surgeon's murder.

"My, my, that's terrible," Crepeau said. "Who do they think did it?"

"The cops suspect a masseuse named Annie Chance."

"So, what the fuck do you want with me?" The Creep demanded suddenly. "You're a lawyer. You'd better not be here with malice aforethought, as they say."

Phil knew he had to be careful not to imply any guilt on Crepeau's part, or he might not get out of this fleabag alive. He reminded himself that his purpose here was only to find a potential suspect X, which he had done, and to establish that X knew Poindexter. He had accomplished both goals. The rest was up to the cops.

"I was named the executor of his estate," said Phil, aware he was attempting to con a con, "and as such, I'm trying to tie up all the loose ends. In his files, I came across a reference to a promissory note for a specific sum. It's at least an indication that Poindexter might still owe money. Since I was in Vancouver anyway, I decided to look for you. I can't wind up the estate until I establish the existence and validity of the note, or at least be able to swear that I tried."

"There are gaps in my memory of my life prior to an unfortunate accident last year," Crepeau said."You probably know more than I do. Maybe Poindick and I were all square and maybe we weren't. How large is that sum?"

Phil had no figure in mind, having invented the whole story. "Close to six figures," he improvised.

Crepeau's cold eyes fixed on Phil, registering nothing.

"However, Mr. Crepeau," Phil added, "I would have to insist that you produce the original note upon which the apparent debt is based. Only then could the estate properly consider its merit. It's a legal necessity, you understand."

"Yeah, well, anything's a nice piece of cash when there's too much month left over at the end of my money," said Clarence, baring yellowing teeth in a lopsided grin.

"I must also insist," Phil continued, "that you produce incontestable proof within thirty days. The matter is urgent and I am desirous of finalizing the estate."

"Jesus, all you lawyers sound the same. Anyway, I anticipate a business trip to Victoria soon." He flashed another grin at Phil. "You may well want to get in on this deal."

"I'm not out to make money at this time of my life," Phil replied. "Thank you just the same."

"You're probably letting the appearance of my current circumstances influence you."

"Perhaps. I did wonder why you're living here. None of my business, of course."

"I'll tell you why," Clarence invented. "I'm about to convince some investors to buy this rat-trap hotel, along with a lot of other adjacent dumps on this street. Demolish an entire square block to make room for some downtown condo development."

"You'd probably have to raise megabucks to do that," Phil said cautiously.

"There's no profit for the owners in providing housing for the poor, so the tab could be cheap. I've raised big sums of money before this, sir, and I can do it again," Crepeau boasted.

"Yes, I'm sure you have," Phil murmured. He couldn't help adding, "That was in the stock brokerage business, wasn't it?"

Clarence frowned, but was cagey enough to curb the anger any reference to his past aroused. "If you know that," Clarence replied, staring directly at Figgwiggin, "then you must know that I had problems in my business and with your profession. So I'll admit to you I made some mistakes. But I've paid my dues, and really, my only fault was a little front running."

"Front running? I'm not familiar with that term," said Phil.

"Against the law, of course, but the trader buys or sells stock for a personal account in advance of an order to buy or sell stock for a client, knowing that the client order will influence the price of the stock and let him liquidate his position at a profit. But I've paid a heavy penalty for my sins and can truthfully say I have seen the fiscal light. I am born again financially. I'd like to cut you in. Give me a chance to put things together properly and then come and see you."

"That sounds good, Mr. Crepeau," said Phil, rising from his chair, "but now I must leave you."

"I'll go through my papers and turn up that note," Crepeau said as he ushered Phil into the hallway. "Mr. Fawcett, you brought Mr. Figgwiggin here, I think it only fair that you escort him safely out of the East Hastings area. I wouldn't want to see you killed as well, counselor."

Phil, eager to make his escape, was halfway down the dingy hall when the Creep called after him, "My reputation may be as dead as the Pope's pecker, Mr. Figgwiggin, but I assure you, I will be on the up and up." Phil waved back at him and continued on his way, trailed closely by Tap Fawcett.

Clarence returned to his chair by the seagull-soiled window and tried to brainstorm his situation. He was going to have to be strong, to smarten up, get back into the game. This business with Figgwiggin, he thought, might be the first step, the catalyst. Unless my mind is still playing tricks on me, he thought, there was never a promissory note, but there was a lot of money involved. I'm going to find out where this joker Figgwiggin lives and where he's really coming from. He says he represents the Poindexter estate, but there's a smell of mackerel rotting in the moonlight here.

The Creep remembered that Dicky boy, that son of a bitch, was one of his problems. Memory had never served him well after that beating, but it came back to him that the bastard owed him big money. The laundryman's dead and I've lost the marker, thought Crepeau, but there just might be some way of getting a chunk back.

It occurred to Crepeau that the redevelopment idea actually had merit. It certainly wasn't the worst scheme he'd ever cooked up on the spur of the moment, and a lot of Vancouverites were getting mighty tired of commuting to the burbs. Thinking about it buoyed Crepeau's spirits. Revitalize downtown Vancouver, that's the ticket. Why not?

Who could he put the bit on? Investors of all stripes were always looking to make a buck. Maybe the Creep could even turn an honest dollar, but even for that he needed start-up money.

Maybe it's time he did some shit-kicking himself, Crepeau decided. Use any aces in the hole he hadn't already flogged to death.

Twenty-three

Phil returned to Gordie Haskins's bungalow in Delta, where his hosts promised him a lift to the next morning's Victoria-bound ferry.

Gordie and his wife Marjorie were lively conversationalists. They performed the well-established marital dance of a couple who had been together for almost fifty years, and the frequent sharp exchanges sometimes shocked even long-term acquaintances like Phil. He was just about to tune out during a conversation about health problems when Gordie asked his wife, "What'd the doctor say about your big, fat ass?"

"I don't know," Marjorie had retorted, "your name never came up."

It was late and Phil was tired from his perambulation on the seamy side of Vancouver,
but sleep eluded him, his brain was too
active. The time on the digital clock—1:32—
stamped itself on Phil's medulla oblongata
with branding-iron effect. Damn, what to do
for a good night's sleep?

He attempted to conjure up a beautiful,
tranquil scene from his past and visualize
himself there again, taking in the sights,
sounds and scents of the place. Soon he was
at the confluence of two rivers where the
Clearwater River ran into the Peace River in
northeastern B.C. The water sparkled in the
sun as it ran across the shining stones of the
sandbar and into the deeper water of the
mother river. He could see the demarcation
line where the clear water met the more
azure green of the Peace, where the big dolly
varden trout usually hung out. The fly line
arced through the air and the black gnat
dropped on the flowing water just where the
lunkers lurked. Strike! A big one hit the fly
and leapt high above the ripples as he set the
hook. A terrific fight before catch and release.

Then take the trail or wade up the
Clearwater, always hoping for the bigger
trout lurking around the next bend. Arrive at
the waterfall on the escarpment, which

blocked further physical passage upstream. How good the fishing must be back up there, where no fisherman had ever cast a line. Stand on the massive outcropping of rock to the side of the deep pool under the falls, in the long evening light, watching Arctic grayling picking bugs and mosquitoes off the surface of the water, rising swiftly up from the depths, sucking the insects in with a gentle smack that sounded like a lover's kiss. The stars come out and it's time to trudge back through the woods to a campfire, where he and his companions pan-fry their catch and talk languidly about life.

Enjoying the vision, Phil was relaxing, almost off to dreamland, with his memories of the good feelings and energy he always obtained from fly fishing, the complete disconnect from daily stress and client contact that was so relentless and wearing.

But the scene only existed in his mind, and the thought of how the Bennett Dam had forever ruined his idyll snapped him out of his somnolence. No more that splendid pool below the waterfall, loaded with grayling and rainbow trout, a fly fisherman's paradise. No more could he stand in chest waders in that fast-moving sun-dappled stream, eagerly casting for trout.

The Bennett Dam had created the largest artificial lake in North America and buried his fond memories under a few hundred feet of water, in addition to creating an environmental nightmare. Wild things no longer inhabited a living river, thanks to the dam and B.C. Hydro. The fish had gone somewhere else, where, he didn't know, but it wouldn't be the same.

What concerned Phil most, the major political scandal, was not what governments did that was illegal, but what they did legally. This made Phil sad, then mad, neither of which was conducive to sleep.

The reminder of his lost paradise plunged Phil into melancholic musing about the eventual death of all things. The Calvinists believed that God had a plan for everyone before they were born, ending in a nasty surprise when they died. God's plan, then, for most people, Phil thought, must be a dose of clap and a second mortgage.

His thoughts shifted to the Poindexter conundrum, and suspects' names tumbled around in his mind: Riley Eldridge, Don Shivagitz, Robert Madigan, Clarence Crepeau and Annie Chance. Any one of them could be a barking mad headcase and have done the dirty deed. Who else was there?

There were some three hundred thousand psychopaths in Canada, comprising about one percent of the population. They were hard to detect, as they were outwardly normal, whatever that meant. A disproportionate number could be found in professions such as banking, law, psychiatry, and politics, where they exercised exploitive power over people and organizations.

Studies showed strong correlations between the behaviour patterns of politicians and criminal psychopaths. Researchers found the criminals relatively easy to study, but experienced difficulty gathering much data on politicians, because they didn't like to be studied. The smartest psychopaths preferred business or politics over a life of crime.

Phil had found some suspects with motivation all right, but otherwise, his failure to make significant progress ate at him.

Two other things were conspiring to keep him sleepless in Delta. The Haskinses were no doubt accustomed to the steady ticking of the godawful grandfather clock in the living room, but how could they stand the continual chiming? Especially when the damn thing didn't work properly. What time was a quarter to *clunk*?

The soprano buzz of a solitary mosquito

tormented him even more than the clock, as it searched the room for blood like the bride of Dracula. He'd seen mosquitoes in the Northwest Territories that could stand flat-footed and make love to a turkey. Delta was no Mosquito Coast; in fact, its citizens boasted about the scarcity of the little bloodsuckers in the area, so why was this sad and lonely bugger bugging him? He had to lay a trap for him—or was it a her? And why was his over-active brain worrying about the sex of a mosquito in the middle of the night?

Leaving only his head and hands outside the bedcovers, Phil positioned one hand a few inches from his face and waited for the bastard to land somewhere on his exposed features. Son of a bitch! The winged harassment had landed on his hand instead.

Shaking his hand slightly, Phil forced the mosquito to fly and again waited until it came in for a landing on this face. In the darkness, Phil took his best guess as to the insect's position, then slapped himself sharply near his left ear. His ear rang for a few seconds, then he heard the mosquito's whine once more.

Phil slammed his hand against his face again just as the clock struck the half hour. Again he heard the mosquito buzz away. To be that tricky, it had to be a female. Fourth time lucky. Eureka! Phil thought. This time he'd either killed the intruder, wounded her badly or broken his nose.

When the pain had subsided, Phil debated trying to fall asleep in the fifteen-minute interval between chimes, or to use the bathroom so he wouldn't have to get up later on. He opted for waiting, since his kidneys were still good and his prostate was working reasonably well. Besides, the toilet was way down the hall.

Impatient with the worry loop his brain seemed intent on creating, Phil tried to recall some of the dirty old songs he and his buddies used to sing during the war. Maybe that would send him off to sleep. He sang softly:

Dinah won't you show
Dinah won't you show
Dinah won't you show your lay-ay-eggs.
Dinah show your legs,
Dinah show your legs
A foot above the knee!
A rich girl wears a braz-ear-aye,
A poor girl uses string,
Dinah don't use anyfing,
Just let's those buggers swing.
A rich girl uses Vaseline,
A poor girl uses lard,
Dinah uses axle grease

And takes it by the yard...

Phil halted. He couldn't remember any more verses. A few seconds later, he launched into another ditty, this one sung to the tune of *Hark the Herald Angels Sing*:

Uncle George and Auntie Mabel
Fainted at the breakfast table,
Isn't that sufficient warning
Not to do it in the morning;
Ovaltine has set them right,
Now they do it morn and night;
Uncle George is hoping soon
To do it in the afternoon,
Auntie Mabel has a hunch
That he'll be coming home for lunch!

At police headquarters the next morning, Harry Muldoon and Wade Cavanaugh held another case conference. Muldoon was ready to bite the bullet. "Annie Chance had the motive, she knew the method and she had the opportunity," he said decisively, staring at the ceiling. "What more do we need?" His eyes came to rest on Cavanaugh, daring the younger man to challenge him.

Wade was silent for a moment, weighing career prospects against honesty. "We've been through this a dozen times," he said, suppressing a yawn.

Muldoon shrugged. "Yeah, sure we have. "But we're starting to look stupid, and both the chief of police and the public want some action. We're going to charge Chance based on the evidence we've got. It's all in the file." He handed a folder to Cavanaugh.

"Get this down to the crown prosecutor's office and try to get an immediate charge approval. I've talked to them already, so they're familiar with the case. Have Thorndyke do the vetting if you can."

"What if he doesn't buy it?"

"Tell him to go fax himself!"

"If you say so," Wade replied, hearing the frustration build in his superior's voice. "But let me play devil's advocate. Any half-assed lawyer Annie hires is going to have a field day with this type of case. He'll flog his bag of tricks around the courtroom and probably have the jury laughing at us in no time."

"Yeah, I know," Muldoon growled. "The bastards learn shit like that in law school. That's how so many guilty cockroaches fall through the cracks. But you can't say what the result's going to be. This murder was so vicious, a jury won't be sympathetic."

"Sarge, that doesn't change the fact that all we have is circumstantial evidence, which is unreliable and open to misinterpretation. We can hope Chance gets convicted, but right and wrong will have less to do with the outcome than who plays the best game in court, or who knows best which legal technicalities to hide behind."

"So now you're lecturing me?" Harry snapped. He had no tolerance for those who disagreed with him. They had no right to their stupid opinions.

"No, Sarge," Wade hastened to reply. "You keep telling me that you think Annie Chance is probably guilty. I'm just saying, a judge is going to tell the jurors they can't convict on probability; they have to be certain beyond a reasonable doubt. And you can bet the judge'll spend at least a half an hour explaining the difference between probability and certainty."

"Point taken. Just the same, we've got to put some pressure on her. Maybe she'll crack and confess, or tell us what else she knows. Let Annie take her chances, no pun intended. That way we're off the hook. I'll swear out a warrant as soon as we get charge approval, then you and I will arrest her personally. Tomorrow. Today, I've had it with this place, so let's you and I do a policeman's exit."

"What's that?"

Harry stood up and growled, "A cop-out."

Twenty-four

The evening sky was overcast and an early spring storm was brewing as Muldoon and Cavanaugh pulled up in front of 1073 Seaquay Crescent. A chill breeze spattered them with raindrops as they walked down the east-side sidewalk of the old mansion where Annie Chance carried on business. A small apartment at the side of the building provided her living quarters.

Wade carried the warrant for Annie's arrest. Muldoon was packing his snub-nosed Smith & Wesson .38 in a shoulder holster made of leather, whose belt slot was low so that most of the holster and the gun were above his waist. That way he could wear a stylish sweater and no one could see the gun lying flat against the swell of his beer belly. As Muldoon rang the bell, both cops noticed that the door was slightly ajar. The sound of the chimes reverberated through the flat, but no one appeared. Harry rapped on the door. They waited on the threshold, then Harry knocked louder. Silence. Constable Cavanaugh pushed and the door swung inward. Muldoon shouted down the hall, but got no reply.

"Looks like no one's home," said Wade, "but why the open door?"

"Gives us reasonable grounds to take a look. We're here to arrest her, in any case." Harry switched on the lights in the gloomy hallway. Everything seemed in perfect order.

From the hallway, they entered the kitchen. A frying pan and a bottle of olive oil were on the stove, and on the table, a dirty plate, steak knife and fork, HP sauce and a ketchup bottle, salt and pepper shakers and a glass with a bit of red liquid in it. Cranberry juice, Muldoon figured.

A plate of six chocolate chip cookies sat beside an open package on the counter, and two coffee cups, the same pattern as the plate, were upside down on the counter. Annie must have been entertaining, or maybe she'd been eating when her visitor arrived.

The open front door bothered him. Few people were so careless these days. They heard a faint sound from somewhere down a darkened inner hallway. Harry froze momentarily, then quickly drew his revolver and motioned to Cavanaugh to back him up. Muldoon flicked a wall switch. The sudden light revealed a small cat walking toward them. "Damn it!" Muldoon burst out. "It's just a little house cat. This business is making me jumpy."

The hall led them into a bedroom with the standard furniture: dresser and clothes closet against one wall, laundry basket in a corner, pictures on the wall. A door on one end of the far side probably opened into an ensuite bathroom. The queen-sized bed was the main feature and it looked slept in. In fact, it was in a state of chaos, with sheets and blankets churned in all directions. A dressing gown lay crumpled in a corner. Harry walked around the end of the bed.

Annie Chance lay face down on the floor between the bed and the wall, naked.

A dark red stain spread across the beige carpet from a large wound on her right thigh. Wade, peering over Harry's shoulder, blurted, "My God, I think one cheek of her ass is missing!"

Harry knelt beside the body. Grasping Annie's long blonde hair, he turned her head to face him. A strangler's victim is not a pretty sight. Annie's lips and ears were purple. There was blood-stained froth on her nose and mouth, and her tongue lolled gargoyle-like out of the side of her mouth. Muldoon noticed that her hands were tightly clenched.

The typical signs of death by asphyxia were present: congestion and patecehiae, the tiny hemorrhages caused by constriction of the neck. A pair of tan pantyhose encircled her neck, the ends pulled tight and held with a knot at the side of her throat, which showed bruises and scratches around the ligature. The scratches, along with Annie's broken crimson fingernails, testified to her attempts to tear away the hose.

"Don't touch anything," Muldoon ordered Cavanaugh. "Call it in. She's dead, but we'd better have an ambulance, too." Wade stepped out of the room to radio in, leaving Muldoon to prowl around the perimeter of the room. The clothing in the closet and dresser was in disarray, suggesting that someone had searched through them.

Wade rushed back a few seconds later. "The mobile crime lab's on the way. They're trying to find the coroner." Wade gazed down at Annie's body and said quietly, "Looks like you were wrong about her, Sarge. Someone didn't want her to talk and got here before we did."

Muldoon's mind was spinning, but he hated to admit that Wade's doubts had been legitimate. "Okay, so maybe she was only an accomplice, but she knew something she wasn't telling. Too bad we didn't make the arrest sooner. She hasn't been dead long, there's no rigor mortis yet."

Waiting for the technical people to arrive, Muldoon inspected the kitchen. The table setting was for one person. The plate and the frying pan on the stove indicated some kind of meat had been fried and eaten, a steak perhaps. The memory of the wound on Annie's backside leaped into Muldoon's mind and he suddenly felt faint.

"Jesus Christ!" he exclaimed, not responding when Cavanaugh anxiously asked him what was wrong. He looked again at the glass. Did the murderer drink Annie's blood? Muldoon backed away from the table, shuddering.

He struggled for control of his stomach and his thoughts. If Annie was innocent, why kill her, when she was so perfect as the fall guy? He could only conclude that perverted sex provided its own motives for violence.

Within minutes the small apartment was a beehive of activity. A group of ident officers arrived, clad in white, fibre-free bunny suits complete with slip-on shoe covers and hoods, to gather the forensic evidence. They would only get one chance to collect uncontaminated clues, and the first twenty-four hours after a death were critical.

It was low-tech, meticulous work, and the officers scoured the place on hands and knees, going over every square inch. They stayed off the beaten track of the floor in the kitchen and bedroom, processing the traffic areas by laying down strips of adhesive tape. The location of each strip was documented, then pulled up to reveal whatever minute fibres, powders, or bits of other detritus had been deposited there. They looked for shoe-tread impressions both inside and outside the house and took video and thirty-five-millimetre photographs of the scene.

Muldoon felt tired. He took out his handkerchief and wiped the sweat from his forehead. "Be sure and use krazy glue in a vacuum," he directed the tech squad.

"How does that work, anyway?" asked Wade, ever the eager student.

An ident officer explained that the glue migrated to the enzymes in human sweat and hardened right on the object, then fluorescent powder was placed on the print and photographed.

An ambulance arrived. Harry knew the cause of death, but felt he needed to determine a precise time of death. Only a forensic pathologist could ascertain that, and the lack of pathologists in Victoria was costing the department big bucks and needless delay. Rather than shipping the body, plus two officers, by ferry to the Lower Mainland for an autopsy, Muldoon decided to fly in a forensic pathologist from Vancouver, who could also provide expert testimony in court later on.

Phil picked up the phone on the first ring. It was Harry Muldoon.

"I want you down in my office pronto, Figgwiggin. Just tell me you're on your way."

"Why should I be?"

"Because if you aren't, I'm having you picked up for obstruction of justice, that's why. Now get cracking."

"Seeing as you asked so nicely, Harry, okay." Phil hung up, mystified. He had no intention of letting the cops take him for a ride, however, so he donned coat and hat and left immediately.

Muldoon wasted little time on preliminaries.

"What did Annie Chance tell you about Poindexter's murder?" snorted Harry, obviously straining to keep a lid on his temper.

Nonplussed, Phil answered. "You must understand, Harry, that if she told me anything, then it's privileged information under solicitor-client confidentiality."

"So she did retain you! I thought so," said Muldoon. "But you piss me off. Your only excuse for that answer no longer exists."

"Why do you say that?"

"Because the woman's dead," Muldoon said bluntly. "Murdered! It's going to hit the news anytime now."

Phil was flabbergasted. "What in God's name is going on here? When did this happen?" He slumped forward in his chair and grasped the edge of Muldoon's desk, his head bowed.

"Late yesterday. And I'm wondering where you were when she was killed, Figgpudding."

Phil was breathing heavily, gasping for air. "I'll ignore that last remark. Where...where did it happen?" he managed.

"In her own bedroom."

"How?"

"Strangled!"

Phil just sat, staring at the floor, trying to regain his composure.

"So let's skip the legal technicalities like client privilege and confidentiality, shall we? You lawyers make me sick with your flim-flam. You were the one who wanted to play the private eye. Said you wanted to know who killed cock robin. So I say you're going to help us now."

"I'm sure you'll recall, I did offer to help the last time I was in this office. The truth is," he admitted sadly, "I haven't come to any conclusion about who murdered Dick Poindexter. My sleuthing attempts haven't born much fruit."

"Are you tellin' me Annie Chance didn't know who did it?"

"No, I'm not, but she said she didn't know who did. So I don't know. I'm saying that if she did know, she didn't tell me."

"Maybe that's because she did it herself, with an accomplice. There's still that possibility."

"She always maintained her innocence with me," Phil said.

"As if she'd do anything else."

"All I can say is that she may have unwittingly set it up, or been set up herself." Phil's long-standing strategy of holding out on cops and prosecutors prevented him from saying more. Particularly to Muldoon, who could probably fuck up a two-car funeral.

His failure to get any details from Annie on how Poindexter was set up—from which the intermediary might have been traced—was bad detective work on his part, and too embarrassing to reveal to Muldoon unless absolutely necessary. He had been right at the point of exploring that aspect of the case, but now it was too late. Phil decided Annie's business records might provide some clues.

"If she hadn't been killed, Sergeant," said Phil guardedly, "she may have divulged something else to me, or remembered something that would've led to Poindexter's killer. She wasn't under arrest on a murder charge, though—"

"I went over there to do just that, but she was already dead," Muldoon interrupted.

"—so I was primarily talking to her about that cockamamie bawdy-house charge your department brought against her. I was looking forward to battling it out in court, if young Snively decided to pursue the matter. Mind you, I was always on the lookout for evidence in Dick's murder. I had my doubts about Annie at first, because of the circumstantial evidence. But I figured until she was charged with murder I wouldn't have to make up my mind whether to defend her. But she asked me to, in relation to the other matter, and by then I believed she was innocent, so I took her on as a client."

"I'll ask you again," Muldoon's tone was harsh. "Do you have any idea who might've killed Annie?"

"Read my lips. I don't know. Not without something more to go on. Now you, Sergeant Muldoon, seized all her business records in that raid on her massage parlour. Isn't that right?"

"House of ill repute. Her clients were getting more ass than a toilet seat."

"Whatever. Like you said, it makes no nevermind now. But if I could look at those records, I might find something that would fit into a couple of things she said and some theories I was starting to develop. Could I take a look at them?"

"Highly irregular."

"Now who's being difficult? How did I ever get the impression that you wanted my help?"

Muldoon stared thoughtfully at Phil for several moments, then said, "You don't know about the cannibal bit, do you? You couldn't, because we're not releasing that information. Remember, this is strictly confidential."

"What cannibal bit?"

Muldoon told him about the rump steak on the kitchen table.

"Damnation! Hard to believe," said Phil, revolted.

"We're dealing with a psychopath."

"There was never any doubt about that."

"The forensics lab didn't come up with any results in the Poindexter case that would form a link to anyone specific. But here's something you don't know, Figgy, and it goes no farther than this room. Even though Chance was strangled, we found a fancy skill saw on the premises. We think it's the weapon used in the Poindexter murder. Forensics say they haven't even had time to check the stuff they bagged: dust, hairs, fibres, drugs, blood-stained material and clippings from her fingernails. So what we get from that saw, I don't know yet. We've had no luck in either of these cases and this is the first promising find. These murders smell as bad as an Arabian wrestler's breechcloth and I'm pissed that it took this long to get any real evidence."

"Well, it bugged me too, so we have that in common, Harry. So, about her records?"

"Okay, you can take a look at them, but it won't do you any good."

"Why not?"

"Because there was precious little to them. I don't think we got all of them."

"When can I look at what you do have?"

"Right now, if you want. Come on up to the exhibit room, Constable Cavanaugh'll show them to you."

"Fine."

Muldoon stuck his head in the exhibit room door. "Wade, let Figgwiggin here take a look at anything he wants to see from the Chance search." Cavanaugh, in uniform again, was pushing various pieces of paper around a large desk, making an attempt to look busy. He rose and hitched his belt a bit higher on his hips, then came around the table to offer an outstretched hand.

Phil shook it. "So, you're Cavanaugh. You've undoubtedly heard about me from Harry. And I've certainly heard about you."

"Nothing good, I'll bet. From Annie Chance, right?"

"She did talk to me about you, yes."

"I know she didn't like me, but I want you to know..." Wade pitched his voice lower and glanced around the room as if it had ears, "I never really thought she was guilty, and also, well, I kind of admired her. A gutsy lady."

"Too bad you can't tell her."

"Yeah, I'm sorry she got snuffed. I'm doing what I can to find out who did it."

"Off the record, do you want to comment

on what your boss just told me about the skill saw you found at Annie's?"

Wade grimaced and pursed his lips. "You know, for what it's worth, I think the saw was too easy. It wasn't there before, unless Tony LeBlanc and his partner did a lousy search, and it sure wasn't there when we raided her party. Personally, I think it was planted."

"It doesn't make much difference now, but we're ad idem there, Officer. Thanks for your honest opinion. Now let's see what you've got in this pile of paper."

Muldoon was right about the paucity of Annie's records. Phil thought he'd be able to compile a working list of Annie's clients, but all he found was a hodgepodge of bills, receipts and the like, which failed to yield any new insights.

Back at home, Phil checked his messages. Mike's voice sounded frantic. "Hey, Figg, where the hell are you? What's going on? Come down and see me asap, all right?" Phil looked forward to hashing things out with Fowler. Two old farts were better than one! Too bad Mike hadn't also been a lawyer. They would have made a good law firm, Figgwiggin & Fowler. Maybe they could have found a third partner, got another fast talker and called the firm Fowler, Figgwiggin and Filibuster. No Liquespittals nor Varlets need apply.

Phil hotfooted it down to Mike's as fast as he could, and filled his buddy in about Annie's death and his interview with the cops. Mike said it was news of Annie's death that had thrown him into a lather and prompted his earlier call.

"What's your take on all of this?" said Mike, "you've had more hard thinking time at it than I have."

"Could you put on some coffee first? Make it strong."

"Sure. Good idea." Mike was agitated and seemed glad to have an excuse to get busy with something. He went out to the kitchen. "Talk to me while I put a pot on."

"Make it strong, would you?" Phil requested again. He leaned against the kitchen door, watching Mike rattle around the mess in the kitchen. "We'll probably never know whether she was running a glorified cathouse or whether she was an accessory to Dick's murder. But either she knew who actually killed him, or the killer was afraid she'd figure it out."

"That makes sense."

"Why else would someone murder her?

She knew too much, so someone rubbed her out, likely the same psychopath who killed Poindexter. Same kind of nut, at least."

"Let me ask you, Figg, if Annie had lived, you would've defended her against the murder charge the cops wanted to lay on her, wouldn't you?"

"Well, I took her retainer in the bawdy house charge. Yeah," Phil added, stroking his goatee, "I would've represented her on the murder charge, too."

"I'll bet her killer figures you for her lawyer overall. And probably also thinks Annie told you all kinds of stuff about the Poindexter murder."

"What are you getting at, Mike?" Phil asked, although he could see where this was leading.

"I'm saying, if they killed her to keep her quiet, you're the next target, Figg. The killer's probably looking for you right now."

"You're right, but how the hell do I find out who it is?"

The intercom buzzed. Mike answered the garbled female voice from below. "Right, I was expecting you. Come on up."

"Visitors?" Phil inquired.

"One, and I'm glad you're here, because I've hired this cleaning lady to do some work on your place as well as mine."

"You what?" asked Phil, one eyebrow raised. "This is no time for—"

"This is the maid from Northern Exposure Domestic Services."

"You never told me you were going to hire a cleaning lady, and I'm not in the mood for—"

"It was supposed to be a surprise."

The doorbell rang and Mike ushered a stunning young lady into his rooms. Both men stared, then Mike remembered to help her off with her trench coat. A dark sultry Latin type, she wore a tight, aquamarine T-shirt over a figure that wouldn't quit. Across her magnificent chest in tiny print was the message *Grow some of your own*.

"I'm Mike, this is Phil, and you are?"

"Sharon Sharalike is what I go by." She spoke with a southern twang. "We don't give out our real names." Or real accents, either, Phil thought. "But you can call me Shari."

She looked quizzically around the living room at the jumble of books, magazines, recording equipment, tapes, old records, and sundry bric-a-brac that littered the place. A didjeridoo stood in one corner next to a banjo. Clustered around the TV sat several large stuffed animals, including a lion, a gorilla, a pregnant moose, and a small buffalo. A large blow-up picture of a naked man playing a piano, an old Valentine's Day card tacked to his ass, graced one wall. Another wall held a picture of a skier being pulled through a plowed field by a tractor. The caption read *Ski Illinois*. The dining room table was covered with small tools, a jeweller's eyepiece, a jar full of handmade marbles and a yo-yo.

Shari performed an inspection tour as the men watched. She circumvented a small coffee table on which sat a small nerdy-looking mannequin in a raincoat. A bulb was attached to his back with a length of plastic hose. Shari reached down and squeezed the bulb. The flasher's raincoat flew open, revealing, among other appendages, a message on his bare chest: *Call when you get work.*

"Ooh, my," said Shari, unfazed. Seeing the hopeless condition of the rug, Shari picked up a piece of pipe which was bent into a curve at one end. A length of chain link had been welded across the space created by the bend. "What's this?" Shari asked, perplexed.

"A Ukrainian chainsaw," said Mike proudly.

"This place could certainly use some work," Shari observed, shaking her head.

Phil chimed in with, "Oh, give me a home where the buffalo roam and I'll show you a very messy rug. This place is a disgrace, Mike."

"I'd better get to it," Shari said in silky tones; then commenced to disrobe right to the buff—no G-string, no pasties—retaining only her high-heeled black shoes. Phil could see she only had one wrinkle, the one she sat on. "Where do you want me to start, Mike?" Shari asked.

Once he managed to close his gaping mouth, Mike coughed, then replied, "How about some low dusting over there below the hi-fi equipment?"

"Certainly, it will be my pleasure," she drawled. Striking provocative poses, Shari stroked the duster across the furniture, and at one point did a backflip, spin and a headstand. Although Phil was as mesmerized by the view as Mike, he noticed the cleaning was more of a cursory tidying up and rearrangement of the mess.

"Young lady, do your parents know what you do for a living?" Phil asked.

"They do," Shari replied, "but then I always was a rebel. My mother cried and my dad went all quiet when I told them."

"You could run into some dangerous situations doing this kind of work," Phil went on. "Not from us, of course," he hastened to add, "but there are some weird types out there, as I'm sure you realize. I've come across some horror stories in my time, beatings, rapes, gunfights."

"I know all that, but I'm careful," Shari responded seriously. "Our company tries to screen the customers. But it pays so much better than welfare, stuffing envelopes or babysitting. Even better than many skilled jobs. There's nothing immoral or perverse about what I'm doing. You guys need house cleaning and I can do a good job of that if you really care."

"What's Mike paying you for this housekeeping scam, anyway?"

"Not me, Phil, you're paying," Mike jumped in. "Remember our deal? This is one of Annie Chance's services. You told me to sign up for all of them."

Phil stroked his bearded chin. "I see. What are your rates, dear, may I ask?"

"A hundred and thirty dollars an hour, which is our minimum amount of time."

"Mike," said Phil in measured tones as he pulled bills from his wallet, "we should let the young lady put her clothes back on before she catches cold."

Shari leaped into her clothes and left, after tucking her fee into her ample cleavage.

"You old son of a bitch, was that really necessary?" Phil growled, torn between annoyance and amusement.

"Didn't you like it?"

"Well, yeah, but not the payment part." He chuckled ruefully, then turned serious. "Listen, Mike, Muldoon's all but convinced Annie Chance told me who the murderer is, and he's not happy that I wouldn't—or that I couldn't tell him."

"You've dug out a bunch of suspects," Mike said flatly. "Don't you have any idea who it is yet?"

"I'm getting close. That's obvious."

"Yeah, maybe too close. Let's bat it around some more."

"I could use some of that coffee first."

"I'll join you. Gotta be ready by now."

Twenty-five

Phil figured his angina was growing steadily worse, but he tried to ignore his predicament. If he felt angina coming on, he used one of the nitrolingual spray canisters that he carried in every coat and jacket. He stubbornly clung to the motto: yesterday's history, tomorrow's a mystery, you can only live for today. A poem he liked even better was:

The floor of the death cell he paced,
He must pay the wages of sin,
The warden said, "You have one hour of grace,"
He said, "Okay, send her in!

By unspoken agreement, he and Mike Fowler seldom discussed the details of their physical ailments or their aging problems, at least not in a serious vein. Following a recent admission to hospital for routine tests, Mike's doctor had told him he had a large inoperable aneurysm just below the renal arteries in his abdomen. If the balloon, a weakened spot in a blood vessel wall, ruptured, the consequences could be devastating. Death now stalked Mike as well as Phil. Youth was a disease from which they'd both recovered, but they knew there was a hospital somewhere from out whose front doors they wouldn't walk. Still, both men remained optimistic that they could delay the inevitable.

It was when he was alone that Phil wondered which one of them would die first, and whether the other would mourn. Was there any need to grieve a full and interesting life? The rapport between the two men was nothing palpable, but did such things have a life of their own? When both were gone, there would be no one to remember, but their friendship was great while it lasted.

In the meantime the crap shoot that was life went on, and Phil suddenly remembered he hadn't picked up his mail for two days. He took the elevator downstairs and removed a pile of flyers, bills, a magazine, financial come-ons from banks and brokers, and a larger envelope from his box.

Back in his apartment, he threw the bundle

on his writing desk, removed his shoes and got into a pair of slippers. After fetching a glass of cold buttermilk from the fridge, he looked at the mail.

Something about one item struck him as strange. The envelope was heavy and slightly bumpy. It bore several stamps and no return address, and the postmark was faint and indecipherable.

A day earlier, before he found out about Annie Chance's death, Phil would have torn the letter open without a thought. Now he was wary. He placed the suspicious envelope carefully back on his desk. Was he being paranoid? It was probably nothing, but he needed Mike's expertise.

A few minutes after Phil called, there was a knock on the door and Mike poked his head in. "What's up?" he asked. Phil explained.

Mike took a long look at the letter before fingering it gingerly. "Have you got a really sharp razor blade?" he asked his friend. Phil went into the bathroom and ejected a new blade from a safety-razor package.

Mike held the envelope steady on the table with a thumbnail at one corner and asked Phil to do the same at the opposite end. Inserting the very tip of the razor blade, he carefully cut the envelope open along the top of the flap. Peeking inside, Mike spotted a layer of tissue paper, then a green wire protruding from between two layers of cellophane. Mike whistled through his teeth. Closer inspection revealed a thin pad of plastic explosives neatly sandwiched within the cellophane.

"There's enough of the heavy stuff here to blow both of us out of this room," Mike said with authority. "Lucky you were suspicious."

"You mean I'm lucky you had the guts to take a look. Thanks. How would that get through the mails?"

"Don't count on the posties to find letter bombs. They handle more than three million pieces of mail a day and the stuff goes through like a blur. They don't have the time to X-ray or inspect every parcel or bulky letter. They do what they can, but unless an alert postal worker knows how to identify a mail bomb, or happens to spot something suspicious, it's going to get through."

"Can you disarm it?"

"Sure. I'll take it down to my place and work on it. You've got to be cautious with explosives, of course, but they're not difficult to handle if you know what you're doing and use your imagination, because every job is different. The sender wants it to arrive intact.

It's only when you open it up wide and start to take out the contents that the thing blows up. This may have a spring-loaded device inside to establish a contact that triggers the explosion."

"Maybe this package wasn't delivered by the regular carrier," Phil mused.

"Hmm. Which would mean that someone knows where you live and has access to the lobby of the building, at least. As Jake once said to the Kid, wouldn't that give a dog's ass the heartburn!"

"Most assuredly, and it doesn't make me feel any better, either."

"Are you going to report this to the cops?"

"Now, there's a good question. Let's consider the pros and cons."

"Someone's got to track down the son of a bitch who's doing this stuff before he gets you, too," said Mike.

A wave of dizziness forced Phil to lower himself slowly into an armchair. Mike, noticing how pale Phil had become, took a seat on the chesterfield. They sat staring at each other, momentarily at a loss for speech.

Phil broke the silence first. "That someone has to be me, because I don't have much faith in the cops. Muldoon would only say it serves me right for messing around in a murder case. The alternative would be to fly the coop—take a long holiday in Mexico."

"Not your style and it wouldn't do any good," Mike declared. "This wacko's likely smart enough to trail you there, or anywhere else, for that matter. In Mexico, murder takes out more people than most diseases. You might as well stay here and take your chances. Anyway, the last time I went to Mexico City, I got caught in a fecal storm."

Colour was returning to Phil's face as he asked, "Fecal storm. Just what might that be?"

"They've got over twenty-five million people there and about as many dogs. No reasonable sewage system in much of the city. Everybody's got to crap someplace, which they mostly do in the streets, particularly the dogs, who leave presents everywhere. It's hot there, as you know. The sun blazes down, drying out all that excrement. The people tramp through the residue, turning it into dust. A big wind comes up and suddenly you're walking through a fecal storm, breathing in all that virus-laden shit. Which also gets into the water system."

Phil's face broke into the semblance of a grin. "I wish you hadn't told me that. But since you brought up the subject, I could use a drink of aqua pura. You want one, too?"

"Sure."

Phil got up slowly and went into the kitchen, where he poured two glasses of cold filtered water from the jug in the fridge. He returned and handed one to Mike. They raised their glasses in a friendly salute.

"I can also tell you how to make a fortune in Mexico out of that same situation."

Phil bit as usual. "How?"

"Get the government to pass a law requiring owners to feed their canines phosphorescent dog food so pedestrians can more easily avoid stepping in their poop."

"You've convinced me not to go."

"Good, because you also gotta watch out for the foo birds there. If they shit on you, don't wash it off under any circumstances."

"I'm afraid to ask why not, Mike."

"Because local lore says that you wash it off on penalty of death. So, what I'm telling you is—if the foo shits, wear it."

"You're incorrigible," Phil said, distracted, "but I wouldn't have it any other way."

"Okay, I'll be serious. What do you figure on doing now?"

"Annie told me when I saw her at the courthouse, that if anything happened to her, I was to take a look at the stuff she stashed in a gym horse she keeps in that basement dungeon."

"I remember it well," Mike interjected.

"Somebody obviously thinks I know whatever Annie knew about Dick's murder," Phil went on. "They didn't want her to talk. Now they think I know something I shouldn't, and I want to know what it is they don't want me to talk about. The question is, should we look that gift horse in the mouth, like Annie wanted?"

"What do you mean 'we,' kemosabe?" quipped Mike.

Phil reacted automatically. "Meanwhile, back at the ranch, the Lone Ranger, mistaking Tonto for a door, shot his knob off! Come to think of it, I'd better go alone. You're better off not being seen with me. Chance warned me to watch my gluteus maximus. Whoever the sons of bitches are, they aren't after you yet, and it's best to keep it that way."

"Before we settle that, there's one other thing. Is taking something that could be evidence from a crime scene legal? What charges could they lay if you do that?"

"Obstructing justice. Harry would dearly love to charge me, but I doubt he would, because Annie was my client. She instructed me to go to her place and get whatever's in that gym horse. There's a will in there, and since she named me her executor, it's a civil matter. My reasons are valid. I'm just doing my best to represent my client's interests by trying to establish her innocence, albeit posthumously, and by acting as the executor and solicitor for her estate."

Mike leaned back on the sofa, shut his eyes and pulled at an ear for a few seconds. "Well, I'm still breathing, so I say we both go. You need help and I insist. When do we go?"

"Late tonight," Phil replied, secretly pleased that Mike wanted in. The cops are all but through at Annie's place, and if they're not, they'll likely only work in the daytime. If Annie had something in her possession that implicated the killer, he'd want to find it, and he might return like a dog to its vomit. If I'm right, we just have to be careful until we get a clue as to who the bastard is. Then go straight to the cops."

"Okay. If we're going to stay up late, let's get a power nap now. Don't forget to lock your door." Mike left for his own digs, taking the letter bomb with him.

y and too heavy," Mike objected.
ed, though he knew Mike couldn't
're right. We'll sit under it. You
ghts while I have a look."
under the horse with some diffi-
noticed a screw-on metal plate.
rewdriver out of his pocket and
1 the panel. "These screws are
easy," he reported. "Means this
off occasionally."
off, Phil thrust his arm through
and felt around inside the hol-
the horse. His fingers touched
ial package, then another. He
undles through the hole and
1 to the floor. Wrapped in can-
vith string, the parcels lay in a
between them. Mike continued
flashlights as Phil untied the
1e bundle and removed the
g.
Phil muttered, looking at what
be a set of books. "Her real
et." He spotted a diary or
among the sheaf of papers.
k look through this while you
the other packet. Then we'll
e where we can see to do this

Twenty-six

"Have you got the flashlights?"
 "Yeah. Do you have the tools?"
 "Yes. It's midnight, let's go."
 Phil parked two blocks away and he and
Mike walked down back alleys to the rear of
the Chance residence on Seaquay. A quarter
moon hid behind the thick clouds marching
slowly across the night sky. The geriatric
prowlers could barely make out the building's silhouetted roofline, which was broken
up by dormers. Tall, leafy arbutus trees deepened the darkness around the house. Moving
slowly in the pitch black, the two timeworn
crocks stepped through the opening in the
boxwood hedge that gave access to the back-

yard. The six-foot hedge provided good cover, and they stood motionless for several moments. The cool night had congealed into a murky charcoal pool around the house. No breeze stirred, nothing moved.

Phil extracted his nitro puffer from his pocket and gave himself a couple of good shots under the tongue. "Don't use your flashlight till we get inside," he cautioned. "Might be someone around."

"It's darker down here than looking up a Mau Mau's muumuu in a coal mine," Mike muttered. "Give me your arm, I can't see a damn thing. And I'm unsteady on strange ground."

Linked together, they crossed the lawn and picked their way around several chairs and a picnic table on a flagstone patio, finally reaching the back door. Locked as expected.

"Wait here," said Phil. "I'm going to check for open windows along the back and sides."

He muttered "No dice" upon his return a few minutes later, but Mike had disappeared. "Where the hell are you?" Phil whispered into the night.

"Up here." The muffled reply came from somewhere above Phil's head. Mike had clambered up the wooden fire escape and was two landings above ground. "Come on

up, there's an o
sage came whis
Phil was une
row stairway
top. Leaning hi
said, "We're
keep the stress

They crawle
the upstairs
Shining thei
stairs. They
descended to
slowly to the

"Maybe I s
as a lookout

"I don't th
here and it's
talking as
shut behin

The dun
their flash
the phone
tre of the
the wall.
padded
thing in
underne
lay it ov
both giv

"Too nois
Phil nodd
see it. "Yo
hold both li

Squatting
culty, Phil
He took a s
started in
coming out
plate comes

The plate
the aperture
low guts of
one substan
pulled the
dropped the
vas and tied
pool of light
to shine the
binding of
outer wrappi

"This is it,"
appeared to
records, I'll
address book
"I'll take a qui
see what's in
take them hom
properly."

Mike unwrapped several layers of burlap from the second packet. manila envelopes were stuffed inside. He removed the elastic bands from one envelope. As he unwrapped it, a wad of paper currency spilled onto the floor. "Jeez, will you look at this, Figg," he exclaimed as he flipped through the twenties, fifties, and hundreds in the envelope. "How much dough do you figure we've got here?"

A low whistle escaped Phil's lips. "If we assume the other envelopes also contain money, we're talking a major amount of cash."

"Do you figure the total's going to be higher than your legal fees?"

Phil gave him a hard look, then laughed good-humouredly. "You take a ball park count while I take a quick look at this other stuff."

"Invisible wages, tips, fiddles and perks, that's what this is," Mike declared. "Happens in every business, everyone wants to make an extra bob or two. They were doing it in Egypt three thousand years before Christ. You can't blame people for trying to cheat the government. Did you read about those RevCan workers who set up bogus accounts and paid themselves refund cheques? They robbed the government to the tune of about five hundred Gs."

"Yeah, I heard about it, but this is no time to discuss corruption in government."

"Right you are."

Phil's mind flashed back to what little Annie had told him about being paid to set Poindexter up. The supposed practical joke had actually provided a pretext for the killer to enter Poindexter's house and murder him. Was this the money? If so, did that make her an accessory before the fact as well as after?

Mike opened another packet, then a third. These were also stuffed with large bills. "This is one helluva stash," he commented. "No way this is all tips and fiddles."

"She did say she'd been paid some money recently. How much do you figure is there?"

Mike peered at Phil from outside the small circle of light. "I can only guess, because the envelopes all have different denominations in them, but I'd say we're talking six figures."

Phil riffled through a few stacks of bills. "I can't see anyone paying Annie that much money just for setting up Dr. Dick. Something else is going on here."

"Damnation," Mike exclaimed, "this bag isn't big enough to carry all this cash. Never mind, I'll stuff the rest down my shorts."

"That'll bring new meaning to the term loaded. There's a lot of other paper here, but we can check it later." Phil began thumbing through the hardcover appointment and address book. Well, what do you know, he thought, our old friend Riley Eldridge. Could be a coincidence. After all, the man was entitled to a massage or anything else he could get from Annie's operation. Then he remembered that Eldridge had hated Poindexter, maybe enough to kill him. "Mike, take a look at this."

Mike squinted down at the book for a few moments, the flashlight beams casting eerie shadows against the styrofoam dungeon wall, then handed it back to Phil. "We'd better do this later, there's not enough light."

"Ssh!" Phil whispered. "What was that?" His head swung sharply toward the stairs.

"What?"

"That noise. Didn't you hear it? Douse the light."

"Didn't hear anything. But then you know my hearing's not so hot these days."

"I heard some sort of clicking. Something."

"You got your nitro spray with you?" Mike asked. "Give me a shot. I'm short of breath."

"Good idea. My heart's racing." Phil got out the spray and handed it to Mike. "We'd better take a couple of extra puffs. We may need it."

Mike took a good hit, then said, "Screw being in your eighties! After seventy, it's just patch, patch, patch!" He fumbled in the dark until the hand gripping the spray connected with Phil's, then he relaxed his grip on the container.

The two men listened in silence, but they heard nothing more.

"Let's stop and analyse the situation," said Mike, still whispering. "You've got lots of suspects for the Poindexter and Chance murders, but you'd have a hard time making it stick to any of them."

"Right, and the cops aren't even investigating them. They don't even know about them," Phil answered.

There was a long pause before Mike continued. "Poindexter didn't have the brains to stop being an asshole and he paid the price. Annie Chance, who could be cited as an accessory, was no girl guide, more likely a depraved woman, to whom Doctor Dick did dirt, just like he did to Eldridge, Madigan, Shivagitz and Crepeau. She ran a very strange establishment. Maybe they were all in the same S & M cult."

"That certainly could be one scenario." Phil stuck his hand inside the second packet, pulled out another hardcover book and

up, there's an open window here," the message came whispering softly down.

Phil was uneasy, but he mounted the narrow stairway and soon joined Mike at the top. Leaning his forehead against the wall, he said, "We're okay so far. I just hope I can keep the stress level down to a dull roar."

They crawled with great difficulty through the upstairs window, emerging in a hallway. Shining their flashlights, they found the stairs. They gripped the banister as they descended to the lower corridor, then moved slowly to the door of the dungeon.

"Maybe I should hang around the main floor as a lookout," Mike offered in a stage whisper.

"I don't think that's necessary. There's no one here and it's better to stick together." Phil kept talking as they headed down. "Pull the door shut behind you. Careful on these stairs."

The dungeon's contents looked ghostly as their flashlights searched the dark corners of the phoney grotto. The gym horse in the centre of the room cast a long shadow against the wall. It was a sturdy piece of equipment, padded on the top and sides. "If there's anything in it, the only access will be from underneath. It might be easier to search if we lay it over on its side," Phil suggested. "If we both give it a shove, it should topple."

"Too noisy and too heavy," Mike objected.

Phil nodded, though he knew Mike couldn't see it. "You're right. We'll sit under it. You hold both lights while I have a look."

Squatting under the horse with some difficulty, Phil noticed a screw-on metal plate. He took a screwdriver out of his pocket and started in on the panel. "These screws are coming out easy," he reported. "Means this plate comes off occasionally."

The plate off, Phil thrust his arm through the aperture and felt around inside the hollow guts of the horse. His fingers touched one substantial package, then another. He pulled the bundles through the hole and dropped them to the floor. Wrapped in canvas and tied with string, the parcels lay in a pool of light between them. Mike continued to shine the flashlights as Phil untied the binding of one bundle and removed the outer wrapping.

"This is it," Phil muttered, looking at what appeared to be a set of books. "Her real records, I'll bet." He spotted a diary or address book among the sheaf of papers. "I'll take a quick look through this while you see what's in the other packet. Then we'll take them home where we can see to do this properly."

Twenty-six

"Have you got the flashlights?"

"Yeah. Do you have the tools?"

"Yes. It's midnight, let's go."

Phil parked two blocks away and he and Mike walked down back alleys to the rear of the Chance residence on Seaquay. A quarter moon hid behind the thick clouds marching slowly across the night sky. The geriatric prowlers could barely make out the building's silhouetted roofline, which was broken up by dormers. Tall, leafy arbutus trees deepened the darkness around the house. Moving slowly in the pitch black, the two timeworn crocks stepped through the opening in the boxwood hedge that gave access to the backyard. The six-foot hedge provided good cover, and they stood motionless for several moments. The cool night had congealed into a murky charcoal pool around the house. No breeze stirred, nothing moved.

Phil extracted his nitro puffer from his pocket and gave himself a couple of good shots under the tongue. "Don't use your flashlight till we get inside," he cautioned. "Might be someone around."

"It's darker down here than looking up a Mau Mau's muumuu in a coal mine," Mike muttered. "Give me your arm, I can't see a damn thing. And I'm unsteady on strange ground."

Linked together, they crossed the lawn and picked their way around several chairs and a picnic table on a flagstone patio, finally reaching the back door. Locked as expected.

"Wait here," said Phil. "I'm going to check for open windows along the back and sides."

He muttered "No dice" upon his return a few minutes later, but Mike had disappeared. "Where the hell are you?" Phil whispered into the night.

"Up here." The muffled reply came from somewhere above Phil's head. Mike had clambered up the wooden fire escape and was two landings above ground. "Come on

Mike unwrapped several layers of burlap from the second packet. manila envelopes were stuffed inside. He removed the elastic bands from one envelope. As he unwrapped it, a wad of paper currency spilled onto the floor. "Jeez, will you look at this, Figg," he exclaimed as he flipped through the twenties, fifties, and hundreds in the envelope. "How much dough do you figure we've got here?"

A low whistle escaped Phil's lips. "If we assume the other envelopes also contain money, we're talking a major amount of cash."

"Do you figure the total's going to be higher than your legal fees?"

Phil gave him a hard look, then laughed good-humouredly. "You take a ball park count while I take a quick look at this other stuff."

"Invisible wages, tips, fiddles and perks, that's what this is," Mike declared. "Happens in every business, everyone wants to make an extra bob or two. They were doing it in Egypt three thousand years before Christ. You can't blame people for trying to cheat the government. Did you read about those RevCan workers who set up bogus accounts and paid themselves refund cheques? They robbed the government to the tune of about five hundred Gs."

"Yeah, I heard about it, but this is no time to discuss corruption in government."

"Right you are."

Phil's mind flashed back to what little Annie had told him about being paid to set Poindexter up. The supposed practical joke had actually provided a pretext for the killer to enter Poindexter's house and murder him. Was this the money? If so, did that make her an accessory before the fact as well as after?

Mike opened another packet, then a third. These were also stuffed with large bills. "This is one helluva stash," he commented. "No way this is all tips and fiddles."

"She did say she'd been paid some money recently. How much do you figure is there?"

Mike peered at Phil from outside the small circle of light. "I can only guess, because the envelopes all have different denominations in them, but I'd say we're talking six figures."

Phil riffled through a few stacks of bills. "I can't see anyone paying Annie that much money just for setting up Dr. Dick. Something else is going on here."

"Damnation," Mike exclaimed, "this bag isn't big enough to carry all this cash. Never mind, I'll stuff the rest down my shorts."

"That'll bring new meaning to the term loaded. There's a lot of other paper here, but risked turning the flashlight back on. "This looks like a diary, and I can see Annie's will here, too. I want to look more carefully at all this stuff before jumping to any conclusions."

"So revenge might have been the motive, but what about the future? Whoever the killer is, he's after you now."

"Muldoon's still trying to pin Dex's murder on Annie and claim she was done in by an accomplice. That way he can close the book on both cases. But you're right, Mike. If I don't find out who killed them, I could be next. Best I can do is share with the cops once I've read this material. The solution's bound to be in here. Time to go, we've been here too long."

"Well, Figg, I can't say much for your talent, but your perseverance demands respect," Mike smiled as he stuffed wads of bills down his shorts and into his shirt. He looked like a pregnant duck.

"So how much do you think is there?" Phil asked again.

"I kinda lost count, but I'd guesstimate over a half million bucks. I think you should take that appointment book and her diary and the rest straight to the cops and let them have a heart-to-heart talk with your suspects. Now, let's screw this horse's ass back on and get the hell out of here."

The horse reassembled, they crossed the dungeon floor and headed up the cellar stairs. Phil grasped the door handle and turned. Nothing. He tried pulling, but the door remained shut.

"Must be stuck," said Mike, shining his light on Phil's efforts. "I really slammed it hard. Let me have a try." He had no luck, nor did Phil when he tried again.

"Mike! Could someone have locked the damned thing from the other side? Is that the noise I heard?"

"Wouldn't that frost your left nut!"

"Or maybe we just locked ourselves in when you pulled the door shut."

"That could be. Or we've got visitors."

"Let's hope visiting hours are over."

"What do we do now?"

"We are in deep shit."

"I'd say about as deep as King Kong's first dump of the day!"

"You're not just whistling Dixie."

"This is turning into a real sapfu." Mike said in disgust.

"A what?"

"Surpassing all previous fuck-ups! Wait, I just remembered, there's a side exit over here on the right. I saw it when I cased the place during the S & M party. People tore out that way during the raid. A set of steps leads outside."

"Listen, if there *is* someone out there, they may not know I brought you along. I think you should find a place to hide."

"Wait a minute," Mike protested, "we're in this together."

"There's no reason for you to be in it at all. Look at it this way. I told you what the doc said about my heart condition. I've got nothing to lose if I can't outsmart this killer."

"Neither have I, Phil. Shit, I'm eighty-four, my prostate may go at any time, I got an aneurysm—"

"Look, if I don't make it, one of us has to be around to tell the cops what happened. Muldoon will never figure it out for himself. I'll go out and see if the coast is clear."

Mike looked around. He didn't remember too many good hiding places from what he'd seen the night of the raid. He decided to duck into a cupboard under the stairs. "Give me the diary and the other papers, too," he said.

Phil handed over the documents, then grabbed Mike's hand and squeezed hard. He opened his mouth to speak, but Mike beat him to it. "I feel the same way, Phil. Let's hope we get out of this jam, but if we don't, then... well, it's been nice knowing you. Get going and good luck."

Phil turned to leave. "Wait!" Mike hissed after him, reaching into his jacket. "Take this, it might come in handy." He handed Phil the letter bomb. "I resealed the flap, but I didn't disarm the bomb."

"You were carrying this around with you?!" Phil was shocked.

"I figured we might need a weapon, and this is better than nothing."

"What the hell am I supposed to do with it?" Phil could barely get the words out.

"I told you, it's not dangerous until you open it wide. You're not going to open the thing, and if this killer sent it to you, he won't, either. But a situation could develop, like where a guy straps it to himself so they can't take him out without killing themselves..."

"A Mexican standoff. Let's hope it doesn't come to that."

The two old friends shook hands and Phil gingerly tucked the envelope into one of the breast pockets that housed his weird filing system. He crossed the floor, turned off his flashlight and quietly pressed down on the safety bar of the exit door. He swung the door open, stepped through and closed it softly behind him. Standing still in the darkness, he listened intently. Moments passed, one by one, into silence. A dog barked in the distance, but he heard no other sounds.

His eyes gradually made out a stairwell, his nose the dank smell of rotten leaves and damp cement. A flight of stairs ran parallel to the basement wall and led upward into the murk above.

Phil took another nitro puff, then a goodly number of slow, deep breaths, and slowly and silently climbed the steps and peered over the top wall. There was no one in sight, no movement. Letting a minute pass, he stuck close to the wall rather than step out onto the lawn under the night sky.

Creeping along the wall, he turned the corner at the back of the house. Darker here. Again he paused, then began to carefully pick his way around the patio furniture, a barbecue and a small shed. The coast seemed clear. As he passed the shed and started to cross the lawn toward the hedge bordering the back lane, his stress less palpable now, he heard the unmistakable sound of a shell entering the breech of a pump-action shotgun.

Before he could turn, Phil felt the barrel dig sharply into the small of his back. His stomach churned and his heart raced.

"Just keep going and no false moves," the man said. Phil thought he recognized the low, gravelly voice. "I hope you found what you were looking for."

"Just what did you think I'd find in there?" asked Phil, trying hard to keep his voice steady.

"I'm asking the questions," the man snapped, driving the barrel of the gun into Phil's spine.

"I didn't find a thing. Hate to disappoint you, but it was a wild goose chase."

"Don't give me that crap."

"All right," Phil admitted, "I do think I've found what I was looking for, now that you've turned up. I didn't think it was you, Madigan, not until I heard you pump that shotgun."

"I'm sorry to hear that," said Madigan. "Your detecting talents aren't much to brag about, are they?" He prodded Phil in the direction of the front street.

"Look—" Phil began as they reached the sidewalk.

"Shut up and keep walking."

A black four-door station wagon was parked down the street, its lights off. The rear door swung open as they came abreast of it.

"Get in," Madigan ordered. Phil climbed into the spacious back seat. His captor followed him in and slammed the door shut.

Two other men occupied the vehicle. The driver and the front-seat passenger were facing forward, their jacket collars up against the unusual chill of the spring night.

Phil could barely make out the driver's profile, but it seemed familiar. "Do you mind if I backseat drive, Riley? I won't really say anything, I'll just talk. I learned that from my driving test with you."

"You're a smartass, Figgwiggin, and you've just failed your final exam."

"Was I ever going to pass your horseshit driving test?"

"Yes," Riley replied sarcastically, "we always pass you old know-it-all farts the third time around. Gotta put you through the hoops first, though. It smartens up your driving skills. Not that you'll be needing them much longer. You know too much for your own good."

What should I do now? Phil wondered. Once a job was fouled up, anything you tried to do to improve it likely only made it worse.

This was now a susfu—situation unchanged, still fucked up!

Twenty-seven

The front-seat passenger twisted to face Phil. Don Shivagitz! Being kidnapped by three of my main suspects is my reward for playing amateur sleuth, Phil thought. "Did you ever notice," he said aloud, trying to still the tremor in his voice, "that the bigger the crowd, the more people are in it?" No response from his captors. "And that small crowds are poorly attended?" Dead silence in the car. "I suspected each one of you singly, but not as a group," Phil blathered on. "It would be ironic, if you bastards weren't such vicious hypocrites."

The car slid silently through the night. "One of you recommends chelation to guarantee my longevity, another wants me to load up on cayenne pepper, grape juice and brown rice and my driving inspector was finally going to give me my licence—"

"You wish," said Eldridge from the driver's seat. "All you old farts should be yanked off the road, permanently."

"—but now you want to kill me," Phil went on, ignoring the interruption.

"That seems to be the way you want it, Figgwiggin," Shivagitz replied. "We all tried to discourage you."

Madigan's voice came from Phil's left. "Have you started the chelation treatments?"

"It doesn't look like I'll have the time," Phil replied. "Someone seems to be missing," he added.

"Who's that?" Riley asked

"Clarence Crepeau, a.k.a. the Creep?" Phil replied. No response, no acknowledgement from the three kidnappers, which meant they didn't know about Crepeau. Phil had been so certain of the Creep's guilt. And he liked Shivagitz. It was dismaying to find out how wrong he'd been about all the players, and frightening to realize that his curiosity was about to get him killed.

Eldridge took the Island Highway through the municipalities of View Royal and

Langford, heading toward Sooke, then turned off onto a narrow side road into the boondocks. Here's where they figure to administer the deep six, Phil thought. He'd never taken the time to devise an epitaph for himself, but he doubted his captors planned to erect a tombstone, anyway. "Where are we going?" he asked aloud.

"You'll find out soon enough," Eldridge said over his shoulder.

"That's it, I've had enough of this baboonery," Phil shouted, losing his cool. "You're all under arrest. Turn around and drive to the police station so Harry Muldoon can read you your rights and cuff you."

"Very funny," said Madigan. "What's the charge?"

"Try kidnapping, conspiracy and murder! You are a combination of persons gathered together for an evil or unlawful purpose. You have made agreements between you to do things that are criminal, illegal and reprehensible."

"Once a lawyer, always a lawyer. They never stop talking," said Riley. "Where's your proof? You haven't got—what do you call it?—a scintilla of evidence."

"It could be inferred from the circumstances. The cops couldn't find any suspects to fit the material evidence they collected, but it'll be a different story if they start investigating you bastards. Which is probably why I'm here," Phil added ruefully.

"You got that right!" Madigan exclaimed.

Increasingly desperate as they bumped over the uneven road, Phil spoke faster. "I don't know which of you is the actual killer; maybe you all are. Ranking you on the psycho scale, I'd say take your pick. And I don't really know where Annie Chance fits into the lineup. I'll hold to the view that she was just an accessory, a patsy, and that you guys set her up—used her in your combined plot for revenge on Poindexter."

"Don't you shysters ever shut up?" Shivagitz demanded. "You think we're guilty, do you? Well, this is your last chance to sway a jury."

"Certainly not of my peers."

"I wouldn't say that," Madigan said. "We're all peeling empty bananas and you're no exception."

Shivagitz spoke in a low sibilant tone. "Now listen up, Figgwiggin, enough of this bullshit banter. Cut out this Sam Spade act, or we're going to make you."

"God, I hope you guys aren't hungry. I don't know if I have enough buttock steaks to feed this whole Boy Scout troop," said Phil with a grim smile.

"What the hell are you talking about?" Shivagitz asked, genuinely puzzled. "Not a diet I ever heard of. Start making sense."

Riley broke in again, "He went to Annie Chance's house to get her records. Search him, Madigan, let's see what he came up with."

"He said he didn't find anything," Madigan replied. "But he's lying, of course."

"Get cracking and search him, then."

"Okay, but put the roof light on. It's dark as hell back here." He ordered Phil to take everything out of his pockets.

"No. Why should I help you?"

Madigan handed his shortened shotgun to Shivagitz, who rested the weapon on the back of the front seat and pointed it at Phil's head.

Madigan flipped open Phil's suit jacket and came across a wad of envelopes, summonses, bills and letters in his breast pockets.

"This is an invasion of privacy, gentlemen, and I'm asking you to cease and desist, or you may regret it."

Madigan ignored Phil's outburst. "Look at the amount of stuff he's carrying," he said in astonishment.

"Yeah, two inner breast pockets. Well, I guess he needs them to haul all that lot," an irritated Shivagitz carped. He was kneeling on the seat and hanging over the back, overseeing the search.

"This is my last warning, gentlemen. I protest the stupidity of most human actions, and particularly yours. I've accomplished what I set out to do—you're all either psychopathic killers or accessories to the murder of Dick Poindexter and Annie Chance. May God have mercy on all you assholes!"

"Shut up and listen," Riley shouted even louder. "We'll tell you if we're guilty when we're damn good and ready. Now what did he find in that goddamned house?" he snapped at Madigan, who was still rifling through Phil's papers.

"There's a lot of summonses here. You're quite a criminal yourself, Figgwiggin, a scofflaw of sorts," Madigan said with a smirk.

"They'll never convict me on any of those charges."

"You may be right there," agreed Eldridge. "And you'll never get your driver's licence. In fact, I'll make sure you never drive again."

Heavy forest sped past on either side of a narrow ditch-lined road. The darkness was just beginning to fade into a blue mist. Riley, ever the model driver, kept his speed down as he negotiated the bumpy road.

Shivagitz fidgeted. "For Christ's sake, let's finish this search. We've got decisions to make."

Phil's mind worked feverishly. This kite's taken too much flak and is going to crash, he thought. He could go down with the plane or bail out. A lot of his old buddies had faced the same horrendous choice in the war. The only difference was that in a car, Phil lacked the height for his chute to open and he risked becoming a flaming candle. He was prepared to die, and comforted himself with the knowledge that he wouldn't have to face the lengthy, painful demise he'd always dreaded. His body's survival instincts revved up: his heart raced, sweat stung his eyes and dampened his shirt, and his stomach was an empty pit.

Phil shifted in his seat so that he faced Shivagitz and Madigan as squarely as possible. They were still engrossed in his papers. Phil braced his feet on the floorboards and slid his right hand behind him onto the door handle. Madigan had the envelope containing the mail bomb in his hand.

"Don't open that envelope!" Phil yelled. "Don't open it."

He pushed down on the latch and shoved hard against the door. As it swung open, he used all the force he could muster to push off from the floor and launch himself as far as he could toward the ditch.

As he sailed out of the car, he heard a *BAR-ROOM!* as a horrific explosion ripped through the quiet night and an intense white light filled the gloomy void.

Twenty-eight

"Stand and Deliver!" The loud cry reverberated in Phil's ears as he sat on an extremely hard seat of a rumbling stagecoach. Horses' hooves clattered to a stop and he heard whinnying in the night. What the devil? He poked his head through the curtains covering the door. A highwayman dressed in black stood in the roadway, pointing a pistol straight at Phil. A pale moon slipped from behind scudding clouds to reveal the robber's face. It was Mel Pratt, Phil's best friend from his youth.

"Why are you doing this, Mel?"

"I'm here to shoot you—a game of snooker," Mel replied, grinning and thrusting a pool cue at Phil.

So Mel was still trying to pull a fast one, as always. Phil looked at the short, crooked cue in his hand. "I'm not playing you with this goddamned stick. Where's the rack?" Phil hunted for his favourite cue in the Connaught Pool Hall, a task made difficult by the thick fog that was rapidly obliterating the scene.

Phil became aware of the sound of laboured breathing and recognized it as his own. He couldn't seem to feel his body, let alone find the pool cue. Where was he? Apparently somewhere behind the giant eight ball that was advancing toward him out of the mist. He realized he'd been dreaming.

A breeze began to push at the haze before his eyes and he fought to see what lay beyond. Mike Fowler's face, peering intently down at him, drifted into focus. It was good to see another old friend. Phil blinked, trying to clear away more of the drifting fog. He saw Mike's lips move, but heard nothing. He stared uncomprehendingly.

Mike leaned forward and spoke more loudly. Phil caught snatches of the sentence, "You...son of a...make it!"

Make what? Oh yeah, life, he supposed. He was still in the here and now, wherever that was. At least he wasn't entirely deaf, but he didn't know whether he could muster the strength to talk. He decided not to try until he was alone. Phil drifted back into the mists of a dreamland he had been occupying for several days.

The next time he awoke he was in a heavy sweat. This time he immediately recognized that he was in a private hospital room. Wires led from his chest to a monitor and an intravenous system was plugged into a vein in his left arm. He wondered what they were feeding him and hoped it was coffee. He could use a caffeine jolt. He felt like a blind skunk trying to make love to a fart.

Gradually Phil remembered bailing out of Riley's car. He began to replay the conversation in the car and the explosion. His thoughts were jumping about like rabbits in his brain, in and out of hidey-holes. It dawned on him that none of his abductors had actually admitted to killing either Poindexter or Chance. Had he fallen into the same trap as Muldoon, making assumptions of guilt? No, there was no doubt the three had intended to kill him. Phil was the only person who suspected them of persuading Annie to leave Poindexter bound and vulnerable to attack. One or all of them must have entered Dick's house later on and killed him.

And yet the thrust of their conversation had seemed to involve a search for something very important to them. Evidence of their complicity?

His thought processes were as slow as a turtle trying to hump an army helmet. It occurred to Phil that the three might have been trying to solve the murders, if only to exonerate themselves. That they didn't know the Creep was irrelevant, but their innocence, at least in Annie's murder, was supported by their apparent ignorance about the cannibalism inflicted on the masseuse. Also, they had failed to recognize the mail bomb. Or was that because of the poor lighting in the car? The envelope had contained a lethal charge, and he'd assumed that one or all of the co-conspirators had sent it. Now what was he supposed to believe? Trying to unravel the mystery made his head hurt.

He had tried to warn the three men about the bomb, but the truth was, he had used it deliberately. He'd thrown himself out of the car and let them take their chances with the bomb. Did that make him a murderer? No, don't go down that street, he chided himself. Even if there was anything to that scenario, it was self-defence. He'd had no intent. He'd been the unwilling instrument of fate.

Eldridge, Madigan and Shivagitz just had to be culpable. There was no other plausible reason for their actions.

Anyway, he had worse things to worry about. Were his injuries affecting his brain? Why couldn't he wake up when there was a doctor around? He had to talk to someone about his condition.

Just then the door opened and Mike walked in. He approached the bed and smiled down at his buddy.

Phil whispered through dry lips, "Why can't I feel anything?"

Mike had to ask him to repeat himself. "They've got you doped up to the eyeballs and taped up to the testicles," he said, "including casts for broken bones. But the docs seem to think they can fix you up."

Phil motioned with his eyes and head to the jug of water on the side table and Mike helped him take a few sips through a straw.

"Why bother?" Phil said, once his throat felt sufficiently lubricated. "What happened? How come I'm not dead yet? I'd made my decision, you know. I was on the midnight express off this mortal coil, damn it! Now I'm what I never wanted to be—a fucking basket case tied to a hospital bed!"

"Who the hell knows what happened, if

you don't?" Mike replied. "They found you in a ditch on a side road out in Sooke. Good thing your head wasn't under water or you would have drowned."

"Drowned?!"

"You were in a ditch full of water!"

The memory of the blast sent aftershock waves through Phil's brain.

"You've had a near-death experience," said a solemn Mike.

"I don't remember seeing any tunnels with bright shining lights at the end. I don't remember floating around on the ceiling looking down at my body."

"You made a soft landing, what are the odds of that? You're one lucky man, my friend."

"The others?" Phil asked.

"All dead," Mike answered, pulling a chair over to the side of the bed, "and good riddance to bad rubbish. The cops had a helluva time figuring out who they were, because after the car blew apart, what was left crashed and burned. Not a pretty sight, I guess."

"And I'm still here. I can't believe it," Phil rasped.

"From what you told me before, these were professional lunatics. I hope you're satisfied, now that you know who murdered Dick Poindexter and Annie Chance. They nearly got you too. So, let's assume you're going to get well," Mike said, determined to stay on the bright side. "In which case, what do you figure on doing next?"

"Minding my own business might be a good idea."

"You'd never succeed. Now listen." Mike leaned in and lowered his voice. "I've been reading Annie's diary. She told you Poindexter set the Creep up because he cheated the doc out of some cash, right?" Phil nodded weakly.

"Well, the diary tells it a little differently. Poindexter told Annie he was holding onto some money for someone else. Poindexter never did tell her who, but you can bet your I.V. it was for the Creep—probably the proceeds of his stock swindle. Anyway, Poindexter was laughing, because he wasn't about to give the money back. So next time Annie's over there rubbing the doc's parts, she gets him all relaxed and goes off to look for the money. And finds it."

Phil could barely make sense of the words as Mike continued. "And that's how she came to have eight hundred and seventy-five thousand dollars stuffed in her gym horse. I've got it hidden at my place, but Phil, we've gotta figure out what we're going to do with it."

"I don't give a shit about the money," Phil said with as much force as he could summon. "Mike, look at me. This is my worst nightmare. I'm not likely to leave this goddamned place and I'm not prepared to live like a cripple. We talked about this."

"Yeah, I know, but don't take that attitude just yet. Not till we find out how bad things are. You might heal up okay. Might take a little while though, and a little money." Mike didn't mention that *No heroic measures* was written on the patient chart at the foot of the bed.

"If I do get out of this hospital—"

"You have to. Who else is going to help me break into whorehouses in the dead of night?" Mike chuckled, a little too heartily. "Now just relax and enjoy yourself. Oh, by the way, I checked Annie's will. It was in her own handwriting. What do they call that?"

"A holograph will."

"She doesn't mention any relatives, she just wants the executor to pick a suitable charity."

"And she did name me as executor?"

"Yes, sole. So what say you and I take the money and split? Go down to some spot like Costa Rica, really enjoy ourselves, live high on the hog for the rest of our lives."

"You mean, rent a luxury condo for a month or two?"

"Well, after you recuperate you're going to need a good holiday."

"Hmm. I'm too tired to think about it right now. But you know, that idea does have some merit." Phil allowed a few rays of hope to penetrate his mind. "We could set up a sort of tontine. The survivor could pick out a charity Annie would approve of, say the Sandy Merriman House for battered women. So, a holiday you say, then the balance goes to charity. I'll have to refer this to my subconscious."

"Okay, I'll tell the nurses you're back in your right legal mind. They'll probably send the doctors in tomorrow to talk to you. As I understand things, you're a mass of bruises, your left leg's broken in two places along with two ribs, your left shoulder's dislocated and you've got a mean concussion."

"What about my heart?"

"They're monitoring it, as you can see," Mike said, waving his hand at the machinery. "To be honest with you, when I talked to the medicos, they didn't think your ditch-diving stunt was going to improve your overall performance. On the other hand, they don't think the heart thing is any worse."

Mike lowered his eyes for a moment, then looked Phil in the eye as he said, "Phil, we're both playing in overtime, so we gotta keep our spirits up. We may not be able to grind it out in the corners anymore, but with our experience we could still score a few goals."

He patted his pockets. "I nearly forgot. I brought the papers we found in the horse's ass. I made copies; always good to be on the safe side. I'll read the stuff as well while you're convalescing." Mike pulled at the side table drawer, which opened with a metallic screech. "I'll leave the originals here, including Annie's diary, so as soon as you're up to it, you can read it, too."

"Thanks, Mike. I'm out of energy... have to sleep..." Phil's voice faded away and his head slumped sideways on the pillow.

Mike stood looking down at Figg for a few moments, his face grey with worry, then departed, leaving Phil alone with his rattling snore. He stopped at the nurses' station halfway down the marbled corridor. Leaning heavily against the counter, he rang the little silver bell.

Nurse Turlock hurried down the hall. No need to wonder about the burnout and turnover rate among nurses nowadays. When was she going to get a break? Had to take one soon, her fanny was dragging. As if the ward wasn't short-staffed already, Velma had called in sick at the last minute and her replacement had failed to show. "I'm voting to strike at the next union meeting," Turlock muttered to herself, "unless they double our wages and hire more staff." She spotted Mike by the nurses' station and wondered what the old fart was doing out of bed.   As her shoes squeaked to a halt in front of him, she realized he wasn't a patient.

Mike spun around when the stocky nurse strode up to him. "I don't know what you're doing here, sir, but I'm going to have to ask you to leave."

"Philip Figgwiggin," Mike said, "in 411. I'm really worried about him."

"I can understand that, but it's eleven o'clock at night. Way past visiting hours."

Mike appealed to her better nature. "I won't be any bother. Maybe there's some-where I could stay. I know how busy you are, short-staffed and all. I could keep an eye on him, help you out." He could see she was weakening. "How's he doing, really?"

"We're not supposed to comment on a patient's condition, hospital rules. But..." Turlock thought it over while Mike's eyes pleaded with her. "He's not in great shape. The next few days will be critical." With over twenty patients to look after, Turlock made her decision. "There's a small staff rest area across the hall," she said, pointing at a door. "It's not used much because we never get any rest. There's a couch in there, and a fridge and table. Or you could use the TV room at the end of the hall."

"Thanks, Nurse," Mike said, his face creasing into a grateful smile. "He's my best friend and he's got no relatives in this part of the world. We kinda only got each other. We never talk about, well, you wouldn't, either, would you? I'd just like to be around, in case, well, you know, if—"

"I understand," said the nurse, compassion in her eyes. "You can stay. Just remember, you didn't hear it from me."

Twenty-nine

Phil awoke again later that night, an old ditty playing over and over in his head:

I'm a rambler, I'm a gambler,
I'm a long way from home,
And if you don't like me,
Then—leave me alone.
I eat when I'm hungry,
I drink when I'm dry,
And if the whiskey don't get me,
Then—I'll live till I die!

He drifted back into a half-sleep. At some point, he heard a soft scrape of metal on metal. It came from the table at his bedside. Turning his head in that direction, he made out a dark figure bending over the cabinet and slowly pulling open the top drawer. A nurse, he thought, but what's she looking for?

"Are you here to give me another shot of whatever dope I'm on?" he said in a low, shaky voice, fighting off his lassitude.

The figure turned and shone a small flashlight in his face. "No, Phil Figgwiggin, I am not." Phil recognized Mary-Mary Quite Contrary Podalchuk's voice. "You're supposed to have had enough sedatives to keep you asleep until morning. I didn't mean to wake you up."

"Aren't visiting hours over for the day, Mary?" he asked, still groggy.

"Not for me. When you've been around hospitals as much as I have, you learn how to come and go with impunity."

"What'd you bring me? Oranges or flowers?"

"Would you believe a get-well-soon card?"

"Ordinarily, yes. But not at this hour." Phil felt his brain jump-start. "So what's in the drawer that warrants your attention?"

"Why wouldn't you stay out of Poindexter's murder?" Mary exclaimed. "I tried to dissuade you, but you wouldn't quit."

"Mary, it was you who put me onto Eldridge, Shivagitz and Madigan. Why would you sic me on them, if you didn't want me involved?"

"Only because they weren't guilty. But your investigation made everything point to them as the killers, and apart from you, there's no one left to prove otherwise."

Phil thought that over, peering at Mary. He couldn't make out her expression in the gloom. "My God, Mary," he burst out. "Not you! Why, for Christ's sake?"

"Not for Christ's sake, Phil," said Mary coldly. "Not even for the sake of the devil. For several reasons, one of which was supposed to be a big pile of money, which I still haven't got! I think you know where it is. You're probably not going to make it, anyway. I'd be doing you a favour if I pulled the plug on your life-support system and stuffed a pillow over your face. Tell me where the money is, or I'll do it."

Stunned by Mary's callous admission, her threats and her matter-of-fact, glacial tone, Phil lay squinting in the dark, fully aware of his helplessness. How could he have misjudged Mary so badly? Once again he was appalled by his lack of perception. He needed to buy some time.

"Tell me this is some kind of spoof. Are you saying it was you and not those psychotic assholes who killed Dick Poindexter?"

"That's right, I did it. With Annie Chance's help. Even if she didn't know I was going to kill him, she did her part."

"You did the murder by yourself?"

"Certainly. I'm strong enough and I know how to operate power tools. It was payback time for that double-crossing prick."

Phil was as shocked at Mary's uncharacteristic profanity as her confession. "So why did you kill him, Mary?"

"I fell in love with him. He promised me the moon, then left me with lunar dust. He cheated on me with Annie."

"But why did Annie help you?"

"There's something you don't know about Annie and I, Philip. We batted from both sides of the sexual plate. We were rivals at first, when Dick dumped me for her, but then we became attracted to each other. True to his colours, Dick soon double-crossed her, too, so we arranged what Annie thought was a bit of well-deserved revenge."

"I didn't think anything could surprise me anymore, but I never figured either of you for lesbians."

"Do you expect lesbians to look like Amazon warriors with double-edged swords? We come in all sizes and shapes of female, you know."

"Okay, I can understand that. You're welcome to your own lifestyle—it's just that I never had any inkling."

"When I was with men, I left my sex life up to them. With women, I chose for myself. Unfortunately, Annie had to go."

Phil's bedsheets were sticky with his sweat and he was feeling sick to his stomach. His right hand hunted under the rumpled covers for the call button. He had to get help and keep Mary talking until someone arrived. His fear rose as he remembered that it often took fifteen minutes before a summons was answered, if it was answered at all. Yet it was his only option.

"Mary, back up a bit, I'm confused. How did Madigan and the others fit into this whole thing?"

"Their motives for hating Dick were real, just as I told you. They wanted their own revenge on Dick, and Annie and I were happy to help them get it. Annie was supposed to strap Dick down to the massage table and leave the door open for them."

"Were they going to kill him?"

"I think they just wanted to give him a good horsewhipping, then leave him there and get out. But I got there ahead of them. I wanted him dead when they came in. When those three psychologically damaged people found him dead, there must have been a great soiling of undergarments. They've been running scared ever since. Hoist on their own petard, as they say. Their presence on the scene was designed to muddy the waters and exonerate Annie, if the police ever charged her. The three men were terrified that they'd be accused of murder, but they were also afraid to pursue it further. Then you came along. Must have been a shock to them, because they knew that whoever they were dealing with meant business."

"I can certainly see that you do. You sent the bomb to me, didn't you?"

"You were going to die anyway, and soon, or so you told me."

This was a nightmare. Mary's manner was becoming more agitated. Phil was running out of time. "What went wrong with the plan, Mary?" he asked.

"We found out about Clarence the Creep, but we didn't figure on you ever finding him. That was a fine bit of detective work on your part, Phillip."

"Thanks." Phil's voice was heavy with irony. "Nice to know I didn't botch everything."

"You couldn't blame Dick for stealing the Creep's money, when you consider that Crepeau was a crook and an embezzler in the first place. Crepeau swindled a lot of cash in that stock deal with the two gold-mining companies. He needed a safe place to hide it, but unfortunately, he chose Dick as his bag-man. Annie and I were biding our time until the case blew over, then we were going to take the money, go off somewhere and live it up. But she wouldn't tell me where she hid it, so I got the message that she was about to double-cross me, too. You read Annie's journal, didn't you? That's how you found out where the money is. Well, I want it."

"All I have is the documentation you're holding in your hands. I didn't have time to read it before those goons grabbed me."

"Don't press your luck, Philip." There was menace in Mary's voice.

"You killed Annie, too, didn't you? I can't believe it. She was a neat lady. I liked her."

"So did I, a lot actually, for some time."

"For what it's worth now, I couldn't see her actually killing anybody. I even figured I could get her acquitted."

"On the story she told you, you probably could have. She was a mixed-up woman, emotionally unstable and intellectually immature. Annie thought love could be hate, that ugliness could be beauty, black could be white and sexual pleasure was tantamount to pain. Those kind of people are a danger to themselves and certainly to others they come in contact with."

Look who's talking, thought Phil. His right hand was still feeling around for the call button. He began to surreptitiously reel in the cord to get to the button.

"She shouldn't have tried to skip out on me," Mary was saying. "We might have worked it out, but when the police kept harassing her, I was afraid she wouldn't hold up if they charged her with murder. She might have tried to make a deal by turning me in. I couldn't let that happen."

"So love doesn't last forever, is that it? I sensed that Annie didn't kill Poindexter. Maybe you told her you were only going to torture him a bit, teach him a lesson, or take the money and laugh in his face. I guess Annie couldn't stomach what you did. Is that another reason you killed her?"

"You should have quit when you had the chance, Philip. Annie was a tool who'd served her purpose. Evil wanders to and fro in this world, seeking whom it may devour. Particularly those who are insecure and maladjusted, and Annie was becoming dangerous. I thought I knew where she'd stashed the money, but it turned out the bitch had moved it again. Pretended it was better if only she knew where it was. And now I think you have it. Tell me where it is or you know what I'm going to do."

"First you threaten to put me out of my misery and next you want to make some kind of a deal regarding money I don't have."

Phil's mind was in as high a gear as he could manage under the circumstances. His law practice had taught him that premeditated murder usually involved one of the great human passions. A tangled mess of greed, sex, love and hate had ensnared all the players in the Poindexter drama. He believed in the existence of evil, but he'd failed to recognize it in the dogmatic, cruel and perverse Contrary Mary Podalchuk.

"I can't help you, Mary," Phil said. Ah, found it! Phil pressed the button and kept his thumb down, hoping someone at the nursing station would see the light or hear the buzzer and react, do something.

"You're lying. Annie would have eventually led you to me. She probably blabbed about everything in this diary. I'm not taking any chances. I'm going to burn all her papers."

"Are you serious?"

"Of course. I don't advocate leaving a record of our activities. Now tell me what I want to know, or I'll pull the plug."

"Why not just slice me open, rip my heart out and eat it?"

"This isn't the time or the place, even though, like the ancients, I believe that by consuming human flesh, one ingests the best qualities of the victim."

Phil's sight had adjusted enough to the dim light to see that the door was slowly opening behind Mary's back. He laughed as loud as he could to cover his rescuer's entry. Phil's laughter ended in a racking cough. "That would've been a fitting end to my legal career," he said, fighting for just a bit more time. "Like I said, Mary-Mary, my heart belongs to you. Suppose I did know where the money is, and I told you? I think you'd still pull the plug."

"Not if you promise to keep your mouth shut."

"That's not likely—I'm a lawyer, remember? Let me think about this for a moment. I'm really not anxious to go until I find out how badly injured I am. If it's bad news, you could come back and still do me a favour by pulling the plug on this ta-pocketa-pocketa machine."

"We haven't got all night, Phil. Make up your mind right now."

"You say you had a lesbian affair with Annie?" The figure quietly approached Mary.

"Right."

"Then can I tell you a joke while I'm making up my mind? You always liked my jokes, Mary."

"All right, go ahead, but this better be good."

"An old cowboy's dressed to kill in a cowboy shirt, hat, jeans, spurs and chaps. He goes into a bar and orders a drink. He's sipping his whiskey when a young lady sits down next to him. After ordering her drink, she turns to the cowboy and asks, 'Are you a real cowboy?' He says, 'Well, ma'am, I've spent my whole life on the range, herding cows, breaking horses and mending fences. I guess I am a real cowboy.' After a while, he asks the young lady what she is. She says, 'I'm a lesbian. I spend my whole day thinking about women. As soon as I get up in the morning I think of women. When I eat, shower, watch TV, everything seems to make me think of women.' She finishes her drink and leaves, and—"

Phil stared in astonishment. Clarence Crepeau stood behind Mary, brandishing a weapon, something long and pointed. What was he doing here? It came to Figg in a flash. Looking for his money, that's what.

The Creep snatched the book and the documents from Mary's hand. She turned to face him and Crepeau shoved hard, slamming Mary back onto the hospital bed, where she landed heavily on Phil.

Phil gasped in pain.

Rolling back off the bed, using both it and Phil as a springboard, Mary launched herself back at the Creep in a frenzy, a banshee's scream on her lips.

The Creep, who was armed with an icepick, flung his arm up in front of himself.

Did Mary impale herself on the pick or did the Creep stab her straight through the heart?

Phil only saw the sudden halt in Mary's forward progress, heard her shriek of surprise and pain as she slid sideways into the wall and slumped to the floor.

The Creep stood over her, a shocked look on his ferret face.

Thirty

As Phil lay helpless, watching in amazement while the horrific scene unfolded, Mike Fowler burst through the door, goosed Crepeau with a stun gun and pulled the trigger. The Creep tap-danced for a few seconds, then flopped onto the floor, writhing as waves of muscle spasms rocked his body.

Mike stared down at Mary, slumped against the wall and at the Creep rolling around in a long trail of blood that spread rapidly across the marble floor.

He walked over to Phil's bed and calmly asked, "What the hell's the punchline of that cockamamie joke? I was afraid if I waited till the end I might break out laughing before I managed to zap him."

"Where was I?" Phil said, weak with relief. "Oh, yeah, the girl leaves and the cowboy orders another whiskey. A tourist couple sits down next to him and they ask, 'Are you a real cowboy?' The cowboy says, 'I always thought I was, but I just found out I'm a lesbian.'"

Wade Cavanaugh watched as Harry Muldoon swung back and forth in his swivel chair, his hands clasped behind his head and a satisfied grin on his face. Wade figured he would have to endure another boastful lecture. It seemed like a good time to pitch Muldoon for promotion to full detective status.

"Crepeau's legal-aide mouthpiece told Thorndyke he's willing to cop a plea if we go for manslaughter instead of murder. What do you think, Wade? Do we go for it?"

"It would save us a lot of time and trouble, boss, and it could end up that way anyway, so why not? Crepeau got into the hospital the back way and grabbed the icepick from the workroom. He had a weapon with him when he went into the room, but he says he had no intention of using it. He could be telling the truth."

"Yeah, claims he just wanted some documents he felt he should have. What that was, he wouldn't say. But do we give a shit?"

"He's holding the icepick out in front of him when Podalchuk counterattacks." Wade illustrated by mimicking Crepeau's movements. "At what point is it a defensive weapon, instead of an offensive one? Whether it just happened, or whether he intentionally stabbed forward with the pick, no one will ever know, but his lawyer's going to deny intent. If the verdict's manslaughter, Crepeau will only serve five to ten."

Wade didn't even have to ask for the promotion. "Thank you, Detective Cavanaugh." When Wade beamed, Muldoon added, "You've got the job for keeps—as soon as I can arrange it."

Wade gave out with just the right amount of gratitude and stroking of Harry's ego.

"The best news of all," Harry exuded happily, "is that this wraps up, in a neat little package, all the other murders and deaths. Exactly which one or more of that bunch of psychotic assholes were responsible for the Poindexter and Chance murders doesn't matter anymore, because all the suspects are dead. We can go back to business as usual. Except for one thing." Muldoon's face darkened.

"What's that, Sarge?"

"That interfering ex-lawyer Figgpudding.

Dumb luck he didn't buy the farm in that explosion along with the others."

"If he had, Sarge, none of the rest of this would've happened."

"Right again, Detective. But if he gets better, and if I can think of something to charge him with that'll stick, I will. He and that Mike Fowler character still know more than they're telling. Fowler's another smartass just like his buddy; it must be contagious. If Figgwiggin thinks I'm going to thank him for fucking around like he did, he's got another think coming."

Thirty-one

"A tall, lean Texan rode into town on a short, fat mule and an onlooker asked, 'Is that your fat ass, Jack?' I can't believe we're here, Phil."

"Neither can I, but here we are."

The two friends were reclining in chaise longues. The balcony of their air-conditioned suite overlooked the hotel pool and the Reserva da Barra Beach. The hotel was just west of the more famous Copacabana and Ipanema beaches in Rio.

"We owe a small vote of thanks to Wade Cavanaugh," said Mike. "I wasn't sure we should vamoose, but when he called, advising you Harry Muldoon might come gunning for us, that was the clincher. It was time to get outta Dodge."

"Not entirely loyal to the new boss, but

Cavanaugh did what he thought was right. I'm glad he made detective."

"Personally, I'm going to be the life of this party even if it lasts till eight p.m."

"If you're only as old as you feel, how can I be alive at a hundred and fifty? I'm wrinkled, saggy and lumpy, and that's just my left leg. This aging stuff isn't for sissies."

With that, Phil picked up the English edition of the Rio daily, while Mike poured two refills from a pitcher of frozen margaritas. With ultra-violet rays no longer a worry, Phil and Mike soaked up the tropical sunshine streaming through the brazen growth of purple bougainvillea arcing over the balcony.

"What's on your mind, Figg?" Mike asked.

Phil looked up from his newspaper. "We could have us another client."

"To replace Annie Chance, perchance?"

"Listen to this," said Phil, lifting an eyebrow. "*Crackdown on unacceptable crime,*" he read. "And guess what the crime is?"

"I'll bite."

"Topless sunbathing!"

"You gotta be kidding. This place is famous for that."

"Maybe the tide's turning. Apparently there's a public decency code in this city requiring that women's breasts be covered.

Twenty officers in full uniform, toting assault rifles, arrested this woman for indecent exposure in a public place."

"Hell, I saw multi teeny bikinis just this morning that left absolutely nothing to my imagination," Mike said.

"Right on. This is a violation of the civil rights of the good female citizens of Brazil. The models and samba dancers of this city have every right to avoid tan lines. After all, in the pre-Lenten Carnival celebrations, all they wear is a little glitter. We didn't come here to put up with this kind of miscarriage of justice, did we?"

"We certainly didn't, counselor," Mike replied, scratching his nose. "Let's find that woman, what's her name?"

"Dolores del Smutz," Phil deadpanned.

"How are we going to get you a licence to practice law in Brazil?"

"I'm an internationally famous lawyer, and I have the bucks to prove it to the local law society. I'm sure they'll have a fee to join, though it may be high, to keep out the riff-raff. Sun worshippers and fun lovers of South America will rally behind the cause. We'll look into this tomorrow."

"You got it, Figg. What else is on your mind?"

Phil put his paper aside and looked off

toward the ocean. "How I got out of that situation alive and managed to recover, I'll never know!"

"You must've been blasted out of that car faster than grandmothers fart their own meatloaf."

"I've never heard anything so loud in my life."

The straight man syndrome kicked in as usual. "Okay, how loud was it?"

"It reminded me of the difference between a saloon and an elephant's fart."

"And what difference might that be?"

"One's a bar room. The others a *barroom!*"

"I should've smelled that one coming."

"And what are you thinking about?"

Mike scratched his scalp, sending up a small flurry of dandruff. "We should find out whether there's a Southern Exposure Domestic Services in this country."

Phil nodded enthusiastically. "Not a bad idea. But guess who pays this time if there is?"

"Pass me the suntan oil, will you? I think my bald spot's drying up."

"I've got good news and bad news on the potency front," Phil said.

"Okay, what's the good news?"

"Viagra, the first pill for impotence. Now available in Canada."

"A damn sight better deal than the Potency

Patch and scrotum shaving," was Mike's quick rejoinder. "What's the bad news?"

"If you're on heart medication, like nitroglycerin, or other drugs for diabetes and such problems, you can't use Viagra. It's dangerous under those conditions."

"Damn shame, Phil, but I can think of another reason why lawyers shouldn't take Viagra."

"I'll bite. Why might that be?"

"All you'd get by giving Viagra to a lawyer is a taller lawyer."

"Another lawyer joke. Very funny!"

"So what if the Viagra's dangerous, it's not a bad way to die," said Mike. "In fact, the French would call it the sweet death."

"However, there is other good news."

"More good news?"

"Another drug company's come up with something called MUSE, short for Medicated Urethral System of Erection. The drug, alpostadil, is for erectile dysfunction," Phil explained. "It affects only the penis as opposed to the whole body."

"So what's the bad news there? Other than we don't have any."

"The drug gives you a natural-feeling erection in ten minutes, but you have to shove this tiny suppository, about the size of half a grain of rice, up your penis—"

"Up yours, not mine," Mike interrupted. "I've been thinking. If we were at our sexual peak in our teens, how could we let so many good years slip through our fingers?"

"Before we lesbians talk about something besides women, I have got to say that gals are much more psychic than guys."

"Why do you say that?"

"Because they're the first to know if you're going to get laid."

"Badda-bing, badda boom!" Mike reached for the pitcher again.

"Who are we kidding?" Phil moaned. "Any woman who'd make love to either of us would have to close her eyes to keep from laughing."

"Yeah, let's face it, at our age, sex is all talk. Incidentally, what's got seven balls and screws you twice a week?"

"What?"

"Lotto 649."

Phil laughed at this sally. "Is there anything serious you want to talk about, Mike?"

"I was thinking of the word 'parlay.'"

Phil repeated the word. "Do you mean, 'Parlez-vous le ding-dong', as in French? Or a parley, to confer with an enemy to settle a dispute or discuss terms? Or maybe to parlay, or bet the original wager plus your winnings on the next race?"

"Yeah, what you said last, that's it. Means to change something into something bigger, doesn't it?

"Yeah, but I don't get what you're getting at."

"Well," Mike said as he scratched his armpit, "this climate's really getting to me. I mean, here we are, sitting on a pile of money. Our luck's running good. I say we try to parlay the cash into something bigger."

Phil reached for a banana from the bowl on the glass-topped coffee table. He pondered Mike's suggestion as he peeled the fruit.

"Let's put our brains to work, Phil," Mike urged. I don't mean anything earth-shaking, let someone with the time and life energy save the planet. We're all ants and here comes the steamroller, but maybe there's something you and I can do."

"You may have something there. Let's think about it tomorrow, but not now."

"Okay. Another thing I'm wondering though, is whether you'd do anything differently if you had to solve the Poindexter murder all over again."

"I never did solve it. Hindsight only makes you realize you never had any foresight. I had about as much luck solving that case as I had of not getting wet while pissing into a stiff breeze."

"Walking around in circles asking for directions, were you?"

Phil didn't answer immediately. "That's about it. I never realized Mary-Mary was a pathological control freak with an axe to grind. Let alone that she was grinding it out of combined jealousy, revenge and greed. Maybe there were even darker reasons, but she was lost in some endless schizophrenia-like interpretation of collective reality."

"Whatever that means," Mike replied cheerfully. He dipped a potato chip into the salsa.

"She couldn't distinguish between physical facts and inner fantasies," Phil explained.

"Hard to believe such bizarre crimes actually take place."

"I told Muldoon that Mary confessed to both crimes, but there's no corroboration, and I doubt Harry believed me."

"She's dead, along with your friends Riley, Bob and Don, so what does it matter?"

"Everybody's dead, except the Creep," Phil said.

"They had the Creep cold in Podalchuk's death, so I ask you again, what does it matter who murdered who? Crepeau won't get out of the slammer till long after we're gone. Muldoon looks good, he's getting great press, and that's probably all Harry cares about."

Phil laughed lightly. "Yeah, and he never even thanked me for my help."

"What do you want, a shit-disturber's medal? Anyway, we've been well paid for the pain, suffering and mental anguish we've endured through this whole thing."

"That sounds like my line," Phil objected.

"Unless you want to give the money to Revenue Canada."

"What, give the feds more money to waste? No way!"

"Doesn't your Methodist upbringing make you feel guilty?" asked Mike.

"Not a bit. You?"

"No. Lucky we weren't raised as Catholics."

"I was, actually. Went to a public school run by the Sisters of Little or No Mercy!"

"You were not. You've still got your ears. Well, your friend Mary certainly fooled everybody, you have to give her that. Wonder what church she went to?"

"She misled me completely, but then so did those other three patsies. It still bothers me, you know," Phil said, stroking his goatee. "I was one lousy detective."

"Mary didn't count on the Creep actually showing up to find his money," said Mike. "And to think, that wad of ill-gotten, laundered dough, originally purloined by

Clarence the Creep, went through his hands and those of Dick the Prick, Annie the Chance and Mary the Contrary. A fat lot of good it did any of them. None of them got to spend one bit of it. We ended up with the whole enchilada. Serendipity!"

"Yeah, and I still can't get over Mary's cannibalism. She really believed she was empowering herself, so to speak, by drinking the blood and eating the flesh of her victims."

"Don't Christians do that in Communion?"

"Mike, that's not like the real thing; it's symbolic."

"How the hell does somebody get that way?"

"She spent some time down in Peru and Mexico in her teens, probably picked up some sacrificial nonsense about the Aztecs then. But to actually do it—like I said, there was a big gap between her actions and any kind of reality. It's like she had no moral compass at all. Even the concept seemed to mean nothing to her. Cold."

Mike thought that over. "I'm just glad I met her and the Creep only once and that I had the stun gun with me. But Jesus, Figg, you were persistent, I'll give you that. You kept her talking, even in your condition. Kept your cool even when you saw Crepeau coming up behind her."

"Thank God you were hot on his heels. Actually, I was scared shirtless. I couldn't do anything else, so I just kept talking."

"True to your legal training. Just proves the old adage, the early bird may get the worm, but the second mouse gets the cheese."

"You sure know how to hurt a guy. But you're right, a lot of people don't know I'm not as smart as they think I am."

"They won't find out any different from me," Mike assured him, "but then what are friends for?" He clinked glasses with Phil, who became thoughtful.

"Maybe," Phil said, "friends help us get a glimpse of who we really are, and what we're doing here on this godforsaken planet we call home. You know, Mike, I really can't imagine not having known you."

"It was providence, old buddy, a bit of good luck for both of us. But hey, let's not get serious, or this conversation will become a real fubar—like the whole Poindexter case."

"A fubar?"

"Yeah, fucked up beyond all recognition!"

"Maybe it *did* do us a fat lot of good."

"Would you say that again?"

"A fat lot of good..."

BOOKS BY HAL SISSON

The Big Bamboozle
_____-03-8 $9.99/$6.99 U.S.

"*King Kong* and the *Planet of the Apes* have an
exciting successor." — *CARPNews*

Coots, Codgers and Curmudgeons
_____-04-6 $14.95/$9.95 U.S.

"Fans of W.O. Mitchell and Greg Clark will find this
book irresistible." — *Stitches*

Garage Sale of the Mind
_____-07-0 $19.95/$13.95 U.S.

More Prairie reminiscences from the authors of
Coots, Codgers and Curmudgeons.

A Fowler View of Life
_____-05-4   *$12.95/$8.95 U.S.*

An affectionate biography of jazz musician Bill
Fowler, who with wife Evelyn ran Seabreeze Guest
Farm on BC's beautiful Hornby Island.

Ask for these books at your local bookstore or use this page to order.

Please send me the books I have checked above. I am enclosing
$____ (add $3.00 Canadian or U.S. for postage and handling for the
first book, $1.00 for each additional book). Send cheque or money
order, no cash or C.O.D.s, please.

Name _____

Address _____

City, Prov/State, Postal/Zip_____

Mail to: Salal Press, Box 36060, Victoria, BC, Canada, V9A 7J5.
Allow six weeks for delivery.
Prices and availability subject to change without notice.

HAL SISSON

was born in Moose Jaw, Saskatchewan. His varied career includes a stint as a reporter for the *Saskatoon Star-Phoenix* and a thirty-year law practice in Alberta. He retired from the law in 1984 to devote time to croquet, marble collecting and writing fiction. He conceived, produced and starred in *Sorry 'Bout That*, the longest running annual burlesque revue in Western Canada. He is the co-author of *Coots, Codgers and Curmudgeons* and *Garage Sale of the Mind* (both with Dwayne Rowe), *Caverns of the Cross* (Arsenal Pulp Press) and *The Big Bamboozle*.